Anne Stormont

Baby Steps

Rowan Russell Books

Also by Anne Stormont

Change of Life

Displacement

Settlement

Fulfilment

Acknowledgements

Thank you to all family members and friends who continue to offer encouragement and support to me and my writing – you know who you are.

Special thanks to my wonderful editor John Hudspith who accepts nothing but the best, and to talented book designer Jane Dixon-Smith who has ensured that the book looks good both inside and out.

And thanks also to Iain Stormont for ruthless proof-reading.

Chapter One

Sophie

Sophie Campbell groaned when the alarm on her phone beeped. It was a Monday morning in early October and she felt like she'd only just fallen asleep. It had been another bad night, lying awake, tossing and turning, desperate for the morning to come but dreading it too.

After a few minutes of listening to the rain pattering on the bedroom window of her Glasgow flat, she forced herself out of bed. At least work would provide a much-needed distraction. She grimaced at her reflection in the mirror as she made her way to the bathroom. Her hair was a tangled mess and her pale face and strained expression made her look older than her thirty-three years.

Once in the shower she let her tears fall. The pressure of her grief had been relentless – with her every day for the past year – but its intensity had been easing slightly. Recently she'd had days and even weeks when she didn't cry. But now, with the first anniversary of her brother, Finlay's, death having just passed, it was back and it was full-on.

As she dried her hair and got dressed she wondered again what had possessed her to take on this latest assignment when her boss, George Brodie, the head of documentary research at BBC Scotland, had offered it to her at short notice on Friday morning. It wasn't even as if it was in her normal subject areas.

She mainly worked on the research for nature and science based programmes. And although she did have a bit of experience on social and cultural ones, she felt she was far from an expert in those fields.

She couldn't help smiling when she recalled how George's pitch had gone. He was at his persuasive best.

Usually when she was summoned to his office, the conversation was brief and to the point. The summoning itself had been normal with George suddenly appearing at her workstation and simply saying, "My office." The offer of coffee and a pastry when she arrived was the first sign that George was going all in.

"Just a coffee, please," Sophie replied, intrigued as to why George was making such an effort.

"Just over ten years now, isn't it?" George said after he'd served up their coffees and they were sitting facing each other across his desk. "Since you joined us here in Research."

"Yes, that's right."

"You've done well, worked hard, learned a lot and displayed a lot of skill. You're a real asset to the unit."

"Thank you. That's—"

"You keen to move on, get promotion?"

"Well, yes, yes I think I am," Sophie said now even more curious. "If the right post were to—"

"Senior researcher job at BBC's Natural History Unit in Bristol, could be coming up in six months or so. Someone like you with your Natural Science degree and all your experience in helping put together outdoor and nature programmes as well as your wider general experience, you'd be ideal. Happy to recommend you for it if you're interested."

Of course she was interested. And George knew it, but all he said was, "No need to respond just now. You can think about it. Let me know."

"Right," Sophie said, certain this wasn't the real reason she was there, but she was interested, nevertheless.

"Good. Now the reason I needed to see you today is I want you to leave what you're working on at the moment and take over another more urgent project."

Sophie was in the middle of researching a feature on the growing popularity of allotments in Scotland's cities for a long-running gardening series. She didn't want to abandon it and besides that she had a deadline to meet.

But before she could respond, George added, "Don't worry about the allotment project. It's well on its way. And your trainee co-worker is proving more than competent, largely thanks to your excellent training and support, so she can take over." George smiled knowingly at her.

Oh, he was good at getting what he wanted, she'd give him that. Flattery, the possibility of promotion, she knew she was being manipulated but she was also intrigued as to what exactly he was asking of her. So Sophie smiled back at him, in what she hoped was also a knowing way, letting him know she knew what he was up to.

George gave an almost imperceptible nod before going on to say, "So, this favour I need," he leaned his forearms on the desk, clasped his hands and leant towards her, "we recently commissioned a documentary television series. It's going to be broadcast UK wide. Obviously all the preliminary research work at a general level has been done. But now, of course, it's down to specifics." George paused to take a sip of his coffee.

"Of course," Sophie said, wishing he'd just get on with it.

"Each programme will tell the stories of injured British military veterans making the return to civilian life. The first programme in the series is to be about a Glasgow-based veterans charity called Revive and some of the people who use its services.

"Unfortunately your colleague, Liz Maitland, who was originally tasked with series research has been signed off on sick leave. She should hopefully be back to work on the subsequent episodes but we need someone to step in immediately to do the research for this first one."

"Right," said Sophie. "And that someone—"

"That someone needs to be you," said George. "You have the experience, efficiency and sensitivity to do this. It'll look good on your CV."

"Okay," Sophie said. But she wasn't sure it *was* okay.

Her boss then went on to show some uncharacteristic empathy when he said, "I acknowledge that the military subject matter could be tough for you. I haven't forgotten that your brother died on active service in Afghanistan, so although I would like you to accept the work, I won't think any less of you if you decline."

"I … I appreciate that," Sophie said before swallowing hard and then clearing her throat. She hadn't expected that. Blunt, insensitive George was definitely easier to handle than this kinder version.

Though, she didn't have to wait for the former version to reappear as he got to his feet, indicating the meeting was over. "Take an hour to think it over," he said, "and then let me know what you decide."

In the end, Sophie didn't need the hour. She was nothing if not professional. This was work. It was nothing to do with her personal life. Besides, as George had said, it would be a good one for her CV especially as the intention was to base and transmit the series across the whole of the UK.

She was also tempted by the Bristol job and so she asked to be informed of any developments on that front. Maybe a fresh start in a new city hundreds of miles away was just what she needed – both professionally and personally.

Her boss, of course, had been delighted to hand over the military veteran's programme brief to her, along with the research carried out so far, and she spent the rest of Friday and much of the weekend getting up to speed. As she did so, she admitted to herself that it hadn't been an entirely head over heart decision to take on this particular job. It had occurred to her that it might make her feel a bit closer to Finlay.

But on that Monday morning as she applied her makeup, she felt a niggle of doubt as to whether that would really be a good thing.

She couldn't face breakfast and settled for a glass of water instead. After she'd rinsed out the glass she glanced around the open plan kitchen and living room. At least with Rick no longer living there the flat was tidy, though there was still a load of his stuff in the spare bedroom. She should really give him a deadline for collecting it all, tell him she'd bin the lot if he didn't.

She'd kicked him out a couple of months earlier, having come home early from work and found him in their bed with a woman she not only knew, but had up until then liked. She'd been shocked, hurt and furious when she found out exactly what her lying, cheating boyfriend had been up to. The boyfriend who she'd financially supported when he couldn't make a proper living as a musician, who'd lived with her rent free for two years, who'd said he loved her. The boyfriend who it turned out couldn't cope with her being distracted by grief. The boyfriend who, as he put it, 'needed to distract and comfort himself' because 'she'd been so wrapped up in herself over the last year and had nothing left to give him'. The boyfriend who'd been having a months-long affair with Lisa, the talented and pretty singer from his band.

It still hurt but at least she could now concede she was definitely better off without him.

In fact, she reminded herself, as she slipped on her jacket, she was better off without any man. After the way things had ended with Rick, someone she'd truly believed she'd loved and who she had thought loved her, she was unwilling to entrust her damaged heart to anyone else ever again.

She was obviously a hopeless judge of character. Indeed, she'd recently decided the whole love, marriage and having children thing wasn't for her. These things would only leave her vulnerable to yet more heartbreak and she was so done with all of that. She only had to look at her parents to know this was the right choice for her. No, from now on, she'd be keeping any sexual interactions casual and for fun only.

After all, she also reminded herself, in every other way her life was as good as it could be. She had her flat, a job she loved and good and loyal female friends – friends who she knew would always be on her side.

She took in a deep breath, rolled her shoulders and straightened her back. She was independent and she was strong. She'd proved she could take what life threw at her – including her useless ex, her estrangement from her mother, and even the loss of her darling brother. She was proud that she was still standing in spite of it all.

'I've got this,' she said to herself as she walked out the door.

With the rain having stopped and the sky clearing, Sophie would have preferred to walk from her flat in Glasgow's Kelvinside area to the city's Hyndland district where the Revive charity had its premises. But she would need to go into the office after her interview with the charity's manager so she took the car for what was only a five-minute drive.

Hyndland was a pleasant, mainly residential area of the city, but even so, for reasons of cost if nothing else, she'd been expecting a charitable organisation like Revive to be housed in a utilitarian concrete box perhaps surrounded by other similar buildings and a gravel car park. But the single-storey, stone-built structure with its pitched and slated roof was much more attractive than that – and the grass and flower beds which surrounded it, along with the tree-lined perimeter, said parkland rather than business park.

As Sophie left her car in the small car park at the side of the building and walked up to the entrance, she realised that her earlier reservations had gone and she was keen to find out more. This was what she did and no matter how tricky the subject matter, this was work. It wasn't personal and it wasn't about her.

She was about to press the buzzer at the front entrance when the door opened and she was confronted by one extremely good-looking guy. He looked like he was in his early thirties, around the same age as she was, and he was the epitome of tall, fair and handsome and oh my what a lovely smile he had. "Miss Campbell, I presume," he said extending his hand.

Chapter Two

Steven

Steven Jackson had finished replying to the emails that always seemed to build up in Revive's inbox over the weekend. He stretched then rubbed the back of his neck before pushing away from his desk and standing up. He flexed his thigh muscles and smiled to himself. This standing up thing – it was still a bit of a novelty and something he'd never again take for granted.

He had a few minutes before his 9.30 appointment arrived. He decided to use those minutes double-checking everything was in order for the tour he'd be giving the BBC's Sophie Campbell. It was amazing that Revive had even been considered and he wanted to present them at their best. He knew how valuable it could be for the charity to be featured in this documentary series and not only that but to also have the work of the centre making up the first episode would be beyond special.

It was when he was on his way back to his office and happened to glance out the corridor window that he saw her approaching. He opened the door just as she was about to press the buzzer.

As he offered the woman his hand, he felt his throat go dry and his heartrate speed up. She was beautiful – small, with long, strawberry blonde hair which she wore tied back in a low ponytail – and her eyes were the most lovely hazel colour. "Miss Campbell, I presume," he said. "I got the email explaining that you'd be coming in place of Miss Maitland. I'm Steven Jackson. Pleased to meet you."

"Pleased to meet you too," the woman replied, smiling at him as she shook his hand. "I *am* Miss Campbell. But please, call me Sophie."

Steven gave a little nod, "And you can call me Steven," he said, realising as he took a step back that was a dumb thing to say. "Please, come in and welcome to Revive."

As he led the way to his office, Steven wondered why his nervousness about presenting the centre in a good light had gone up a gear and now seemed to include presenting himself in a good light too. He didn't think he had any expectations of what a researcher from the BBC would look like so he wasn't sure why he felt so surprised and unsettled as they shook hands. Yes, she was a very good-looking woman – but it wasn't like it was the first time he'd encountered that. It was more than that. There was something else going on. Something he hadn't experienced for quite some time.

"Would you like a tea or a coffee before we start?" Steven asked after hanging up Sophie's coat.

"No, I'm fine, thank you. There's a lot I need to see and ask about. We should probably just get started."

She was right. This was work. Nothing more. "Of course," he said. "I thought I'd do a brief presentation on what Revive aims to do and how we go about it, and then give you the guided tour so you can see us in action."

"Sounds good," Sophie said, reaching into her bag for her notebook and pen. She also took out her phone and popped it in the pocket of her trousers. "Do you mind if I record here and there? I'll tell you if and when I am, check it's okay first, especially if there are other people around, but for remembering room layouts and interiors I find video is easier than trying to scribble notes."

"That's fine," Steven said.

Doing the presentation on how Revive was set up and worked helped Steven to regain his focus.

He began by explaining that he'd started working there as

manager six months previously and that as well as the paid staff who, like him, were all former members of the military who'd seen active service, there was also a team of local volunteers who helped to keep everything running.

He outlined the services that Revive provided saying that it gave its users practical support – be it financial, physical, or emotional. He explained that the charity also offered work opportunities, opportunities to learn new skills, to socialise, to get fit physically and mentally and generally helped in whatever ways were necessary to ease the return to civilian life.

He went on to tell her that the charity's day-to-day costs were funded by grants from the government and from The Veteran's Foundation but that it was also reliant on fund-raising initiatives and personal donations.

"Yes," Sophie said, "I was wondering about funding. How on earth does the charity afford a place like this?"

"Ah, Revive hasn't always been housed here," Steven said. "After it was originally set up in 2003 to support local veterans of the Iraq war it was in all sorts of temporary accommodation, from former shops and offices to portacabins. None of them were ideal and all of them curtailed the services that could be offered."

"So what changed?" Sophie said.

"Long story short – sort of." Steven paused to grin at Sophie, glad to see she seemed genuinely interested and that he didn't seem to be boring her. "This place became available. It's a 1930s building and it was originally a primary school. It came up for sale when the school merged with another one in the area and moved to a nearby newly built campus. Revive's board members could see it had the potential to be the ideal premises.

"So, a major fundraising drive was launched, and that along with two very generous donations from a pair of philanthropic Scottish billionaire businessmen, meant Revive became the building's proud and greatly relieved new owners. And so, with those two main benefactors also covering the cost of renovations and alterations, we now have an attractive, accessible, multi-use space that exactly fits our needs.

"An amazing achievement," Sophie said and Steven couldn't believe how pleased he was that she thought so

"I think so," he said, aware he was grinning like an idiot. "It also helps that we have first-class board members running the show and keeping an eye on the finances. They all share a clear and common vision of how we should proceed and we have a practical and achievable plan of action in place for the next couple of years." Steven took a swig of water from a glass on his desk before sitting back.

"It all sounds impressive," Sophie said. "So how about a tour so I can see if the place lives up to your excellent description?"

The smile she gave him made his throat go dry and he took another gulp of water before saying, "It would be my pleasure."

He began the tour by showing Sophie the various meeting rooms and offices. He then took her to see the workshops and studios, the gym and the therapy rooms, and he finished by letting her see the kitchen, the café and the shop. He pointed out that the café and shop also had their own shared entrance from the car park so that members of the public could make use of them without having to come through the centre itself.

He also introduced her to many of the people there. Some of them told her about themselves and there were several people in that group who Sophie said would make ideal participants in the documentary. She asked them if they'd be willing to be interviewed as part of it and she promised the ones who agreed that they'd be contacted as part of the follow up to her visit.

"This is amazing," Sophie said as they stood looking round the shop. She seemed impressed by all of it but the shop got the strongest reaction. "Everything for sale here has, at least in part, been made here at the centre?"

"Yep, the jewellery, the art and craft work, the pottery, the clothes, and the fresh bread and cakes are all made here by vet- erans who make use of the facilities, workshops and classes that we offer. The makers are paid for the goods they provide and that in turn generates a small but steady income for the centre."

"So as well as a place to receive help to get over trauma, a place to come where you'll meet other people who've been through similar experiences, the centre also provides users with a workplace and a sense of purpose."

"Precisely," Steven said, smiling at Sophie's understanding. "Look, why don't we grab a coffee in the café and we can continue our conversation there." He pointed in the direction of the café's internal doorway. "We'll still be working after all," he said, his smile now slightly cheeky as he referred to Sophie's earlier refusal of his offer in favour of getting started.

"Hmm, yeah, I suppose I can allow that," Sophie said, putting on a semi-serious face, the twinkle in her eyes showing him that she knew he was teasing her.

"Oh my goodness, that's so good," Sophie said. They'd found themselves a table in the pleasingly busy café and had been served with their coffee and cake order. She'd taken a bite of the slice of chocolate sponge and now had her eyes closed as she groaned with pleasure. A sight and a sound that had Steven finding it very difficult to keep his mind on his job.

He was still staring at her when she opened her eyes and looked into his. "Sorry," she said, looking slightly embarrassed. "I didn't have any breakfast and this …" She pointed to the cake. "This is definitely hitting the spot."

His throat had gone dry again. "You shouldn't skip breakfast," he said, his voice only just avoiding becoming a pathetic croak. "Most important meal of the day."

"Yeah, I know," Sophie said, looking serious all of a sudden. "I've … I've sort of lost my appetite a bit lately."

"I'm sorry to hear that," he said, resisting the urge to reach for her hand. "You've not been ill, have you?"

"No, no nothing like that." She looked embarrassed again.

"Well you seem to have tracked it down now … your appetite," he said.

She nodded, still frowning to herself, and oh, how he wanted to soothe that frown away.

"So," he said, deciding to get back on a professional track. "The café and the shop are proving to be great assets. They both allow the local community to offer its support but not just in a 'giving to charity' sort of a way. There's something in it for them if they can make a purchase and that gives a certain dignity and pride to us as the providers."

"Yes, I can see that," Sophie said, also seeming to have got her professional vibe back. "And I should think for military folks, so used to giving their service, it must mean a lot to them to be able to continue to give and to not just be on the receiving end of the good works of others."

"That's it exactly," Steven said, his smile wide. He loved how this woman had instantly got what they were about here at Revive. "It's what attracted me to work here myself."

Sophie nodded. "And you're willing to be interviewed on camera about all of it and about yourself?"

"Yes, if it will help raise our profile, I'm definitely up for that," Steven said.

"Right then," said Sophie, "let's go back to your office and you can tell me more about exactly how you came to work here."

Once they were seated facing each other across Steven's desk, Sophie began by saying, "So tell me a bit about your military service and how you came to be honourably discharged."

Steven couldn't help noticing that Sophie looked uncomfortable as she asked. He thought it might be because she was squeamish about the possibility of hearing about how exactly he'd been wounded. So he decided to keep the gruesome details to a minimum.

"I was in the army – Black Watch, 3rd Battalion. It was early last year. I was serving out in Afghanistan, had been there for three months in Helmand province. Me and my unit, we were out on patrol one morning. All seemed quiet. A young lad was watching us come down the street, then at the last minute as we approached him, he ran away. We decided to follow him, thinking there might be something going on. That's when it happened …" his voice trailed off as he took a moment.

"When what happened?" Her voice was quieter and he saw that Sophie had now gone pale.

"An IED, at the side of the road where we were walking. My comrade stepped on it. It went off. He was killed instantly. I was badly injured. And now after many operations, a ton of physio and lots of therapy, here I am."

Sophie nodded. He could see her swallow before she spoke. "And here … how did you end up here?"

"Nearly a year later, when all the treatment was over, I came back here to my hometown, back to living with my folks. I had no idea what I'd do next. But what I did know was I needed a job, a reason to get out of bed in the morning, and I needed to get a place of my own. Long story short, I heard about this place not long after I came home, began as a volunteer, applied for the manager's job when it came up and that was that. I felt useful again and I was able to get a flat nearby. So although this job's maybe not what I want to do for the rest of my life, it certainly rescued me coming along when it did. Truth is, I love this place and I'll be grateful for it, no matter what I end up doing long-term."

Sophie nodded again. For a moment she looked as if she was going to ask him something else but then seemed to think better of it. She sighed as she sat back in her chair.

"I hope you don't mind me asking," Steven said, "but are you okay? Only you look very pale?"

"What? Oh, yes, yes I'm fine sorry. Probably just hungry again. Like I said I didn't have any breakfast and the effects of the cake must have worn off." She attempted a smile that didn't quite make it to her eyes.

Steven glanced at the clock on the wall. It was nearly noon. "Look, why don't I take you to lunch? Not here. We could sneak out to a nice wee Italian I know. It's just round the corner and—"

"Oh no. No, that's … I have to go … get back to the office."

Steven himself paled when he saw how horrified she looked as she stumbled to her feet. She grabbed her coat and bag and almost ran for the door. He went to get up but she waved her arm at him. "No need to see me out. Production team will be in touch." And with that she was gone.

"Right, okay then," he said to the empty room, not only baffled by her quick exit but also realising he was way too disappointed that she was so reluctant to have lunch with him. After all, as she'd reminded him, this morning had been work not pleasure and besides that he'd only just met her. So why did her rejection matter so much? And why had she been so uncomfortable when he talked about his injuries? It wasn't as if he'd told her the worst of it.

Chapter Three

Sophie

She made it back to the car without throwing up but it was a close thing. Once inside the car, she took a minute to steady herself. Then, as the physical effects of listening to Steven talking about how he was injured abated, the emotional ones set in.

Tears ran down her face as she thought about her brother. Finlay had also encountered an IED while serving in Afghanistan but unlike Steven he hadn't survived the blast. Finlay, her much-loved little brother, who grew up to be a Royal Marine, was blown to bits aged only twenty-four, obliterated from her life as his own one ended. A year on, the loss and the hurt were still excruciating.

Sad and upset as she was, she also felt angry with herself. She'd been unprofessional ending the meeting like that. What must Steven have thought? She should have stuck with the allotment job. She'd believed she was strong enough to come to Revive, and for the most part it had been fine. She'd been genuinely interested in and impressed by the people she'd met. And the nature of the practical and positive work they were doing meant that listening to them hadn't been difficult. But talking with Steven shifted things up a gear. Suddenly it became all too personal and all too painful.

It had been an error of judgement accepting the assignment but, as she prepared to drive away, she decided not to be too hard on herself. At least she'd done enough to come up with a report and recommendations for the programme team. Job done. It wasn't as if she'd have to come back here and she wouldn't have to see Steven Jackson ever again. It was fine.

Except that last part wasn't fine. She liked Steven. He was clearly passionate about his work and about the charity in general. He was a committed professional and he was also a good communicator. She could definitely see why, with him at the helm, the charity would be successful in achieving its aims and she also knew that he'd come across well on TV. She also had to admit she hadn't just liked him on a professional level or out of admiration for what he was doing. He was actually a lovely guy. Not only amazingly good-looking with his cropped blond hair and stunning blue eyes but also interesting, interested, and kind

Nevertheless, she knew nothing could come of her attraction to him. And as she drove to her office at the BBC's Glasgow headquarters at Pacific Quay, she reminded herself of why that was, of how from now on she planned to guard her heart

The rest of the week at work was busy but it was also routine and uneventful compared to Monday which suited Sophie just fine. She wrote up her summary of her visit to Revive, listing her recommendations regarding who to interview and what to feature, and attended a report-back meeting with the production team. Her contribution was well-received and the production team would be taking it from there.

She then moved on to carrying out the preliminary and desk-based research for the further five episodes that would make up the series. That way when her sick colleague returned to work she could hit the ground running. As well as that, she started on her next scheduled project which involved looking into possible candidates for a feature documentary on Scotland's female scientists past and present. She also remained available to the junior colleague who'd taken on the allotment project research.

Life away from work had been fairly quiet, just the way she

liked it. She spent that week's evenings much as she had for the last six months – at home in the flat, mostly reading or binge watching a TV drama series, but she found it hard to focus on either pastime. She was restless in a way she hadn't been before and she wasn't sure why. Just when she'd thought she was coming to terms with things and that she was okay with how her life was now, something else seemed to be niggling away at her. Something she couldn't quite fathom.

In between struggling to follow the kind of bingeworthy series that normally held her attention, or to retain the storyline in the crime novel she was currently reading, she had a phone call from her dad.

He lived in Edinburgh and although they didn't see each other often he did make sure to call her from time to time.

"I'm fine, Dad, honestly," Sophie said in response to her father's concerns that she might be feeling down. "Yes, Finlay's anniversary was hard, just as it would have been for you. But I'm okay, been busy at work and you know, just getting on with things. Anyway, what about you and Carla? Got any holiday plans in the offing?"

"Hmm," her father said.

Sophie knew she knew she wasn't fooling her father. He was after all one of Scotland's top lawyers, a senior advocate serving in the highest courts in the country. He knew avoidance when he heard it. But he let it go and told her about a winter cruise he and his wife would be going on over Christmas.

He returned to a more difficult topic before the end of their conversation when he said, "Have you been in touch with your mother recently?"

Sophie knew that on this subject only an honest answer would do. "No, I haven't. Like I said I've been busy with work … and stuff. But I'll be in touch with her soon."

Her father didn't push her on it, but she knew that even though her parents were divorced, he'd be wishing she had reached out to her mum.

What she didn't tell him was that her mother had been in touch with her several times during the last week. In fact there had been daily texts since Finlay's anniversary asking her how she was, begging her to get in touch. She hadn't replied to any of them. She was way too angry to do that.

Her only other social contact had been with her best friends Lainey and Paula. The three of them had been friends since their student days at Glasgow university when they'd shared a flat and a whole lot of other experiences.

Paula and Sophie shared an extra bond as Paula's brother, Dean, had also been in the military and served in Afghanistan. So she and Paula had supported each other during the worrying times when their brothers had been on active duty. Dean had, however, survived. He'd left the army and was now back living with his wife and two children in Glasgow and running his own business. Sophie knew Paula was sensitive to the fact that her brother had survived while Sophie's hadn't, but Paula also always seemed to judge things right when she talked about either of their brothers – something that made Sophie love her friend even more.

Both Lainey and Paula had messaged Sophie off and on during the week, following up on the contact they'd had with her on the ghastly anniversary, checking she was okay and begging her to come out with them. In the end it had been Lainey who had called her on the Friday evening.

"Hello, Ms Hermit," Lainey said brightly when Sophie gave in and answered. "How the heck are you?"

"I'm good," Sophie replied with as much enthusiasm as she could muster.

"No, you're not," Lainey said.

"No, I'm not." Sophie knew that while she could sort of fool her father and he'd play along, Lainey and Paula were an entirely different proposition.

"So, what's up? Is it Fin? You still hurting as bad?"

"Yes and no," Sophie said. "It's partly that and partly other stuff."

"Okay, you're going to need to be a bit more specific if I'm going to have a hope of making it better for you."

"That's just it," Sophie said. "I'm not sure what it is myself, so I don't think you can help me. I think it's something I'm going to have to figure out for myself."

"Oh no you don't," Lainey said. "You've been dealing with things on your own for long enough. The occasional coffees, the even more occasional pub nights, and the few evening visits we've shared at each other's homes in recent months don't count. You're going to come out with Paula and me tomorrow night. We're going to have a proper night out. We're going to eat, drink and be merry and you're going to share how you're feeling and then Paula and I are going to offer lots of helpful advice which you're going to act on."

"I don't know—"

"Ah, but I do. We have a table reservation at Great Western Gourmet and there's a taxi booked to pick you up at 7.30. So, make sure you're ready. See you there." And with that Lainey hung up. A text followed a few minutes later. It was from Paula and all it said was, 'don't even think about not turning up'.

As she got ready for her Saturday night out, Sophie found that she was actually looking forward to it. Lainey was right. She had become a hermit and it wasn't healthy. Okay, so she'd been hurt and wasn't looking for romance, and yes, she still had to cope with her grief, but neither of those things meant she should continue to hide away. Her friends were right. She needed to get back out there, to stop hiding from the world. It would be easier said than done and would take time and effort but going out that evening would be a start.

So, for the first time in ages, she made a conscious effort to look her best. She took time over her makeup and left her hair down. Instead of her usual casual and comfy jeans, she went for a smarter tight-fitting black pair and the new green cashmere sweater she'd treated herself to on a trip to the shops earlier that day. She added her leather jacket, tan knee-high boots and a pretty scarf and she was good to go.

"Good to see you've not let yourself go completely," Lainey said, grinning as she stood and leant across the table to hug her when she arrived at the restaurant. "Nice jumper," she added as Sophie shrugged off her jacket and sat down next to Paula.

Paula too gave her hug. "Yeah, seems like you actually managed to make a bit of an effort. We thought you might turn up in your PJs." She giggled before hugging her again. "Mind you, we'd have been okay with that if it meant we got to see you."

"Too right we would," Lainey said, pouring Sophie a glass of prosecco and passing it to her. "It's been way too long."

"Aw, thanks, you two – I think." Sophie smiled.

"To us!" Lainey said, raising her glass. "Besties forever."

Sophie and Paula clinked their glasses with Lainey and each other and repeated the toast. Paula also proposed a toast to Finlay's memory, which for Sophie was amazingly touching and she wasn't afraid or ashamed to let her tears fall as they clinked glasses again.

It wasn't long before the three of them were laughing and chatting away like the old friends they were, and in that way truly good friends do despite time apart.

As they ate tasty salad starters with garlic bread, followed by delicious pasta main courses, they caught up with how work had been going for the three of them.

Paula told them about some of the stuff she and her Primary Three class had been doing recently.

"I don't know how you're still standing," Sophie said after Paula told them about the latest round of paperwork she'd had to complete. "Wrangling all those seven-year-olds every day and doing all the prep and paperwork too."

"Yeah," Paula said. "As I've said before, teaching can be very stressful but I love it, not the bureaucracy, of course, but being with the children, seeing them learn and grow – it's really special."

"Speaking of children learning and growing," Lainey said, "How's your wee Molly doing? Got any recent photos to share with us?"

Paula smiled. "You mean photos that I haven't already bombarded you with?" Paula dug her phone out of her bag. "Molly's doing great," she added as she scrolled down her phone screen looking for any as yet unshared pictures of her eighteen-month-old daughter. "Here you go," she said, passing the phone to Lainey who held it so that Sophie could also see the screen. "That's the newest dozen or so."

As she looked at her friend's family photos, Sophie felt an unexpected stab of jealousy along with that vaguely unsettled feeling she'd recently been experiencing. Looking at the mixture of father and daughter, mother and daughter, and parents and daughter photos confirmed what a strongly bonded unit Paula's family was. It was clear from the expressions on the adults' faces just how much they loved their daughter and, in one particularly poignant selfie of the three of them, where Paula's husband was looking at his wife not the camera, it was also clear just how much he loved her.

She was happy for Paula. Her friend had married a good bloke and normally Sophie loved seeing photos of her friend's little girl as well as seeing her in real life. It wasn't as if she envied Paula for being a wife and mother. So why the weird feeling?

Probably just biology, she told herself – her ovaries reminding her the clock was ticking and that she'd recently met an attractive and eligible man. A basic urge that her rational and logical brain should and would ignore to protect her wellbeing.

"Aw," said Lainey, as she handed the phone back to Paula. "Molly really is adorable. And what are you and Martin like? So obviously very much in lurve." Lainey laughed and batted her eyelashes as she clasped her hands together under her chin.

"Yes, we are actually." Paula's smile was wide. "Despite being permanently knackered, Martin and I love being parents and we actually love each other more than ever."

Lainey mimed throwing up before grinning at Sophie and nodding in Paula's direction, "That could be us too one day, if we're not careful."

Sophie managed to force a smile before taking a big gulp of wine.

The conversation then turned to what was going on with Lainey. In response Lainey shared a couple of success stories from her caseload as a social worker working with children and families in one of Glasgow's most economically deprived areas. Then she confirmed that although Neil, the latest in a long line of men in her life, was a nice guy, he wasn't 'the one' and so she would soon be breaking that fact to him.

When it was Sophie's turn to update her friends on what she had going on, she told them about her visit to Revive, and Paula said she'd heard of the charity from her ex-soldier brother.

"Of course, Dean doesn't have to use their services, being one of the lucky ones who returned unscathed from active service," Paula said, looking at Sophie and squeezing her hand as she said it. Sophie squeezed back, giving her friend a small smile. "But he's friendly with some of the veterans who volunteer or work there – I think he actually served with a couple of them – so I know he's visited a few times and he's done some fund-raising too."

"And you were okay?" Lainey asked, turning to Sophie. "Going to visit the charity, given the nature if its work, it wasn't too painful for you?"

"No, no it was fine. Like I say it was all very interesting, positive and professional." Sophie tried not to dwell on how hearing how Steven had been injured affected her. Much as she loved and trusted her friends, she certainly wasn't going to share the other feelings he stirred in her. It wasn't as if they'd be leading anywhere.

"Oh, and speaking of my brother," Paula said, "I hope you're both remembering you have an invite to his fortieth birthday party in three weeks' time."

Sophie's heart sank. She had forgotten. It was one thing getting back out there with Paula and Lainey, but she wasn't sure she was ready to go to a party. It wasn't as if she knew Dean all that well. Indeed she suspected she and Lainey had probably only been invited at Paula's suggestion.

"I had forgotten actually," Sophie said. "Sorry, maybe it's best if I—"

"It's not surprising you forgot," Paula said. "You've had a lot on your mind lately."

"Yes," Sophie said. "So, I don't know that I'm in the right place to go—"

"Oh, no you don't, lady." It was Lainey who interrupted this time. "Tonight is only step one in your social rehabilitation. We can tick 'coming out with your besties' off the list. Next step is to get out there with other people, other *men* people." Lainey raised an eyebrow.

"But I don't—"

"No buts," Lainey said raising a hand to stop Sophie's protest. "You're coming. You're going to drink and dance the night away and you're going to knock the socks off every eligible guy in the room." Lainey turned to Paula. "There will be single eligible men there, right?"

Paula frowned. "Eh, I suppose so. I don't know all his friends or who exactly is invited. But yeah, he must have some single mates, mustn't he?"

"He better," said Lainey. "Anyway, whatever, I've booked the three of us a spa day on the day of the party. Hair will be cut and styled, nails will be painted, faces will be made up. So, we can all be looking at our hottest and best – and while Paula is reminding Martin why he married her, you and me can have some fun." She wiggled her eyebrows at Sophie and then grinned a wicked grin.

"Okay, okay! Sophie couldn't help laughing. "You win." She knew when she was beaten.

Chapter Four

Steven

Steven checked out his appearance as he splashed on some aftershave. He'd been to the Turkish barber round the corner from his flat that morning and so his hair was short, just the way he liked it, and he was clean-shaven. Then in the afternoon he nipped into the city centre and bought himself a new pale blue shirt and a pair of dark navy chinos.

Shopping for clothes wasn't something he enjoyed since his injuries complicated the process of getting something that was both comfortable and which fitted. He did have a reasonably smart set of clothes for work, but his off-duty wardrobe was mostly jeans, joggers, tee-shirts and hoodies. And, as he rarely went to social gatherings, other than work-related ones, his wardrobe was decidedly low on party wear.

Parties were also something he didn't normally enjoy. He had once upon a time, but nowadays what with all the standing around and small talk with folk he'd probably never see again, they didn't feel worth the trouble. But this one was special. It was Dean's fortieth after all.

Dean Watson had also served in Afghanistan at around the same time as Steven although he'd been in a different unit and was stationed in a different province. They hadn't actually met until both were out of the army and back in Glasgow. It was at Revive that they'd been introduced to each other.

Dean was a big supporter of the centre, both in terms of raising awareness and raising funds. He was now a successful businessman with his own IT company and so he rubbed shoulders with other successful and influential people – people he roped in to help with the fundraisers he'd initiated. He'd organised and taken part in several money-raising events for Revive including one which involved running a marathon, doing a triathlon and climbing Ben Lomond, the closest Munro-sized mountain to Glasgow, all in one weekend. But as well as all of that, on a personal level Dean and him had quickly become good friends, and it was a friendship Steven truly valued built as it was on a lot of common ground.

So, Steven decided not only was he going to the party, but he was going to do his best to enjoy it. As he confirmed his intention by smiling at himself in the mirror, his phone beeped on the bedside table.

Picking it up, he saw it was a text from the birthday boy himself.

Looking forward to seeing you tonight. Don't even think about not coming. There will be good beer, good tunes and some rather lovely single ladies.

Steven smiled. Dean knew him too well, certainly as far as his enthusiasm for attending parties went and his liking for a decent ale. Good music was fine by him too although he doubted he'd be dancing. As for the mention of lovely ladies, all that did was bring to mind, for the umpteenth time, a particular lovely lady.

The gorgeous woman he met a month ago was back in his head yet again. The smart, beautiful and intriguing woman, the woman he couldn't stop thinking about. He knew her part in the BBC project with Revive was done but he couldn't help wondering if he'd ever see her again.

The upstairs function room at the pub in Glasgow's west end was already full when Steven arrived. A DJ was getting set up and the party guests were either standing around the empty dance floor in groups chatting or sitting at the tables around its edge. He spotted his host along with some other familiar faces at the far end of the bar.

"Ah, it's the fashionably late Mr Jackson!" Dean called out, grinning when he saw Steven approaching.

"I like making an entrance," Steven replied, smiling back and trying to relax.

"So good to see you, man," Dean said before embracing him. "Thanks for coming."

"Wouldn't have missed it." Steven slapped his friend on the back.

"Yes, you would if you thought you could get away with it."

"Hmm, yeah," Steven rubbed his chin as if pondering. "Maybe I would."

Dean nodded and looked suddenly serious. "Means a lot that you're here – that we're both here."

Steven nodded back. They both knew the full meaning of what Dean was saying. It was good to be at the party but it was even more amazing to be alive. Steven resolved to remind himself of that fact more often.

He needed to lighten up. This was a party, for heaven's sake. He wasn't going into battle, even if it felt a bit like it.

He took a breath. He could do this. "Happy Birthday, old yin," he said, smiling again as he reached into the inner pocket of his leather jacket and pulled out an envelope. "Rude card and a voucher for two to dine out at Great Western Gourmet. Oh, and you don't have to take me as your plus one."

"No danger of that," Dean said grinning. "I'll be picking someone far prettier than you, i.e. my darling wife, Emma, to accompany me. But thanks for the gift. I'll add it to the pile and open it later. Now the first drink is on me. What can I get you?"

While he waited for his drink, Steven was greeted by two of

the guys that he'd recognised earlier. They too were ex-army and users of Revive, so the banter was easy and light-hearted.

"Here you go," Dean said when he returned with Steven's beer. "I better go and mingle. You should do the same. In fact, come with me. You can say hi to Emma and the kids and I'll introduce you to my sister and brother-in-law to get you started."

It was as they approached the people Dean had mentioned that Steven saw her. She was standing on the edge of the group looking as if she'd rather be anywhere but where she was right now. He almost froze on the spot as she turned her head and met his gaze. He knew he was staring, and he also knew he shouldn't, but he couldn't help himself.

His evening had taken a sudden turn for the better. Sophie Campbell was here at the party, and in that short, sleeveless, figure-hugging black dress with its deep V-neck, and with her hair swept up so that just a few tendrils hung down, caressing her neck, she was even more stunning than he remembered.

As he was greeted by Emma, Steven tore his gaze away from Sophie. He returned Emma's greeting and after a brief chat with her and the children, twelve-year-old Gracie and ten-year-old Andrew, Dean began the introductions.

Steven shook hands with Dean's sister, Paula, and her husband, Martin, and then with a tall blonde woman named Lainey – short for Elaine apparently.

"And this," Dean said, extending an arm in Sophie's direction, "is another friend of Paula's—"

"Sophie Campbell," Steven interrupted, his gaze locking with Sophie's again as he offered her his hand and grinned at her like an idiot.

Was that a blush he saw on her cheeks as she shook his hand and smiled back at him?

"Lovely to see you again, Sophie," he said with a little bow of his head, before reluctantly releasing her hand from his.

"Good to see you too," Sophie said, still smiling and yes, definitely blushing.

Steven became aware that the others in the group had stopped talking and were looking at him and Sophie.

"You two know each other?" Dean said, raising an eyebrow at him.

Steven glanced at the others. Paula and Lainey were staring at Sophie in much the same way Dean was now looking at him.

"Yeah, Sophie," Lainey said. "How come you've kept this lovely guy a secret?"

Sophie glared at her friend who smirked back at her. "Yes, we know each other," she said. "And it's not a secret."

"Yes," Steven stepped in. "We met about a month ago." He looked at Sophie whose discomfort was obvious. "I see your glass is nearly empty. Why don't we go to the bar and I'll buy you a drink?"

"Good idea," Sophie said, looking relieved. She grabbed hold of his hand and indicated he should lead the way through the crowd.

Once he got over the shock of holding hands with Sophie, Steven couldn't resist looking back over his shoulder at the group they'd left behind. Yes, they were all staring after them.

"Thanks for the rescue," Sophie said as they arrived at the bar and she'd let go of his hand. "But I can take it from here. You don't really have to buy me a drink." Her expression was serious now and her earlier look of discomfort was back.

"I know I don't have to, but I would like to. And I hope you don't mind me saying so, but you look like you could do with one."

The sadness he saw in her lovely eyes as he returned her gaze made him want to take her in his arms, to stroke her hair and to soothe that sadness away. For a brief moment it felt as if there were only the two of them in the room.

He had to take a breath and clear his throat before speaking again. "So, what would you like?" he asked. Sophie now seemed miles away, a slight frown creasing her brow as she appeared lost in her thoughts. "Sophie," he said softly, leaning in towards her.

She gave a small jolt and looked up at him, looking into his eyes, then at his mouth and back into his eyes again. "What?" she said.

"Drink?" he said.

"Oh, yes, right. I'll have a chardonnay please."

"Okay," Steven said as the DJ started playing. "Why don't you go and grab that table for two in the corner, away from the noise."

"You can tell me it's none of my business," Steven said when he joined Sophie at the table and handed over her drink, "because it isn't really, but you don't seem all that happy to be here."

"God, is it that obvious?" Sophie took a gulp of wine.

"Not a party person?" Steven smiled at her.

"You could say that. I mean I'm not anti-social, not really, at least I didn't used to be. But now big groups, lots of people I don't know, making small talk ..." Sophie swept an arm round to indicate the room. "It's not where I really want to be."

"So why come?" The irony of his question wasn't lost on Steven given his own earlier reservations. Reservations he was now delighted he'd overcome.

"Lainey and Paula, they sort of forced me into it. Oh, don't get me wrong, they're my dearest friends. I know they have my best interests at heart and I know they think I need to get out more. They said it would do me good and I wanted to believe them but ..." Sophie fiddled with one of the beer mats as she looked down and frowned.

"But now you wish you hadn't let yourself be persuaded?"

Sophie sighed and gave him a wry smile. "Yeah, exactly. I'm a grown up after all. If I want to spend my spare time in my pyjamas, eating ice cream and binge-watching boxsets rather than being pressured into nights out where, and I quote, 'I might meet a handsome, sexy and available guy', then I should be left to do just that."

"Well, you've met me – again," Steven said grinning at her.

"And although modesty forbids me from claiming to be in the first two categories on your friends' list – I *am* available." Steven covered his face with his hand as Sophie laughed. He enjoyed the sound even as he squirmed in embarrassment. "And that wasn't meant to sound quite so needy."

Sophie reached across the table and patted his hand, "Aw, not to worry. No shame in being single but I'm sure there's a woman out there who will snap you up if that's what you want. Besides, scoring one out of three on the list isn't so bad." She laughed again.

"Ouch," Steven said, sitting back and crossing his hands over his heart. "I'm hurt." But he wasn't at all. He was enjoying seeing Sophie slowly relax, liked that she'd opened up to him about how she hadn't wanted to come to the party. He hoped he could find out more about this woman who was sitting across from him shaking her head in amusement.

"So how about you? Are you a party animal, Mr Available?" Sophie asked before downing the last of her wine.

"Eh, not exactly. Back in the day, yeah, but not so much now, not since …" He paused to take a mouthful of beer before continuing. "To tell you the truth I almost didn't come this evening either."

"So, why did you?"

"Dean – I wanted to be here for him. He's a mate, a good bloke, former comrade too, although we didn't meet while on active service. We actually met at Revive. He's done a lot of fundraising for the centre, but besides that, he's been one hell of a support to me as I've struggled to … to get my life back on track."

Sophie frowned. "Back on track?"

"Yeah, like I said, I was badly injured in Afghanistan. Handling the effects of that and adjusting back to civilian life, it's not been easy. And Dean, he's been there for me."

"I see," Sophie's voice was soft and the compassion in her lovely eyes made Steven swallow hard.

He reached for her hand and she linked her fingers with his as they looked into each other's eyes. "And I'm bloody glad I did come and that you did too. Because I haven't been able to get you out of my mind since that day at the centre."

Chapter Five

Sophie

Sophie couldn't quite believe how the evening was going. She felt dazed, her thoughts all over the place, and all that resolve she'd only recently found seemed to have packed up and gone.

In fact the only thing she was sure of was that Steven Jackson made her feel things she'd never felt before. He looked amazing in that blue shirt and she had to force herself to stop staring at how the muscles in his upper arms were stretching the shirt's sleeves to their limit. Then, when he held her hand and confessed how he hadn't been able to stop thinking about her since they'd met she'd been completely thrown. Her heartrate had gone into overdrive as she'd looked into his gorgeous eyes and then let her gaze fall to his mouth, his lovely and very kissable mouth, and all she could think about was how much she wanted to be in his arms.

"Oh," was all she was able to say in response to his confession.

"Indeed." Steven let go of her hand, sat back and sighed. He closed his eyes briefly before he spoke again. "Sorry, I didn't mean to blurt out what I've been feeling. Please, forget it." He drained his glass and looked as if he was about to get up. "You should probably rejoin your friends and I should probably just go."

"No!" Sophie's shout made several people look over at them.

She lowered her voice, "I'm sorry. You took me by surprise that's all. Truth is," she took a breath and couldn't believe what she was about to say, "Truth is I've been thinking about you too … a bit."

Steven visibly relaxed before letting out an exaggerated gasp. "Only a bit! And again I'm hurt," he said laughing.

"Well, okay then, maybe more than a bit." Sophie could scarcely recognise the sound of her own giggle. When was the last time she'd done that?

"That's encouraging," Steven said. "I actually thought you didn't like me that much, you know, after the abrupt ending to our meeting at Revive. I asked you to come to lunch with me and it seemed like you couldn't get away quick enough."

Sophie felt a deep blush of embarrassment as she recalled how she'd fled that day. "It was nothing personal. I just had to get back to the office. Sorry if I came across as you know …" Her voice trailed off. It didn't feel like the right time to tell him the truth, to tell him about how hearing about his injuries had overwhelmed her with memories of her brother.

"Hey, it's no big deal," Steven said. "Don't beat yourself up." He took a sip of his beer before continuing. "So, would you like to meet up sometime? We could go out to eat or catch a movie, or both?"

"Oh, I can't … that is I don't …" Sophie sighed, realising how torn she felt. She liked Steven, that much she had to admit, but that was her treacherous heart talking. "My last relationship, it didn't end well and I have other stuff going on too. In short, I'm not in an emotionally good place right now."

"I'm sorry to hear that. And the last thing I want to do is put more pressure on you. All I'm asking is to see you again, to spend a bit more time with you. What do you say?" His eyes, his beautiful eyes, looked deep into hers.

"I don't know. Maybe …"

"Look, why not give me your phone. I'll put in my number. You don't have to give me yours and then, after you've thought about it, you could get in touch and we could meet up."

"Well …" Sophie was tempted.

"Please," he said. "You've nothing to lose. It'll be your call. Pardon the pun."

Sophie couldn't help smiling back at him. She reached into her bag and opened up her phone at the contacts page before handing it to him. "Go on then. But I'm not making any promises."

Steven tapped his details into her phone, a huge grin on his face as he did so. When he handed the phone back to her another giggle escaped as she looked at the screen. "Mr Available – really? That's what you're calling yourself?"

"I'm Steven Jackson to everyone else, but to you I'm Available, Steven Available." He wiggled his eyebrows and his grin was the most beguiling it had been so far.

"Okay lady," a voice cut in. "You've had long enough hiding over here. Time to come and join the party." Sophie looked up to see a slightly inebriated looking Lainey standing over them. "And it's also time you spilled on why you didn't tell about meeting this gorgeous man. Though I can see why you'd want to keep him to yourself. Paula and I need to know *all* the details."

Sophie stood up, grabbed her bag and took Lainey's outstretched hand. She had to get Lainey away before she said any more embarrassing stuff. She mouthed 'sorry' at Steven who also got up. "Yeah," he said, "I should probably go and mingle a bit too."

For the rest of the evening she only got glimpses of Steven. She danced with Lainey and Paula and thanked her lucky stars as she did so that the music was so loud it made talking pointless. And between dances she managed to keep their brief chats on safe neutral territory – mainly because Paula's husband was sitting with them and Lainey kept disappearing to dance with any bloke she spotted on his own.

Sophie realised she'd probably drunk more than she should have. So, when the DJ took a break and the opening of the buffet was announced, she decided to get some food, hoping it might soak up some of the alcohol. It was while she was at the buffet table that she had a brief chat with Dean.

"Thanks for coming," he said as they waited in line.

"Thanks for inviting me, you really didn't have to, but I know Paula can be persuasive."

"She certainly can but I didn't need any persuading. I know how much you and Lainey mean to my wee sister and I wanted you to be here. I just hope you're enjoying yourself, although I have to say you certainly seemed to be enjoying talking to Steven."

Sophie could feel the blush flooding her cheeks. "Yes, it was good to meet up with him again. He seems very nice. We met at Revive. I was there as part of my job, researching for a programme the BBC is planning."

"Oh, yes," Dean said. "I've heard about the programme, been contacted by a colleague of yours actually to see if I'd be willing to take part, talk about my fundraising role."

"Ah, right, yes, I did ask Steven at our meeting to send in the names of benefactors who he thought might be willing to be part of the documentary. And as for Revive, I have to say I was really impressed with what I saw there when I visited."

"Hmm, I think Steven was really impressed with what he saw too."

"Oh no, it's nothing like that."

Dean raised a sceptical eyebrow. "If you say so. But going by how he was looking at you, it appears that for Steven it is very much 'like that.'"

Sophie cringed. "You were watching us – along with Lainey and Paula too I bet."

"Can you blame us? You announce you know each other and promptly disappear." Dean's smile was warm and teasing.

Sophie shook her head and smiled back at him. "Yeah, well, Steven could see I needed rescuing as soon as the fact that we'd already met was established. And I really needed to get away from my dear friends' scrutiny."

"I could see that," Dean said. "But for Lainey and Paula you scuttling off only—"

"Only added fuel to the fire of their curiosity."

"Exactly," Dean said. "For what it's worth and I know it's none of my business how you or Steven feel but I can say unreservedly Steven Jackson is one of the good guys."

"I'll bear that in mind," Sophie said, her plate now loaded up with food. As she turned to walk away, Dean had nodded and offered her a brief salute.

Noticing that Lainey was deep in conversation with the guy she'd had several dances with earlier, Sophie joined Paula and Martin who were already tucking into their own helpings from the buffet. She was relieved and grateful that Paula didn't return to the topic of Steven and had simply asked her if she was okay and if she was enjoying herself. Sophie had answered yes to both questions.

With the DJ taking a break and most people sitting eating, Dean took the opportunity to make a speech thanking everyone for coming and for his birthday gifts. His wife, Emma, then proposed a birthday toast.

After that, as the music began playing once again, it seemed to Sophie like a good time to leave. She was okay and she'd enjoyed herself but she suddenly felt exhausted. So she called the local taxi company before saying her goodbyes to Paula and Martin – who assured her they'd see Lainey safely home.

After collecting her coat from the cloakroom, she had a quick look round the function room before she left. Her heart lifted when she saw Steven looking back at her. He waved, before grinning and waving his phone at her.

Chapter Six

Steven

Steven felt optimistic and excited about the prospect of dating Sophie. His optimism was made even stronger when he reflected on the fact that a hidden link between them had brought them together again. It reinforced the 'meant-to-be' feeling he'd had since she'd walked into his workplace. Yes, he liked her. He liked her a lot. And he sensed she liked him too as they'd spent time together at the party.

He got it that she was reluctant to commit to anything, even a date, having recently come out of a relationship that she said ended badly. And then there was the unspecified other stuff she'd mentioned, something Dean alluded to when he phoned him a couple of days after the party 'just to check in with him' as his friend put it.

As well as thanking Steven for coming to his birthday celebration, something Dean again acknowledged had been out of Steven's comfort zone, Dean also mentioned Sophie. "You're a dark horse," he said. "Sophie told me at the party how you met through work at Revive. How come I didn't know that?"

"Like you just said," Steven replied. "It was work. There was nothing to report."

"Yeah, right," said Dean, and Steven could hear the smile in his voice. "Looked like more than that when you were reunited. You looked smitten, man."

"Yeah, well, even if that was true, she wasn't keen on taking things any further. She's getting over a breakup and she said there other things she's dealing with too."

"Right," Dean said, "but for what it's worth I'd say don't give up on her. From what I hear from my sister, Sophie has had a lot to contend with, and that's her story to tell, but I wouldn't say any of it would be a deal breaker. I definitely saw a spark there when she was with you."

"Hmm, I don't know about that," Steven said, wondering again what exactly it was Sophie had been through, what had caused that sadness he saw in her eyes. As he and Dean ended their call, he realised just how much he wanted to be there for her as she dealt with whatever was troubling her.

Oh yes, he'd got it bad.

At first he checked his phone often, at work, at home, first thing in the morning, last thing at night. But there was never any message from Sophie. Somehow he got through the week. Fortunately work was busy which helped a bit and by Friday he decided he wasn't going to hear from her. So when a couple of his colleagues asked if he fancied a pint or two after work on Friday evening, he said yes.

He tried to drown his sorrows and he also tried to take on board the advice from his well-meaning co-workers about plenty more fish and all that – after he drunkenly confessed what had made him such a grumpy git all week. But it didn't work. He woke late on Saturday morning with a very sore head and an equally aching heart.

He hauled himself into the shower and afterwards, as he drank a strong black coffee and looked out of his living room window at the park across the road, he wished he could go jogging. Going out for a run used to be his de-stress method of choice. But that was before. Now, although not impossible, it wasn't an easy option and he'd yet to investigate it fully. But he could go and punch out some of his disappointment and frustration.

So he grabbed his kit and set off for Revive's gym. At first as he hit the punchbag his primary aim was to push all thoughts of Sophie away, then his mind moved on to trying to accept that it was probably just as well she wasn't interested. He'd been kidding himself really.

He'd had girlfriends in the past. And, yes, he'd been out with a few women since his discharge from the army. But none of those relationships had lasted significant amounts of time. All of them had ended amicably and none had left him broken-hearted. Sure the lasting legacy of his injuries had the potential to be an issue for some prospective partners but so far that hadn't seemed to have been the case – or at least nobody had said so to his face. And he certainly wouldn't want to be with someone who judged him on that basis.

He was more than his wounds. Though, if he was honest with himself, there was also a small part of him that dreaded telling Sophie about them. What if, for her, it was a deal breaker?

But right then, Sophie didn't know the details of what had happened to his body, so it wasn't that which had put her off. It was clear he'd simply misjudged her level of interest in taking things further. End of. And with that, he slung a final few punches before quitting and heading home.

His muscles ached from the workout as he took his second shower of the day, but he did at least feel slightly better mentally. Sophie had been a lovely dream, a very pleasant but temporary fantasy of what might have been.

He managed to resist looking at his phone even when it beeped a couple of times as he put together some lunch. He hadn't looked at it since first thing and he decided that was best. If it was important, he knew that any of his contacts – be it his parents, friends or colleagues – would call him if there was anything they needed to say. Emails and text messages could wait.

After lunch he returned to the living room window for more thoughtful gazing. He watched as some local community council members built the bonfire for that evening's Guy Fawkes fireworks party. It was something he still had mixed feelings about – all that fire and loud bangs. He'd only been living in the flat for six months so this would be his first time in close proximity to such an event. It would certainly be a test of just how effective his PTSD therapy had been. He sighed as he turned away from the window.

He thought about ringing Dean or one of his other mates, seeing what they were up to, if they wanted to hang out. But then he thought that most of them would probably want to be spending time with their partners and their children. It was Saturday afternoon, family time for most of them, and he was thirty-three, not some teenager at a loose end.

Besides he didn't usually get bored at weekends. Normally after he'd done the necessary household chores and got some food shopping done, he'd listen to music or play a video game. He'd sometimes visit his parents, or even catch up on some work. And on a Saturday night he might go to the pub with whichever of his mates were free, or more often than not, he'd chill out with a takeaway, and a beer or two while watching some movie or travel series. But none of those things held much appeal that day.

He realised as he stood at his window that he really did want more. He also realised that he'd been subconsciously suppressing what his heart truly desired due to a fear that none of it would happen.

But since meeting Sophie it was as if he couldn't suppress his dreams any longer. His therapist would be proud if she knew and he could imagine her punching the air as he at last acknowledged that he owed it to himself, to the fact he'd survived, to follow his dreams.

Of course there were things he'd done before that he couldn't do now. Things like being able to go for a long cross-country trek without suffering for it afterwards or running marathons.

And although he lived in an ideally adapted flat, staying overnight with friends and family or going on holiday brought complications that had to be worked around. He could also only drive an adapted car. But he was okay with all that.

However, there were other things he hadn't truly given up on. He'd like to ride a bike, to learn to swim again, maybe even be able to dance at parties – not that he'd been much good at that before. And he'd like a job where he could be outdoors a lot of the time.

He also hoped that one day he'd find a woman who he could love and who would love him. He wanted children and he liked to think that one day *his* weekends would be taken up with family, just like his friends' weekends were.

Steven sighed as he slumped down on the sofa. He was an idiot, an overly romantic, overly optimistic idiot. Yes, he could have dreams and he could pursue them. And, okay, he might still meet someone who could be *the* one, but it clearly wasn't going to be Sophie. He allowed himself a bit of a wallow but then he reminded himself once again that he was lucky to be alive. And that, along with recommitting to pursuing his dreams, was more than enough.

Telling himself to get a grip, he got up and set about cleaning, tidying and doing some laundry. Next it was a trip to the super-market and, as it was around five o'clock by the time he got back, he grabbed himself a beer and flicked on the TV.

He'd just settled down on the sofa to watch the post football game analysis and catch the Scottish Premiership scores from that afternoon's matches when his phone rang.

He didn't recognise the number and thinking it was probably some scam caller he almost didn't accept the call. But when the phone continued to ring he pressed answer. "Yes? Who is this?" he barked.

"Hi," said a female voice. "I ... sorry ... is that Steven?"

Steven swallowed. "Yes, yes it is." His heart was hammering. He knew that voice.

"Oh good. I thought I'd reached Mr Angry rather than Mr Available, who come to think of it hasn't exactly been available today. Don't you ever check your messages?"

"Sophie?" he asked. Although he knew it was her.

"Yes, it's Sophie."

"You sent me a message?"

"Messages plural. But when they got no response I decided to give you one more chance and call you. Sorry if it's a bad time."

"No, it's good. It's a good time. Sorry about sounding angry there. I thought you were calling to tell me I owed thousands in income tax and you needed my bank details."

"That *is* one of the reasons I was calling, but I'll get to that in a moment." He could hear the smile in her voice and it made him smile too.

"Right," he said, as he too smiled.

"I was wondering if you weren't doing anything this evening if you'd like to maybe meet up?"

"Right, yeah …" His voice seemed to have all but disappeared and he had to pause and clear his throat.

"It's fine if you're busy, or if you don't fancy it. I was just thinking a drink maybe or something …"

"No, … that is no, I'm not doing anything. And yes, I'd like to meet up. I'd like that very much."

"Good, that's good," Sophie said. "So, do you fancy a drink or getting something to eat?"

"Either or both," Steven replied, his voice back to normal and a huge grin on his face. He moved back to stand at the window. It was dark outside now but he could see that the bonfire had been lit and families were already assembling in the park. "Actually," he said, "how do you fancy a bonfire and some fireworks first? It's all kicking off at my local park in about half an hour. Then afterwards we could grab that drink and some food."

"Okay, that sounds good. Can't remember the last time I was at a fireworks show."

"Great, I'm in Hyndland, near the Revive centre. I'll text you the address. It's a flat but I'll meet you at the stair door and the park's just opposite. Or I could pick you up if you like."

"No, no there's no need. I'm not that far away from you

actually, just across the river. I can walk it in fifteen minutes or so."

"That's great. Text when you're on the final approaches."

"Okay, I will. Oh, and just one more thing."

"Yeah?"

"I'm going to need those bank details." And with that she giggled and hung up.

Chapter Seven

Sophie

Sophie smiled a nervous smile as she read Lainey and Paula's 'good luck' and 'you go girl' messages sent just before she set off to walk to Steven's. The messages also included demands for a full report back the next day. They were almost more enthusiastic than she was. Almost.

It was down to her friends' persistence and encouragement that she was doing this. The previous evening, following several messages during the week, Sophie obeyed orders and went to meet Paula and Lainey at one of their local bars. She knew it was useless to argue when she got the text from Lainey telling her to be at the Dram Fine bar at 7.30pm that evening. Her friends would only turn up at the flat if she didn't show.

"Ah, here she is, the secret keeper, the writer of evasive texts, the avoider of calls," Lainey said, smiling as she nudged Paula.

"Good evening to you too," Sophie replied, laughing as she approached the booth where her two friends were sitting. A bottle of prosecco in an ice bucket had already been delivered to the table and Paula poured her a glass as she sat down.

"Okay," said Lainey as Sophie took her first sip of the fizzy stuff. "To the agenda for tonight's meeting." She mimed looking at list. "Oh, just the one item." She looked at Sophie and raised an eyebrow. "The matter of why Sophie Campbell did not share with her besties that she met a hot man a few weeks ago, a man she fancies and who fancies her."

Paula shook her head and smiled at Sophie as she said, "The case for the prosecution."

Sophie paused to take another sip of her drink before she replied with the speech she'd been rehearsing ever since the summons. "In my defence, there really was nothing to report. It was work. Remember I said I went to the Revive veterans charity, the one your brother has been involved with, Paula?"

"Yes," Paula confirmed.

"Steven's the manager there. So we met, talked shop. He seemed nice. But that was it."

Paula let out a gasp. "I asked my dear brother at the party how he knew Steven. He said he was a fellow ex-soldier. He never mentioned Revive. If he had I'd have made the connection."

"Anyway," said Sophie, just wanting to get the speech over with. "We had no reason to expect we'd ever meet again. So it was a surprise to see him at Dean's party. It would have been rude to ignore him so I didn't, and for a while we sat together and chatted. And that's it. Case closed." Sophie sat back and folded her arms. "Now can we please change the subject?"

Lainey wagged a finger at her. "So you expect us to believe that do you? That that's all there is to it? Because it seemed to Paula and me, and I'll bet everyone else who saw you two together at the party that the mutual attraction level was off the scale."

"No!" Sophie squirmed as she lied. This was too much. She looked towards the door. Could she make a run for it?

Paula rubbed her arm. "Hey, relax," she said. "Of course we can change the subject. I'd love to spend the next half hour sounding off about a bitch of a parent I had to deal with today. But before I do, and for what it's worth, what Lainey is *trying* to say in her assertive but well-meant way ..." Paula paused to give Lainey a meaningful look that got an eye roll and a stuck out tongue in return, "what she's trying to say, is Steven seemed like a great guy and we're guessing you thought so too. We'd love to think you might see him again, get to know him and you know ..."

"Oh, I know," Sophie said. "And I love that you both care. But we have no arrangement to meet again."

"What, nothing?" Lainey spluttered. "No exchange of contact details, no promises to call?"

Sophie felt the blush rising from her neck and making her cheeks burn. She knew it was futile to lie. "Eh, no, not exactly," she said.

"What does that mean?" Lainey narrowed her eyes.

"He gave me his number and he left it up to me if I wanted to contact him."

"Yes!" Lainey clapped her hands together. "Please tell us you're going to call him, arrange a hot date."

Sophie shook her head. "No, I … I can't. I'm not ready for a new relationship. Don't know if I ever will be." Sophie drank what was left in her glass.

"Woah," Lainey said, her voice softer now. "It's not about a relationship. Not yet anyway. All I'm saying is go for it. Go on a date with the guy. Have fun. I dare you."

As Sophie looked from Lainey to Paula, took in their expectant expressions, and realised how much her friends cared about her, she felt a sudden surge of optimism, of daring even. Nobody was more surprised than her when she said, "Okay, you're on. I'll contact him tomorrow."

As soon as she ended the call to Steven, Sophie messaged Lainey and Paula to let them know she'd fulfilled the dare. She then scrambled to get ready. She knew it was her own fault that she was rushing. She really should have contacted Steven earlier but it had taken her all day to work up to it.

She did one last check in the hallway mirror before putting on her quilted jacket. She decided that her hair, which she was wearing loose, and her makeup were fine. She looked okay in her smartest jeans and navy sweater. |In fact she looked more than okay, she looked good.

But then, as she stepped out of her flat and headed downstairs, her enthusiasm started giving way to nervousness.

What had she been thinking? Had she really asked Steven out on a date? She took a deep breath. No, she hadn't. It wasn't a date. She was done with dating. It was two new friends meeting up to watch fireworks and grab a bite to eat. Nothing more.

He was standing under a streetlight and she spotted him waving as she turned the corner. She waved back.

"You found me then?" he said, grinning at her when she arrived in front of him.

"I found you," she said, smiling too at how those words sounded and realising he looked even better than she remembered. It was a cold night and she was glad of her warm sweater and cosy jacket. So she knew that the shiver she felt as they stood under the stars looking at each other was down to anticipation and not the weather.

He offered her his hand. "Shall we?" he said, nodding in the direction of the park.

She slipped her hand into his and even though they were both wearing gloves, she liked how it felt there. She did, however, notice a slightly strange rhythm in the way he walked but she put that down to unfamiliarity.

They joined the crowd around the bonfire. It seemed like most of the neighbourhood had turned up. There were people of all ages, some in groups, some couples. There were dads with toddlers on their shoulders, mums urging slightly older children not to run off, and grandparents sharing out sweets. Her being here too with Steven made Sophie smile into the darkness.

They watched the bonfire for no more than a couple of minutes before Steven said, "Do you fancy a hot chocolate? There's a stall over there." He took a couple of steps in the direction of the stall as he spoke.

Sophie wondered if she was imagining it but he seemed a bit on edge. Whereas she enjoyed looking into the tall flames and breathing in the smell of the woodsmoke while listening to the wood crackling as it burned, she was aware of a restlessness in

Steven. He seemed unable to stand still and kept looking away from the bonfire and when she tried to get a bit closer to it, he hung back and muttered, "Here's fine."

She thought it was either he didn't like crowds, he was nervous or regretful about meeting up, or she was indeed imagining it. But he seemed fine at Dean's rather crowded party, he'd definitely been keen to see her again and when they met just a few minutes earlier he'd appeared genuinely pleased to see her.

So, she decided that she was imagining it and said, "Ooh, a hot chocolate sounds good. I'll come with you."

"Great," Steven said before turning away and setting off so quickly she thought she might have to run to keep up. And there it was again, that slightly strange gait he had when walking.

Once they both had their hot drinks, Steven led the way over to a bench beside what looked like the main path through the park judging by how broad and well-lit it was. The bench also had its back to the bonfire. "Is this okay?" Steven asked. He ran a hand across his brow as if wiping sweat away which was weird on a such a cold night. "Just thought it would be nice to sit down." He cleared his throat.

No, Sophie thought revising her earlier decision that she was imagining it. He really did seem tense. She sat down beside him. For a few moments, they sipped their drinks in silence. Then a huge cheer went up from the crowd and several loud bangs went off, followed by fizzing and whistling sounds filling the air. Sophie jumped to her feet and turned round, before stepping away from the bench. She looked up as lots of bright sparkling colours exploded in the sky beyond the bonfire. The first volley was followed by several more. It was spectacular. "Wow!" she said, turning and expecting to see Steven at her side. "Isn't it—"

But he wasn't at her side. He was still on the bench, his paper cup leaking hot chocolate while he hunched over.

"Steven," Sophie said, immediately going over to him. He didn't look up. She laid her own cup on the arm of the bench before bending down and putting a hand on his shoulder. "Are you all right?"

He recoiled from her touch, lifting a hand as if to protect himself. She took a step back. "Steven?"

Slowly he sat up and turned to face her and there was just enough light for Sophie to make out the pallor and the sheen of sweat on his face. "Sorry," he said. "This was a bad idea. I shouldn't have … I shouldn't have come." He pushed himself to his feet and appeared to steady himself before adding, "I need to go home."

"Okay," Sophie said. "I'm sorry you feel that way." She took both their cups and dumped them in a nearby bin as her mind whirled at this rather rapid brush off. "Better you realise it now, I suppose." Steven's hand was over his mouth. He wasn't going to throw up, was he? "I guess I'll be going then." She turned to walk away.

"No!" Steven's voice boomed out. "Please, don't go."

Okay this was getting weirder by the minute. She stopped and looked back at him. "But you—"

"Please, I can explain." He walked towards her. "Come back with me to my flat. I just … I need to get indoors."

"I don't know. I'm not sure I …"

"Or the pub, we can go to the pub if you prefer …"

Sophie thought for a moment. Her first impressions of this man had been good, okay, more than good. She'd seen him at work. He was a friend of Dean's. It was her who had contacted him. Her gut told her he could be trusted. Or was that her feckless heart?

"Look, if you're feeling unwell you shouldn't be going to the pub. You should go home. So should I. But I could call someone, Dean maybe …"

It was then that a second round of fireworks were let off. Sophie could have sworn she saw Steven flinch. Was that fear she saw on his face? "I promise I'm not ill," he said. "But I do have to go." He reached into his pocket and took out his wallet. "I can see you home in a taxi. I'll pay."

"I can get myself home and I don't need you to pay." Sophie

tried and failed to keep the annoyance she was beginning to feel out of her voice. Steven raised his hands in a surrender gesture as more fireworks exploded overhead. He began walking away from her, heading back towards the park gates. "Text me when you get home. Then feel free to block me if that's what you want." And with that he picked up the pace.

"Wait," she called as she ran after him. "Steven, wait, I'm coming with you." He nodded to show he'd heard her but he didn't slow down.

It only took a few minutes to get back to his flat, a few minutes during which neither of them spoke. Sophie sensed that Steven wasn't able to hold a conversation right at that moment especially as he seemed to be finding it hard to breathe. She wondered if he was asthmatic and if so why he didn't have an inhaler on him.

She followed him into his tenement block and in through the door to his ground floor flat. Steven didn't even stop to close the front door behind them so Sophie did it for him. She followed the now agonised sound that was coming from the room on the left of the hallway. She found Steven sitting on a sofa in the dark, his head in his hands, his breathing still coming in gasps but it was slower and quieter now and he seemed to be focussed on deliberately easing it. She spotted a lamp on a side table and switched it on before sitting down beside him. He still looked pale but the earlier sweating seemed to have stopped.

"Can I get you anything?" she said.

Steven took a couple of controlled deep breaths before replying. "No, thank you, I'm … I'm good." He gave a slight smile before leaning back, his eyes closed and his head tipped towards the ceiling. The fireworks were still going off but they sounded much more distant now.

As she watched him, Sophie could see Steven start to relax and his colour coming back to his face. It was only then she realised what she'd just witnessed.

"Thank goodness for double glazing," Steven said as he opened his eyes and sat up.

"Yeah," Sophie said gently. "That way the volume of the loud bangs is reduced and they don't cause a panic attack."

"You guessed, then?" Steven said.

"Took me a while but I got there in the end."

"I'm so sorry," Steven said. "I thought I could do it, cope with the flames and the bangs but seems I was wrong. It felt like I was back there, back in Afghanistan, back at the … the explosion."

"There's no need to apologise." Sophie reached for his hand and squeezed it. "It was brave of you to even consider it knowing it could prove difficult."

"Don't know about brave," Steven said, leaning back. "Stupid more like." He began hitting his forehead with the heel of his hand. "Stupid, stupid, stupid."

"Hey," Sophie said softly, catching hold of his hand. "Stop beating yourself up." And when he turned back to look at her, he seemed so sad that she just wanted to hold him. "Would … would a hug help?" she asked.

A small smile played on Steven's lips, on his lovely just-asking-to-be-kissed lips. "I think it might," he said.

She moved closer and put her arms around him and he responded by gathering her up in his. She breathed in the wonderful masculine scent of him, enjoyed the feel of his hard chest pressing against her and had to remind herself that she was supposed to be comforting him not imagining what it would be like to have her face pressed against his skin rather than his sweater.

"It's okay," she said, giving him a squeeze, "it's okay."

Chapter Eight

Steven

He wouldn't have blamed her if she'd left him in the park but he was so glad she hadn't. It was great that she was still with him let alone being so kind and understanding.

But being held and comforted by Sophie was a form of sweet torture for Steven. Being this close to her, feeling her hair brush against his face, feeling her breasts pressed against his chest as she stroked his back in a soothing and friendly gesture, well it wasn't quite having the effect she probably intended. The panic attack had passed, his months in therapy were working, but now his body was aroused in a quite different way. Once again he was struggling to get his breathing under control, only for very different reasons.

Sophie pulled back and looked up at him. "You sure you're okay?" she asked. "Only you seem to be … that is your breathing, it still seems to be …"

For a moment her beautiful eyes looked into his. She bit her lower lip in an almost irresistible way before running her tongue across it. Could she see what he was thinking? Did she want him to kiss her as much as he wanted to do it? No, he was kidding himself. Of course she didn't want him to kiss her. She'd just seen him at his most pathetic. She was just being kind. He moved out of her arms and stood up. "I'm fine, really, I am." He ran a hand over his head before rubbing at the back of his neck.

"Thanks again for coming back with me. You must think I'm a right screw up. And I'm sure this isn't what you had in mind when you got in touch so, please …" he held his arm out in the direction of the door, "don't feel you have to stay."

Sophie frowned at him as she too got to her feet. "Don't presume to know what I'm thinking or feeling because you're wrong." She sounded well pissed off.

"Sorry, I—"

"Stop apologising! Stop doing yourself down!"

"Okay, I—"

"No, listen to me," Sophie said holding a hand up as she ordered him to be quiet, "and I'll tell you what I'm thinking and feeling. I'm thinking you're an incredibly brave man and not only because you were a soldier. It's way more than that. You're incredibly brave to have fought back after being injured. Not only have you had to recover from whatever physical injuries you suffered, you're also having to cope with the mental scars too, all while doing a great job at Revive and getting on with your life. But you know the most amazing thing?"

"No," Steven looked down at the floor, his voice sounding hoarse and his mouth feeling dry as he spoke.

"You're not afraid to let your vulnerability show. It must have been hard for you deciding to go to the bonfire knowing what the sights and sounds could trigger but you did it anyway. And when the worst happened you handled it."

Steven felt both embarrassment and relief all at once. "Right. So I'm amazing, am I?" He allowed himself to look up again and he saw tears in Sophie's eyes. Eyes that were now looking directly into his.

"Yes, Steven, yes you bloody well are," she said as a tear ran down her cheek.

"Hey," Steven said. "Please don't cry. Not on my account." He stepped nearer to her before lifting a hand to her face and gently wiping away her tear. He wasn't sure but it seemed as he did so that she leaned her face against his hand.

She put her hands on his shoulders and was once again pressed against him. She tipped her head back to look at him. He saw uncertainty in her eyes but then she looked as if she'd made a decision as she said softly, "Can I ask you for a favour?"

"Anything," he said his voice hoarse again.

"Kiss me."

He didn't need to be asked twice. He smiled at her. "I think I can oblige," he said as his fingers tangled in her hair and he pressed his lips to hers. Her hands moved around the back of his neck as he kissed her and she most definitely kissed him back. He didn't know how long they stood there, their mouths joined, tongues and lips exploring. It was Sophie who ended it. He felt her move back a tiny bit and her lips curved upwards against his.

He opened his eyes to look once again into hers. She was looking right back at him a wide grin on her face.

"Was that okay … are you okay?" he asked.

She nodded, still grinning away. "Best kiss ever," she said.

He laughed. "Is that so?" he said, resisting the urge to punch the air. "I was just thinking the same thing."

"Really? That's good," she said with a mischievous smile. "But I do have one complaint …"

"Oh you do. And what would that be?" Steven asked, still holding her in his arms.

"You promised me food and drink earlier and so far I'm not seeing any evidence of either." She raised an eyebrow at him and her slight pout just made him want to kiss her again.

"Yeah," he said. "I admit I seem to have got a bit distracted. But I'm not sure I can take all the blame for that."

"Okay, whatever." Sophie rolled her eyes as she giggled and stepped out of his embrace. She glanced over her shoulder at the living room doorway. "Kitchen, fridge and wine that way, are they?"

Steven did his best to ignore the effect that giggle was having on him and resisted the need he felt to grab hold of her, take her back to the sofa, and to finish what that kiss had started. "Eh, yes, just across the hall. But you sit," he said, indicating the sofa. "I'll get us drinks and there's some takeaway menus on the coffee table. Have a look and see what you fancy."

This time Sophie's laugh came out as a small snort as she wiggled her eyebrows at him.

"Right," Steven said clearing his throat before saying any more. "Drink? I have wine, white or red, beer, and I think there's some whisky in the—"

"A white wine, please," Sophie said.

Fifteen minutes later they were sitting side by side on the sofa once more. Their pizzas were ordered, they were enjoying their drinks, and Steven was just about coping with the force that was Sophie. He took longer in the kitchen than was necessary when getting Sophie's wine and a beer for himself. He needed a moment to regain some control over his emotions. In the short time since they got back to the flat, he'd gone from overwhelming terror to almost overwhelming sexual desire, to amusement and back to that sexual desire again. While he knew he could handle the terror, deeply unpleasant as it was, he wasn't nearly so sure he could handle his feelings for Sophie. She was amazing and he was falling – falling hard and fast. But if this evening was going to lead anywhere, there was something else he needed to share with her before they moved beyond that first kiss, if they ever did.

He decided to leave it for now though as he wanted to continue to enjoy her company for as long as possible. If this was going to be his only time with her he was determined to make the most of it. So he was happy to chat with her about how the preparations for the documentary on Revive as well as the rest of the now fully commissioned series were progressing. This led to asking her to tell him more about her job at the BBC.

He loved watching her as she talked. He loved watching her eat. He loved how relaxed she looked sitting cross-legged on his sofa as they laughed and chatted.

It was around ten-thirty when she got to her feet. He offered her a coffee but she refused saying she'd never sleep if she had coffee now. He had to stop himself from saying the last thing he wanted her to do was sleep.

"It's time I was going anyway," she said. "I ordered a cab earlier when you were clearing away our plates. It should be here any minute."

To say he was disappointed didn't begin to cover it but he knew this was for the best. Yeah right. He stood up too. "Okay, good," he said. "Good that you've ordered a cab that is, not that you're leaving. I don't want you to leave, although it's fine, of course, you can leave … sorry …" he paused, aware he was rambling like an idiot.

"Hey," Sophie said, coming up to him. She stroked his face with her hand. "It's fine. I've enjoyed our time together very much, although I'm sorry going to the bonfire caused you distress. Thank you for the pizza and the wine … and the kiss."

They stood for a moment, looking at each other. Steven wondered if she might be going to kiss him again and when she didn't make a move he wondered if he should take the initiative this time. It was the sound of the door buzzer that spared him from making a decision. He grabbed the intercom handset and told the cab driver his passenger was on her way before turning to Sophie who had joined him in the hallway. "So, thanks for coming tonight and for not … for not running when things got a bit weird with me."

Sophie put a finger to his lips. "Things didn't get weird. Things got honest and I like that." She then replaced her finger with her mouth and he got lost in yet another of those awesome kisses. When she broke away, she put her hand on his chest and looked into his eyes. "Thank you for this evening," she said. She stepped past him, pulled open the front door and stepped out into the corridor. "Call me when you're ready and we can arrange to meet up again."

Chapter Nine

Sophie

When she reflected on it the following day, Sophie didn't quite know what to make of her date with Steven. The first factor contributing to her confusion was that word 'date'. When had them meeting up officially become a date?

She'd spent the whole week after Dean's party fighting her reservations but she'd not been able to get him out of her head. Her resolve not to start a new relationship had begun to waver even before her friends' intervention.

Then not only did she give in and call him, but she also went on to ask him to kiss her. Then at the end of their evening together when she'd told him to call her, it seemed her resolve was gone completely.

She was glad she hadn't let him push her away when he had the panic attack and she meant it when she said that she'd enjoyed their time together. She was also sure the feelings of attraction were mutual.

The truth was she had no regrets, especially about kissing him, indeed she'd been tempted to take things further and struggled to walk away. It was only due to the remaining small but sensible voice in her head that she'd been able to do so and, she had to admit, she really liked Steven. She wasn't put off or in any way daunted by his PTSD. In fact his openness and honesty about it only increased her admiration of him. After her experience with Rick, honesty, or rather the lack of it, would always be a deal breaker for her.

So where did that leave her? Where did it leave her and Steven? At first, she hoped it left them on the brink of something good, something that could be casual but fun, that would run its course and leave neither of them with any regrets. So she began by hoping he would call her and that they'd take it from there.

But over the next couple of days the doubts returned and Sophie wondered if she was being fair, fair to herself and fair to Steven.

Surely she owed it to herself to stick to the no new relationship rule. She really shouldn't be putting herself at risk like this – the risk of losing anyone else. Then there was the chance she'd be leaving Glasgow, going for a new job and a fresh start hundreds of miles away.

But even more than that, wasn't risking Steven's wellbeing by getting into a relationship with him a really selfish thing to do? Not only was she not looking for anything serious, and he might be, but she also came with so much emotional baggage. Didn't Steven deserve better?

And on it went until she couldn't stand it any longer. It was about the middle of the following week when she had a word with herself.

First of all, she resolved to stop checking her phone every five minutes for a missed call or text from Steven. There weren't any. That was probably a message in itself. The message being that Steven had reservations just as she had and he was going to respect those reservations.

Secondly, it was time to share. After ignoring the first lot of text messages from Lainey and Paula wanting to know all the details of how Saturday had gone, she decided it was time to respond. She tried to keep her replies non-committal but her friends were having none of it.

So, knowing the girls had her best interests at heart despite their insatiable nosiness, and that it would be good to get their take on how she was feeling, she asked both of them round for a girls' night-in on the Thursday evening.

"You asked him to kiss you!" Lainey screeched when the three of them were settled down in Sophie's living room and armed with wine and snacks. Sophie had just shared that part. She didn't give them all the details about Steven's reaction to the fireworks but she did share everything else about how the evening had gone, including how much she liked him, and including that first kiss.

"Yes, I did, I asked him and he did it. He kissed me. And later we kissed some more. And I got the feeling he liked it as much as I did."

"But that was it?" Paula said. "It didn't go … you didn't go any further?"

"No, no further," Sophie said. "Not that I didn't want it to. I'm … He's…" Sophie shrugged in desperation as she struggled to express how she felt.

"Hot?" Paula said, laughing.

"With a sexy smile and you fancy the pants off him," Lainey added.

"Yeah, that." Sophie laughed too as she blushed.

"So, why didn't you, you know, have your wicked way with him?" Lainey asked, wiggling her eyebrows.

"I don't know." Sophie sighed. "I think maybe we shouldn't go there."

"What?" said Paula.

"Yes, what?" Lainey repeated. "Let's get this straight. You like him. He likes you. Not only that, you fancy each other as well. You're both single. You've been on a date. You've kissed. But you don't think you should pursue it. Why the hell not?"

"What she said," Paula added, nodding in Lainey's direction as she fixed her gaze on Sophie.

"I…" Sophie sighed again. "It's complicated, after Rick—"

"After Rick, you need to move on," Paula spoke gently. "Not all men are like him. Don't let Rick spoil your future."

"And nothing's guaranteed but it seems Steven is worth taking a risk on," Lainey said.

"Maybe, but maybe it's me, me who's the risk for Steven. He's been through a lot, you know. He has PTSD from when he was injured in Afghanistan."

Both her friends nodded sympathetically. "Poor guy," said Paula.

"Is he getting help with that?" Lainey asked.

"He's had therapy and he says most of the time he has it under control and he knows how to cope when it overwhelms him." Sophie paused for a moment wondering if she should say more.

Of course Lainey noticed. "What?" she said. "Did something happen when you were with him?"

Sophie told them all of it. The visit to the bonfire, Steven's response to the fireworks going off and then the aftermath. Her friends both agreed with her that going to the event in the park had been a brave thing for Steven to do, and that it had been even braver of him to open up to Sophie.

"But what I don't get," said Paula, "is why him having PTSD makes you think you'd be a risky proposition for him?"

"Because I'm an emotional basket case. There's the grief thing and there's the Rick thing. I'm over Rick in the good riddance sense, but I'm not over how he treated me. Steven deserves someone who's strong and calm and sorted."

"Sounds like you displayed all three when he needed you to," Paula said. "It also seems like he was willing to take the chance and go to the fireworks because he was going with you."

"So maybe you could look at it another way," said Lainey. "Maybe you'd be good for each other."

"Hmm, maybe," Sophie said. "But lately I've come to the conclusion I don't want a serious relationship or marriage or any of that. I really think I'm better off single. And besides that I might be moving down south in the new year, there are openings at the BBC coming up in Bristol. So starting a relationship, even if that's what I wanted, would be stupid."

Lainey shot a wide-eyed look at Paula, a look that Paula returned. "Okay," Lainey said, dragging out the word as she turned her attention back to Sophie. "There's a lot there in what you just said, and believe me, we'll address your desire for permanent singlehood along with you moving away at a later date. But for now, as regards you and the lovely Steven, you're jumping ahead a bit, aren't you? It's early days and it doesn't have to be all heavy and serious and tied into long-term commitment. You could just relax and enjoy it in a, you know, light-hearted way."

Paula nodded her agreement before saying to Sophie, "Anyway, leaving the long-term to one side, how did you leave things with Steven at the end of the night?"

"I told him to call me which was stupid in view of what I've just said. Anyway he hasn't called and I can see now, even though I like him a lot, that it's for the best." Sophie shrugged, trying to look as if it didn't matter.

"It's only been a few days," Lainey said.

"Yeah," Paula added, "I bet he'll be in touch before the weekend, desperate to see you again. You should definitely say yes. Go out with him, take things slow, don't make any big decisions yet, just see how it goes. Have some fun!" Paula lifted her hands and shrugged her shoulders as if to show what she was suggesting was no big deal.

"And if he doesn't call," said Lainey, "you could actually call him. Find out what he's thinking, take it from there."

After her evening with her two friends, two wonderful friends who always had her back and who she realised she was very fortunate to have, Sophie felt a lot better, could see things more clearly, could take herself a little less seriously.

There was no doubting that she really liked Steven. She enjoyed his company and he seemed to be one of the good guys. Maybe they could have a just-for-fun relationship. Maybe they could indeed be good for each other while it lasted. Her possible move to Bristol was six months away so why not enjoy that time.

It would be silly to put her life on hold on the basis of something that might never happen.

So she resolved to keep an open mind. If he called her, she would agree to another date. As she mulled all of this over she realised she was smiling. She was feeling something she hadn't felt for some time. Hope.

But then as the weekend passed followed by the whole of the following week, and she still hadn't heard from him, her hope began to wear thin. It seemed the optimism she'd felt after talking things through with Paula and Lainey was fragile at best and it wasn't long before she was beating herself up for being such an idiot.

She was also baffled. Steven had made the first move, said he liked her. In spite of that he hadn't put pressure on her and he'd left it to her to initiate their first date. He'd seemed reasonable and trustworthy. But then after their date, when she in turn left it to him to get touch about a second one, he blanked her. One date and he'd changed his mind.

She really was so stupid when it came to men. She hadn't seen Rick for what he was until it was too late. Then with Steven she'd deluded herself once more and left herself open to being hurt all over again.

Enough was enough. She had to stop this now. Without pausing to think about it some more, she grabbed her phone and blocked Steven's number.

Chapter Ten

Steven

Two weeks had passed since Steven spent that eventful evening with Sophie. Two weeks since she asked him to call her. Two weeks during which she was never far from his thoughts – thoughts about how kind and understanding she'd been, thoughts about those kisses, and thoughts about how much he wanted to take things further with this beautiful, sexy and caring woman.

He felt a glimmer of hope when they'd met again and spent some time together at Dean's party, and he acted on it, encouraging her to call him and arrange a date. But maybe it had been a selfish thing to do. He'd a like serious relationship – one day. But that was the point. The time wasn't right yet.

He wasn't yet completely healed – part of him would never be – and not only in the way she already knew about. He was coming terms with that but could Sophie? It was true she'd been great about the PTSD so maybe it *was* reasonable to expect she'd be okay with the rest.

Or maybe his dreams should remain just that, dreams, and he should continue with the more realistic plan A and stick with casual for the foreseeable. Would Sophie be up for that? Even if she was, could he keep it casual? So his thoughts went on. Round and round getting nowhere. He was well and truly stuck. He couldn't bring himself to hope but he also couldn't bring himself to give up. And so he did nothing.

* * *

As he'd done on that Saturday morning two weeks before when he'd been waiting for a call from Sophie, he tried diverting his thoughts with chores and shopping. But the diversionary tactics didn't work and all the second-guessing he was subjecting himself to was doing his head in.

It was as he was putting away his grocery shopping just before lunchtime that his phone rang.

"Dean, hi," he said. "What can I do for you?"

"Call her. That's what you can do." His friend sounded grumpy.

"Sorry?"

"Just call her, call Sophie, and get my sister off my back."

"Okay, but …"

He heard Dean sigh. "Look, I know it's none of my business but it's Paula, she's been on at me to speak to you. It seems Sophie's been expecting a call from you, something about a date you two went on recently, and since then nothing."

"Ah, right," said Steven, guilt pricking at him.

"So it's true then? I thought maybe Paula got it wrong. Two sides to every story and all that."

"Yes, it's all true." It was Steven's turn to sigh.

"Want to talk about it?"

"No … yes … maybe."

Dean chuckled. "Right, that's decisive. Should I stay on the line?"

Steven took a deep breath. When he was finished telling Dean the whole story and had shared how he felt about Sophie along with his reservations about taking things further, he already felt a bit better. He knew what he had to do.

"Do it, mate," Dean said as if reading his mind. "Tell her everything. She deserves to know what you're thinking and she deserves to have her say too. One thing I know about you, you're not a quitter. You have to see this through, even if this thing between you isn't going anywhere, it's not fair on either of you to leave things hanging."

"Yeah, you're right. I'll call her and thanks, mate. I needed this kick up the backside."

"Yeah, you did. But besides that, I kind of feel responsible for you two." Steven could hear Dean's smile in his voice.

"Responsible, how?"

"Well it was my party that brought you together, without that your paths might never have crossed again after your first meeting."

"That's true," Steven said, also smiling now.

"So what are you waiting for? Bugger off and call her." With that Dean ended the call.

Muttering to himself that there was no time like the present, and with only the slightest hesitation, Steven pressed the call icon beside Sophie's number. But once connected, the call went straight to voicemail. He lost count of the number of times he tried again. It was the next morning, after several more failed attempts, that he had to admit that his initial suspicion was correct. It felt like a punch in the gut. Sophie had blocked his number.

His anger at himself for messing things up threatened to overwhelm him and he'd just decided to go to the gym to work off some of the adrenalin coursing through him when his phone rang.

When he saw who it was he almost didn't pick up, but he knew he couldn't avoid this particular caller indefinitely.

"What?" he growled into his phone.

"And hello to you too," Dean said with a chuckle. "Someone sounds cross."

"Sorry, mate. It's me, I'm an idiot and I'm angry with myself. Was just about to head to the gym to take it out on the punchbag."

"Has this got anything to do with Sophie by any chance? I was calling to check. Did you call her?"

"Only about a hundred times. No luck. Seems she's blocked me. Can't say I blame her."

"Ah, right. I'm sorry to hear that but don't be too hard on yourself."

"Why not? It was … she was …" Steven sighed. "Sophie was the best thing to happen to me in … in forever, and I was too scared to tell her that and to give us a chance."

"Maybe she'll change her mind. You never know."

"Why would she do that? No, it's over, over before it even started."

"Yeah, well, I suppose all I'm saying is maybe don't give up on her yet."

"Whatever." Steven was back to growling. He took a breath, reminded himself that Dean was being a supportive friend. "Look I appreciate you calling and you know, being on my side, but I really need to get to the gym. So if there's nothing else—"

"Well there is actually. Emma's out with a couple of her friends this evening, the kids are both away on sleepovers, so since I suspect you're free this evening I thought you and me could go out too, get a couple of drinks, grab a bite to eat and have a talk about things."

"I don't know, mate," Steven said not feeling at all sociable. "I'm not—"

"It's not optional," Dean said. "It's for your own good. So I'll see you at 7.30 at the Trattoria and I'll be round to break your door down if you don't turn up."

"Okay, okay," Steven knew when he was beaten and he found himself smiling as he gave in. Lorenzo's Trattoria was a local Italian restaurant and a favourite of his. Yes, Dean knew exactly what he was doing. "I'll be there for the drinks and the food but no promises about the talking thing."

Taking it out on the punchbag at the gym that afternoon helped with the anger he felt towards himself. But he still felt regret and embarrassment at not having contacted Sophie, along with sadness that he'd not be seeing her again.

Nevertheless, during the short taxi ride to the restaurant,

Steven found he was looking forward to the evening out. He hadn't been out socially for the last fortnight and meeting up with Dean would give him a chance to not only get out of the flat but also to get out of his own head – and stop torturing himself about Sophie.

The booth arrangement in the Trattoria meant he couldn't see if Dean was there yet when he gave his friend's name to the waiter who greeted him. The waiter led him to the table and stood to one side to let Steven sit down.

Steven was frozen to the spot. "Sophie?"

Sophie was seated in the booth frowning at her phone. She looked up when she heard his voice. "Steven?" She looked and sounded as surprised as he was. But before he could say anything his own phone buzzed in his pocket. It was a message from Dean.

Sorry, mate, it's a setup and no, I won't be joining you. Paula's idea when she heard Sophie had blocked you and I agreed with my sister that it was time you two got talking. Enjoy your meal.

"What the hell?" Steven said as he reread the text before turning his attention back to Sophie.

She waved her phone at him. "I'm going to murder Paula," she said, but her frown had been replaced by a hint of a smile. "She called earlier, said her husband has a bad cold and had bailed on a dinner date they had here with Dean and his wife. She persuaded me to come along in Martin's place – told me to give Dean's name if I got here first as he'd made the booking. Seems apart from the booking part, the rest was all a big fat lie."

Steven grinned as he thought about his friend's trickery. "And I'm torn between wanting to murder Dean and wanting to thank him. May I?" he said, indicating the seat opposite Sophie.

"Yeah," she said, shrugging.

"Everything is okay?" said the rather puzzled and concerned

looking waiter. After they'd both assured him that it was, he gave them menus, took their drink orders and left them to it.

At first they'd chatted rather awkwardly about work and other safe topics. It wasn't until they'd got their drinks and placed their food order that Steven took a gulp of his beer followed by a deep breath and began the conversation they really needed to have.

"I'm sorry I didn't call you," he said. "It's not that I didn't want to."

"Really?" Sophie looked both sceptical and cross.

"Yes, really. I was being a coward about … about stuff. Then Dean got on the case and pointed out I wasn't being fair to you and that I should tell you about my doubts and concerns about us taking things any further." Steven paused to take a breath as Sophie's intense expression changed to one of hurt.

"Right," she said, before looking away.

He reached for her hand but she pulled it away. "I did call you, in the end, after I spoke with Dean. I called lots of times yesterday and earlier today but the calls never got through."

"I blocked you. Seems I was right to do so." Sophie took a gulp of her wine. "And this … this is a bad idea." She grabbed her bag and jacket and was about to get up.

"No, Sophie, please don't go. You've every right to be angry—"

"Yes, yes I do. All you had to do was call like you said you would. You could have explained and I'd have understood. But instead you left me dangling." Sophie sat back. "Look, I get it, I do. You were right to have doubts. I had them too. I'm a mess and I don't have a good track record with relationships." She sighed, her expression full of regret. "I don't know," she continued, "Maybe if we'd met at another time … maybe then—"

It was then Steven had a moment of clarity. Sophie was thinking the same way he had. She was thinking it was the timing of their meeting each other that was off. But what if … "Maybe there's no right time. Maybe there's just an opportunity here and now and it's down to us to take it or not." Steven reached across the table and took her hand in his. For a moment Sophie looked down at their interlaced fingers and he could he feel her tensing, but when she didn't pull away, Steven took that as an encouraging sign. "I want to be with you, Sophie. I think we could be good together. And although some of my PTSD symptoms still linger, I am getting better, and it was great that you weren't fazed by my difficulties at the bonfire. But—"

"I told you I admired how you dealt—"

"Yeah, yeah I know," Steven said. "But there's other stuff … stuff that happened to me in Afghanistan when the IED went off. I've come to terms with the changes that it's meant, and none of it is going to stop me living my life. But I also know it's only fair to share the full extent of my injuries with you before we go any further as it might change how you think of me."

"Okay," Sophie said, looking concerned now. "So why didn't you just come out and say it, call me and tell me the full story and take it from there?"

Steven sighed. "Because, I guess, I'm a bit of a mess too. I dreaded telling you, dreaded that it would put you off me and I was scared at the prospect of not seeing you again, so I chickened out, put off calling you, left you … left *us* in limbo." He saw her shoulders relax and then she was looking into his eyes, a slight smile twitching at her lips.

"So we're two messes who, if we did get together, could make one big mess," she said.

"Or maybe we could clear up each other's mess and start afresh." Steven smiled as he stroked the back of her hand with his thumb and gazed into her beautiful eyes, while a hint of something that felt like hope stirred in his heart.

"Hmm, maybe, I don't know …" Sophie held his gaze. And was that hopes of her own that he detected in her expression?

It was then that the waiter reappeared with their food and Steven had to reluctantly let go of Sophie's hand. "Okay," he said when the waiter had gone, "how about we relax and eat and then go back to my place and talk some more?"

Chapter Eleven

Sophie

Some kind of mutual but unspoken agreement between them meant that, as they ate their pasta, they restricted their conversation to safe topics such as a new crime thriller series on Netflix that they were both enjoying, and the merits of the Mediterranean diet. And as they did so Sophie found it hard to believe they were there in the restaurant together or that she was feeling quite so relaxed.

It wasn't until they were back at Steven's place that Sophie braced herself for the much more difficult topics she and Steven were about to discuss. Steven went straight to the kitchen to get them both a drink and her phone pinged as she sat in the living room waiting for him. It was a text from Paula and she couldn't help smiling as she read her friend's latest message.

Sorry, not sorry – enjoy your evening xxx

"You're smiling. That's a good start," Steven said as he set their drinks down on the coffee table and joined her on the sofa. "You looked like you wanted to kill me earlier."

"Ah well you'd be right, but you'll need to take your place in the queue because I'll be going after Paula and her brother first." Sophie was still smiling as she indicated her phone. "That was her messaging me with an apology of sorts."

"

Steven nodded and took a sip of his beer. He looked more serious now. "Maybe," he said, speaking softly, "you won't want to kill any of us after we've talked. Would you like to go first?"

"Okay," Sophie said reaching for her wine glass. She took a couple of sips from it before turning to face him. "I like you Steven. I liked you right from the start. After we met again at Dean's party, I wondered if fate, or whatever, was trying to tell me something. I fantasised about us taking things further, about us having a relationship. Then after our evening together my doubts and reservations, the promises I'd made to myself not to get involved with you, with any man, they all seemed to vanish. And for a time so did my doubts that I'd be good for you."

Steven appeared horrified by that last remark and looked as if he was about to say something.

"No, let me finish." Sophie lifted her hand to stop him talking. She had to get it all out. "I did waver about whether I was doing the right thing letting my guard down but in the end after a lot of thought and talking to Paula and Lainey, I was prepared to risk it. I realised it didn't have to be all serious and intense, we could just go on some dates, get to know each other, have some fun together for however long it suited us." Sophie paused and drank some more wine.

Steven's expression was now anguished. "And then I didn't call." He rubbed his hand over his mouth and chin before leaning forward, his elbows on his knees, his head in his hands.

"No, you didn't," Sophie said. "But you did me, you did *us* a favour. Yes, like I said, I wish you'd called and just told me you didn't want to take things further instead of leaving me wondering. But then I figured your failure to call was a clear message in itself, and it proved I'd been wrong about you, about how you felt. So I blocked your number and decided to get on with my life." Sophie sighed as Steven continued to sit with his head in his hands. "Would you like me to leave?" she said, horrified to feel tears starting to run down her face.

Steven sat up quickly. "What? No! Definitely not." He caught hold of her hand in his and when he saw she was crying he used his other hand to wipe at her tears with his thumb. "Please, please don't cry. I hate myself enough already for the way I've treated you. I'm not normally such a coward." Then as she looked into his eyes Sophie saw her own pain and distress reflected back at her.

She couldn't be sure who initiated what happened next but as she leaned her face against the hand Steven was using to wipe away her tears, he slipped it around the back of her neck, pulling her to him. She tilted her head, desperate to feel his lips on hers. Then, as she looked up again and into his beautiful eyes, he did what she yearned for and he kissed her. He was tentative at first but when she groaned in pleasure, he responded with a growl of his own before their kiss became more passionate and demanding.

For Sophie, time seemed to stand still and everything around them felt like it faded into the background as all that mattered was being kissed by Steven. Eventually they stopped. They stopped and stared breathlessly into each other's eyes.

It was Steven who spoke first as he gently cupped her face in his hands. "That was awesome," he said, smiling down at her.

"Mmm," she said, smiling too. "The new best kiss ever."

"So," Steven said as they both sat back and he took hold of her hand. "You said before that you'd been prepared to risk it, to risk there being an us until I … I let you down."

"Yes, I was. I'd told you up front I'd recently been in a relationship which, when it ended, left me hurt. I also told you I had other things going on that made me reluctant to commit to anything but you weren't put off and you left the decision about us taking things further up to me. I liked that you did that and yes, like you, I delayed getting back in touch. But unlike you, in the end, I did and it felt like the right decision until …" She broke off, turning away as tears threatened yet again.

"Until I let you down," Steven said again. He looked stricken as he rubbed the back of his neck with his hand.

"Just tell me, Steven," Sophie said softly. "What is it you need to share with me?"

He nodded before leaning forward. Sophie could only watch in silence as he rolled up first one trouser leg to just above his knee, followed by the other one. "As you know I can walk … took me a while to get the hang of it after what happened. I've had to swap running for going to the gym and doing boxing and weights at least for now. I have a couple of other sets of prosthetics for different activities and terrain. I have adaptations here in the flat to make life easier – like the amputee-friendly set up in the shower, for example. And I have my no-feet-required car. So, as long as I take care of what's left of my legs, I'm good to go under my own steam."

He sat back and looked at Sophie. "So there you have it. Not exactly the body beautiful but it still serves me well and I know, having survived that IED makes me one of the lucky ones."

Sophie hoped he hadn't seen her flinch before he tilted his head back, closed his eyes and let out a long sigh. She reminded herself this wasn't about her or what she'd lost. It was about Steven.

She moved to kneel on the floor in front of him. She stared momentarily at the prosthetic limbs which were attached just below each of Steven's knees before raising her hands and gently stroking the skin at the edge of both stumps. She felt Steven give a small shudder and looked up to see him watching her. "You were wrong, you know," she said. "This—" she paused to nod towards where her fingers continued their stroking. "This was never going to be a deal breaker. What you've suffered, lost and have recovered from, it just makes you and your body even more beautiful."

Steven stretched out his arms towards her. "Come here," he whispered, his expression full of tenderness as tears now ran freely down his face.

Before she had a chance to speak, or even think, he tipped her chin up and pressed his lips to hers once more. As before, their kiss was deep and full of passion and they were both breathless when they eventually broke apart. "Wow," Sophie said as she ran her tongue along her swollen lips. That was … that was even more awesome than before."

Steven continued to hold her close as he looked into her eyes. "It's you that's awesome, Sophie. Your empathy, your kindness, your positivity. I don't know what I've done to deserve you but I do know I want to give us a try if you're still up for it."

Sophie shook her head even as the pangs of longing this man generated in her flooded through her. She pulled away from him. "I don't know about positivity. I'm an emotional disaster. As I've said there's baggage from my last relationship. Then there's the fact that I don't speak to my mother. And on top of all that I'm grieving the loss of my brother."

"Your brother? Your brother died?"

"Yes, Finlay, my younger brother, he died just over a year ago. He was only twenty-four. He was a Marine. Like you he served in Afghanistan only he wasn't one of the lucky ones. He didn't come back. Like with you it was an explosive device …" Sophie broke off unable to go on.

"He was killed when it went off?" Steven said softly.

"Yes, apparently, he threw himself towards it, absorbed the worst of it and saved several of his comrades by doing so."

"He sounds like an amazing guy. I'd like to hear more about him … when you're ready to share."

Sophie nodded as Steven reached for her, pulling her close once more. "I'm so sorry, Sophie," he said.

After a while of crying in his arms, Sophie pushed back. "I still miss him terribly, still can't believe he's gone," she said before pausing to blow her nose and wipe away her tears. "Sometimes I can handle the grief, other times it's overwhelming." She drained the last of the wine from her glass before going on. "So where does all this soul-baring leave us, Steven?"

"Do you trust me?" Steven said.

"Yes, yes I do."

"Good. And I trust you. I trust us, that we can support each other as we give this *us* a proper go. No big commitment, no pressure. Like you said, we can just have some fun together. So what do you say?"

Sophie tried to speak but only a sob got out as her tears fell.

"Hey," Steven said, rubbing at her tears again. "Please, no more tears."

"I warned you," Sophie said, as she managed a sheepish smile and pointed at her face. "Emotional mess."

"You saw me, I was doing the messy crying thing too" Steven said. "Like you said earlier we can either be one big mess together or, like *I* said, we can maybe help each other clean up." He looked into her eyes before pulling her in for yet another incredible kiss. Then, when they stopped to catch their breath, he said, "I'll take that as a yes."

Chapter Twelve

Steven

Once again it wasn't easy letting Sophie leave on that Saturday night after they'd kissed and made up. He would have given anything to take her to bed and to stay there with her for the rest of the weekend. But quite apart from his physical need to be with her, there was the need to get to know her better as a person. He wanted to find out more about her life, about the hurt she'd suffered, more about the loss of her brother, about her breakup, and the nature of the difficulties in her relationship with her mother.

He recognised that all of that would and should keep for another time. He told himself just to be grateful that they were talking again and that he'd been given another chance. So he did his best to hide his disappointment when, after lots more kissing, Sophie finally pulled away from him and said that she'd better call a taxi.

"Yes, right, okay," he said trying to keep his voice even and normal.

"Don't look so sad," Sophie said as she took her phone out of her handbag. "It's been an eventful evening and I need to go home and sleep."

Steven ran his hand across his head and rubbed the back of his neck. "Yeah, sorry, it's just—"

"I know," Sophie said softly, her gorgeous eyes looking into his. "I know, and part of me feels the same. Part of me wants to take you through to the bedroom and order you to give me the best sex ever …" She paused and smiled in a way that just about drove him crazy and he laughed as he recalled how she'd proclaimed his first kisses to be the best kisses ever.

Then with a more serious look on her face she continued. "But I want … I need—"

"You need time. Time to process."

"Yes," she said. "That's exactly what I need. And I love … I love that you get that." She reached for his hand and held it tightly as she used her other hand to call the cab company.

He was glad he didn't have to respond immediately to what she'd just said. His heart had skipped a beat and was now hammering in his chest. For a split second he thought she was going to say she loved him.

After she'd made the call she let go of his hand and got to her feet. "Right," she said, "taxi's on its way. Oh, and you're unblocked on here." She waved her phone.

"Okay, that's good," he said, as he too stood up. But while it was good she'd unblocked him in that sense, he wanted so much more. He reached for her hand. "Sophie—"

Before he could say anything else she'd reached up and put her finger to his lips. "Shh," she said, grinning. "We've done enough talking for now. So, please, just shut up and kiss me."

He didn't need to be asked twice. Sophie pressed into him, her hands on the back of his neck, and moaned as he did as he was told. "I'm sorry," she said when they came up for air. "Sorry I'm not staying."

Steven pressed his forehead against hers before straightening up and saying, "Like I said, I get it. You need time and you want to take things slow. That's fine by me."

Steven meant what he said – when he said it. He got that she wanted to move slowly as they explored a possible relationship and he intended to stick with that being fine with him. But after a restless night where he couldn't get Sophie out of his head, his intention was already wavering. It was early when he called her.

"Hello," she said, her voice sounding sleepy. "What time do you call this?"

"Ah, sorry, I didn't think I just needed …" Steven ran out of words as he mentally kicked himself. So much for taking it slow.

Sophie gave a little laugh. "A girl needs her beauty sleep, you know."

"I know," he said, before quickly adding, "not you! You're beautiful without … you don't need your beauty sleep … but some girls, some people do. For you it probably just makes you more beautiful. I mean …" He moved up from mentally kicking himself to punching.

Sophie was properly giggling now. "Okay, enough with the smooth-talking chat up lines. To what do I owe the honour of this charming wakeup call?"

Steven took a breath. "I was wondering what you were up to today. Wondered if we could meet up."

"Ah, that would be good but I can't. I'm sorry."

"Oh, right, sorry." Steven now gave himself an actual hit, as he smacked his palm off his forehead. He was an idiot. "I shouldn't have called, not after I assured you I could be patient. Just, please, forget it and—"

"No, no Steven, don't. There's no need to apologise. It's not that I don't want to see you. You're not going too fast, honestly."

"You do want to see me? This isn't too fast?"

"Taking it slow, you and me, it's not about us not seeing each other. We need to see each other in order for whatever we might have together to develop. The slow thing is about me not wanting to rush into another serious relationship right now."

"Okay." Steven was smiling now, mainly with relief he hadn't blown it with Sophie already.

"And me not seeing you today, it really is because I can't. I've got to get organised for being away next week. There's a proposed series about Scottish scientists coming up and I've got the research brief to do. So I need to pack and prepare my notes, and the flat could do with a bit of a clean-up too before I go."

"Ah, right I see. Where are you off to?"

"Tomorrow I'm going to Edinburgh, to the National Library. I have some research time booked along with an appointment with one of the archivists. Then I've got university visits starting in Edinburgh and then on to St Andrews, Dundee and Aberdeen before finishing up at Glasgow on Friday."

"Sounds full on." Steven sighed. Didn't seem like he'd be seeing her anytime soon.

"So, I'll be ready for some fun next weekend. Do you like Indian food? I could try and get us a table at The Garam Palace. It's my favourite place to eat Indian."

"Oh, really? I thought you'd want to relax."

"Yes, I do," Sophie laughed again. "Stuffing my face with delicious food is one of my favourite ways of relaxing. So what do you say? Want to join me?"

"Yes, yes, that would be great." Steven was now grinning as another wave of relief hit.

"Good. I'll let you know when I've made the reservation."

"Great," he said, his confidence restored. So restored that he went on to joke, "Oh, and before you go, what are your other favourite ways of relaxing?"

Sophie giggled. "Ah, you'll just have to wait and see, all part of taking it slow." With that she ended the call.

Steven could feel his heartrate increasing as the taxi pulled up the door of restaurant in Glasgow's city centre. The week since he'd since last seen Sophie had passed painfully slowly and his anticipation levels were high.

He spotted her as soon as he got inside, already seated at a table near the back. She must have been watching the door because she immediately stood up, waving and smiling at him and a grinning waiter indicated he should go straight to the table. As soon as he got to her, he kissed her on the cheek, briefly enjoying the feel of her skin and the unique scent that was Sophie before they both sat down.

A slight flush appeared on her neck and face. Steven smiled at the thought he'd caused that blush as he said, "It's good to see you, Soph."

"And you," Sophie said, her own smile showing him she meant it. She also seemed slightly nervous, shy even. She passed him a menu before going on. "I do love the food here. Have you been here before?"

"No, I haven't actually. I'm ashamed to say most of my experience of Indian food is from the takeaway round the corner from my flat." He looked around him as he spoke, taking in the amber-coloured walls, the elaborate ceiling roses with beautiful chandeliers hanging from them, the polished wooden floors and the quality table linen. This long-established and obviously popular restaurant was definitely a cut above. "It looks great. I'm sure the food will be too."

"So let's order," she said. Steven followed Sophie's recommendations for a shared plate of pakoras to start, followed by garlic chicken chilli Balti for his main. She also said she'd share some of her main dish of chicken Mughlai if he agreed to share his with her.

After they'd placed their order and a waiter had brought their drinks, Sophie still seemed nervous. She fiddled with her napkin and kept glancing at him and giving him small, uncertain smiles. In an effort to put her at her ease Steven said, "So tell me about your week. It sounded like you had a lot of work to get through."

"It was great actually. I was able to source all sorts of interesting information for the series, quite a few bits and pieces that most people won't have heard about. The archivists and academics were all amazing, really interesting and helpful." Sophie paused to take a sip of her wine. She already looked more relaxed than she had a couple of minutes before.

"So it was a worthwhile trip?"

"Definitely." Sophie nodded. "I've got lots to share with the production team and several ideas about how to develop the themes."

"What sort of ideas?"

Sophie looked surprised. "You really want to hear all this?"

"Yes, I do. I want to get to know more about what's important to you and, from what you've told me so far, your work clearly is."

"Okay then." She smiled at him. "You asked for it."

So Steven sat back and enjoyed just watching and listening to her as she filled him on some of the facts and stories she'd unearthed on Scottish scientists. Her eyes shone and her rate of speech increased, reflecting her enthusiasm not only for the work she'd carried out during the last few days but also for her job in general. She paused briefly when their starters arrived but then continued as they ate. Her earlier nervousness was well and truly gone. It was only when he asked her about her career ambitions she seemed to hesitate and look slightly tense.

"Oh, I'm not sure exactly," she said. "I could go for promotion or move from the general research areas I work in now into something more specific. But no definite plans at the moment." She took a gulp of her wine before going on to change the subject. "Anyway enough about me. How's your work going? I hear the crew have started filming with you."

"Yes, yes they have. It's been an interesting experience, very different for all of us at Revive, a bit stressful, but mostly enjoyable." Then as they ate their delicious main courses he went on to tell her a bit more about the interviews her colleagues had carried out with him, his staff, and some of the veterans who used Revive's facilities and services.

When they finished eating, and were rounding off their meal with a pot of Indian tea, Sophie said, "So, better than takeaway?"

"Way better," Steven agreed. "Best ever category, like our kisses." He grinned then wiggled his eyebrows at her.

Sophie laughed and Steven wallowed in the sound. "Good," she said, before signalling to the waiter to bring the bill.

Just as they finished their tea the bill arrived. Before Steven could move, Sophie grabbed it and said, "My invitation, my treat."

"But—"

"No, I insist. You can pay next time."

"So there's going to be a next time then?" Steven said, grinning at her.

"Oh, I reckon so," she said smiling back at him.

Chapter Thirteen

Sophie

When she got into bed that night Sophie lay awake thinking over how the evening had gone. She'd definitely missed Steven while she'd been away and it was good to be with him again.

She started off the evening feeling nervous, wondering and hoping they were doing the right thing, hoping Steven wasn't having second thoughts. But then he was so attentive, showing a genuine interest in her. She was touched that he asked her about her week away and what it had involved. Rick had never shown much interest in her career, other than the income it provided to support his lifestyle. In fact, as she thought more about it, she realised he'd only shown any interest in what was going on with her when there was something in it for him. Sometimes he even got jealous if she had anything going on in her non-work life that didn't include him.

Steven though didn't seem to be fazed by the fact she had things going on in her life that didn't include him. He was fine when, in the taxi they were sharing to get home to their respective flats, he asked if he could see her again the following weekend and she had to say no. She smiled as she recalled the conversation.

"Ah, I'm afraid not," she said. "I'll be in Edinburgh next weekend. It's been an annual event for the last decade, me and my oldest friend Lizzie meet up every year at this time. We've only ever had to cancel once and that was last year, after Finlay, when Lizzie came and stayed at the flat with me instead. But it's back to our usual this year. We book into a posh hotel, do a bit of Christmas shopping, get a bit of pampering, a proper girls' weekend, you know the sort of thing."

"Not really," Steven laughed. "I've been known to do a bit of Christmas shopping, usually last minute, but as for pampering, posh hotels and girls' weekends, I can't say I do know about such things."

Sophie laughed too. "Fair enough. Although I can recommend getting a spa treatment, facial, hair, nails, massage, the lot. It's very relaxing."

"Hmm, I'm sure it is. But I reckon, out of that list, I'd probably just go for the massage." Steven wiggled a suggestive eyebrow at her and then momentarily distracted her with a wickedly sexy grin.

She shook her head at him, with a pretend look of disapproval on her face. "Anyway, Lizzie and me have been friends since being in the same class at primary school. She lived round the corner from me in Edinburgh when we were growing up. Nowadays she's married, a mother of four and lives in Fife so we don't see a lot of each other. But our December get together back in the city is a chance for a proper catch up."

"Sounds good. So what about the weekend after that for us? If you're free on the Saturday you could come to mine, I could cook us some dinner."

"You'd cook?" she said smiling.

"Don't sound so surprised," he said. "It's the twenty-first century, you know. Just like women can operate machinery and drive cars, men can actually cook and look after themselves."

She swatted his arm. "Yeah, yeah, I just didn't have you down as a home cooking type. And I must admit it's not one of my strengths."

"Well I've been told I'm not at all bad at the meal making thing. So how about it? You willing to risk it?"

"Definitely," she said.

When the taxi arrived at her flat, Steven asked the driver to wait while he walked Sophie to the tenement door. There they said their goodbyes and the goodnight kiss they shared was amazing.

So as Sophie lay in bed afterwards reliving that moment, she put her fingers to her lips and smiled. It really had been a perfect evening. In fact the only blip was when Steven asked her about her work ambitions and she'd felt a bit awkward. The possibility of the move to Bristol in a few months' time was causing her some inner conflict and she definitely didn't want to discuss it. So she kept her reply very general and moved the conversation on.

For now all she wanted was to live a fuller life than of late and to have some fun. So, maybe Steven could be the perfect person to help her do that. Maybe she just needed to trust him and herself and go for it.

Her week at work was busy as always. She completed and presented her report on the research she'd carried out for the scientists programme and then moved on to begin work on a piece about Scotland's forests and woodlands for a long-running nature show.

Having put in more hours than she was paid for by the time Friday came around, she felt justified in leaving early. She'd taken her weekend bag with her to work in order to go straight to the train station from the office. And by six o'clock that evening she was hugging a very excited Lizzie, in the lobby of the Waverley Grand hotel in Edinburgh city centre.

"I've checked us in," Lizzie said waggling the key to their twin room. "So let's go up and get this party started."

They had dinner within walking distance of the hotel at a popular restaurant on George Street and it was while they were eating and sharing a bottle of champagne that their catch up really got going. Lizzie filled Sophie in on the latest news from her busy, but very happy sounding life and it was as she did so that Sophie realised how much she'd missed her friend. Lizzie updated her on her life with her husband, Gary, as they combined parenting their six-year-old twin boys, and four-year-old and two-year-old daughters, with running their family business. Listening to all of it, it struck Sophie how Lizzie, with her characteristic blend of optimism mixed with realism, had always had a positive and steadying influence on her.

"I don't know how you do it all and keep that mix of energised and relaxed you always seem to have," Sophie said.

"Oh, don't get me wrong, those are all the edited highlights that I just gave you. Believe me, there are moments I'm so tired I could fall asleep standing up and there are other moments when I feel like punching a hole in the nearest wall. But that being said, I wouldn't change a thing. And I know that makes me a very lucky lady."

"I don't think it's all down to luck, I reckon you work pretty hard at it all and you seem to thrive on it too."

"Yep, I definitely do. Gary and me, we've always been a good team, we do our best to make it all work. But that's enough about me. How are things with you? And don't fob me off with the same non-committal answers you gave me back in the hotel room."

Sophie couldn't help smiling at Lizzie's warning. She held her hands up in a gesture of defeat. "Yeah, yeah, I know."

"You said you were fine but I'm sensing you're not, not really. I know you've had a difficult year what with Rick and everything, and I know from when I called you at the time that the recent anniversary of losing Finlay was very tough on you. Is it that? Or have you got other stuff on your mind?"

"No, it's not Rick. Yes, I'm hurt and angry at what he did but I'm starting to let go of all of that. He's not worth the energy. And Finlay, well yes, it was hard coping with the anniversary but I had lots of support from you and my other friends, and I got through it. I suspect the grief will never go away and I don't think I want it to. But you're right it's neither of those things that's filling my head space at the moment."

"I knew it! Your recent texts and calls have seemed evasive to say the least. So tell me."

Sophie knew that just as with Lainey and Paula, there could be no fobbing off, as Lizzie put it. If anything, Lizzie was even more astute than her other two friends and she'd spot any fibs or omissions a mile off. It would be pointless to try and hide anything and besides that she didn't want to. She also knew she'd get a calm and considered response.

So, fortified by good food and a couple of glasses champagne, and with a pot of decaf coffee and a plate of shortbread ready to share, she told Lizzie all about meeting Steven and how things had developed since.

Lizzie listened and said little, but her smiles and nods showed she was pleasantly surprised. There was no Lainey type shrieking. But there was also none of Paula's more slow and considered approach either. As Sophie listened to Lizzie's take on things, she silently marvelled at how fortunate she was to have three such different but equally amazingly supportive friends.

"Right," Lizzie said. "Here's what I think. And can I just begin by saying 'go you.'" She grinned at Sophie and raised her coffee cup as if she was offering a toast.

"Thanks," Sophie said, smiling back. "You don't think I'm making a big mistake, then?"

"No, I don't. The mistake would be to hide away, to stay stuck where you are and to let life pass you by. Rick hurt you badly but you can't let him win. It's fine to be aware and protect yourself but you also have to be realistic. No relationship comes with a guarantee. But the good ones … well, they're good. And of course you're feeling fragile after losing your brother, but don't you think he'd want you to really live your life to the full?" Lizzie paused to drink some coffee and take a bite of shortbread.

Sophie nodded. "I've never actually told anyone else this but I sometimes hear Finlay's voice. Not in a creepy, haunty, ghosty way or anything, but like a whisper in my head. It's usually when I've got something on my mind, a decision to make, that sort of thing. Anyway, I hear him saying 'I dare you' like he did when we were kids."

"Wow," Lizzie said. "That's brilliant. Good on you Fin!" She briefly raised her eyes skyward. "It's like I said. Life's a risky business but avoiding all the risks is no life at all."

"So, you don't think I'm mad then? Getting involved with Steven especially with the added complication it might only be for a short time if I get this Bristol job?"

Lizzie's laugh was kind as she reached over and squeezed Sophie's hand. "What are you like? Complication really is your default setting at the moment, isn't it?"

"Yeah, I suppose it is."

"Just keep it simple. Steven sounds like a great guy. And I'm going to need to see a picture of him by the way. Anyway, here's how I understand things are between you." She began to count off her list on her fingers. "One, after three dates you like each other a lot and have become friends. Two, you've *both* agreed to take it slow. Three, neither of you is intent on forever at this stage. I take it I'm correct?"

"Yes, sounds about right."

"So it's simple. No need to look too far ahead. No need to *complicate*. Plunge in and enjoy."

The following morning Sophie and Lizzie headed out to do some Christmas shopping. They stopped when they couldn't carry any more. Sophie didn't needed to buy a lot of gifts but Lizzie, as always, had a huge list for her children alone and so Sophie offered her services as packhorse.

After a light lunch back at the hotel they headed for the spa to begin their afternoon of pampering. Sophie sensed it wasn't just the effects of the facial and full body massage that were making her feel so relaxed. Nor was it solely due to the pleasing effects of freshly manicured and painted nails, or the blissful scalp massage which preceded her cut and blow dry. Talking to Lizzie also helped her feel somehow lighter. Her friend helped ease her doubts about getting involved with Steven. Keeping things simple and going for enjoyment was the way to go.

By the time of their shared brunch on the Sunday morning Sophie and Lizzie were well and truly caught up and before they knew it was time to check out of the hotel and head home. Once at the station they shared a long hug as they said their goodbyes.

"Thanks for everything this weekend, for listening and helping me get my head straight," Sophie said as they embraced.

"Thanks to you too for listening to all my mummy woes," Lizzie said.

Sophie gave a little laugh as they stood back from their embrace. "Listening wasn't a problem. Offering any helpful advice, that was harder."

"Oh, you didn't do too bad. And you never know, maybe one day I can help *you* out in that department."

Sophie rolled her eyes. "That so isn't going to happen. I told you, no kids on the horizon for me."

"Whatever. One day maybe, you never know. But for now remember what I said as regards getting back to living your life. With your mum and with Steven, with all of it, take it slow and listen to your heart, and above all enjoy it."

Chapter Fourteen

Steven thought a lot about Sophie during the week following their date at the Indian restaurant. Over the weekend he considered getting in touch with her to tell her so. In the end he didn't, deciding it would be better to leave her in peace and let her enjoy her time with her friend uninterrupted.

Work kept him busy. Along with all the usual stuff there was the hours long planning meeting with his colleagues for the coming year. This was followed by a somewhat tedious but necessary budget meeting. Then there was yet another meeting this time with two members of the BBC production team to finalise the details of the late January, early February filming schedule at Revive. This last one though hadn't been in the least tedious and left him feeling fired up for getting the programme made.

He also had a night out with his two best mates from school. They went to the local pub where they watched a football match on the big screen and enjoyed good craic and even better craft beers.

So it wasn't until late on the Sunday afternoon when he guessed Sophie would be home from Edinburgh that he fired off a text.

Hi, hope you had a good week and that you enjoyed your weekend away. Been thinking about you, missing you too. Looking forward to seeing you on Saturday if you're still up for trying out my cooking. Can you get here for around 7pm? xxx

It didn't take Sophie long to get back to him and he grinned as he read her message.

Lovely weekend thanks. Yep, definitely still up for risking my life and sampling your cooking. See you on Saturday xxx

As the following weekend approached, Steven's anticipation and impatience levels rose. He couldn't wait to see Sophie.

He was up early on the Saturday morning, wanting to make sure he had everything prepared for the evening. He cleaned the flat, went shopping and got as much of the meal prepared ahead of time as he could. Then it was time to shower, shave and change and await Sophie's arrival. He couldn't remember ever feeling so excited, anxious and nervous about cooking for anyone. But then this wasn't just anyone. This was Sophie.

She arrived right on time. Her smile as she came into the flat told him she was as pleased to see him as he was to see her. "Hello, you," she said sounding almost shy. She handed him a bottle of wine before shrugging off her coat and hanging it on one of the wall hooks.

Steven swallowed hard as she turned back to face him. She looked stunning. The short black dress, the high heels, her hair pinned up revealing that creamy neck, and the lipstick on those luscious looking lips, it was almost overpowering. For a moment all he could do was stare.

Eventually, though, he managed to speak. "Hello, you look … you look amazing," he stuttered.

"Why thank you," she said smiling. "I reckoned since you were going to all the effort of cooking, I should make an effort too."

"Right. Well … please come through, everything's ready."

"Wow," Sophie said when she saw the table. "A proper table-cloth and napkins and those lovely candles too. It all looks so pretty."

"I'm glad you like it. I kind of wanted it to be a bit special, you know, not having seen you for a couple of weeks and this being the first time we've done this, that you've come here and I've cooked for you …" he ran his hand through his hair, aware he was rambling on, not sure why he felt so nervous.

"Hey, relax," Sophie said, putting her hand on his arm and stroking it. "This isn't a test. And I'm touched you've gone to so much trouble." She looked up at him and for a moment he was lost. He didn't know who made the first move but the next thing he knew they were kissing. It was a long, passionate and all-consuming kiss and left both of them breathless.

"Well if your cooking's as delicious as your kissing, I'm in for a treat," Sophie said when they finally managed to stop. Her voice had a huskiness to it. A huskiness that only ramped up the levels of desire he felt for this beautiful woman.

Sophie giggled as she looked at him. "Eh, Earth to Steven, what does a girl have to do to get fed around here?"

He resisted telling her exactly what he'd like her to do, instead saying, "Yes, right. Please, take a seat and I'll serve up."

"That looks yummy," Sophie said as he served her up a slice of lemon cheesecake for dessert.

"It is but I can't take the credit," Steven said. "Puddings, baking, all that sort of stuff, beyond me I'm afraid. I got it at the wee bakery round the corner. They do some amazing stuff."

"Not a complete domestic god, then." Sophie laughed before taking a bite.

"I'm afraid not." Steven put on a sad face.

Sophie laughed again. "Seriously, though, you are actually a pretty awesome cook. Like I said earlier that smoked salmon starter and the beef stroganoff they were both delicious and I'm seriously impressed."

The conversation had flowed easily between them through-out the meal and it continued to do so when they were settled on the sofa together drinking coffee.

Steven told her what had been happening at work. He told her about the preparations for filming and his hopes that Revive would benefit from the exposure the programme would bring. Then when he went on to tell her about the centre's plans for the year ahead. Sophie said, "I saw it the day we first met. You really love your job, don't you?"

"I do," Steven said. "While I'm fairly sure I don't want to do it forever, it came along at exactly the right time, a time when I'd no idea who I was anymore. It showed me I can still make a positive difference and, in its own way it's given me back some hope for my future."

"So there was a time when you had little hope?" Sophie asked.

"In the early days, after the explosion and my comrade dying. There was the guilt that I'd survived mixed with the fear and shock at losing not only a significant part of both legs, but my career and the future I thought I was going to have too. All of that along with the PTSD … it all made me wish I had died too." Steven paused to take a breath. "Sorry," he said as he allowed the tears to fall, amazed yet again at how comfortable he felt letting Sophie see his more vulnerable side.

"There's no need to apologise," Sophie said as she moved closer to him and squeezed his hand. "I know what it is to feel desperate. I just wish I'd handled it half as well as you have."

"Ah, but you didn't see me at my worst, you didn't see me fall apart and then struggle to get myself back together again."

"You've done really well," Sophie said. "Whereas me, I feel like I'm still struggling. Losing Finlay, it was awful, and the way he died …"

"I know, I know," Steven said, pulling her to him and holding her as she sobbed into his chest. He knew only too well that her brother had died in the most horrible way.

Eventually her sobbing ceased and she looked up at him. He

gently wiped at her tears and his heart twisted at seeing her so distressed. "Tell me," he said softly.

"At first, after he died, I just shut down. I had to be signed off work. I shut myself away, wouldn't talk to anyone. I hardly remember the funeral, no idea how I got through it. Then, like you said, along came the guilt that I was still here and Finlay wasn't. And there was also this aching sadness. But the worst part is the anger."

"Anger at who? At Finlay?"

"No, well maybe a bit of anger that he got himself into such danger. I'm more angry at life, at the unfairness of it, but mainly I'm angry with my mother."

"Your mother? So, is that the reason you don't talk? You're angry with her about your brother's death?"

"Yeah, mainly." Sophie sighed. "A few years ago, after my mother divorced my dad, she left Edinburgh and went back to live on the Isle of Skye, back to the house where she was born and grew up. She said she was going back to look after Grandma but I knew that wasn't the only reason. She admitted as much, said she needed to get away, away from her old life with my dad, away from the city. But it felt like she was also getting away from me.

"She said she'd miss me but I couldn't help feeling, if that was really true, then why leave? She said that I was welcome to visit anytime. But you know how it is. I was busy. And Skye's a bit of a trek from Glasgow so I only went up a couple of times. Last time was just before Finlay..." Sophie swallowed.

"Anyway, on that visit she just seemed so settled, so happy with her new life. She had the croft with the sheep, cows and hens to look after, she could still do her job as a writer and illustrator of children's books and she had Grandma to keep her company. It didn't feel like she needed me. I called her out on it, we argued, she tried to explain but I wasn't having any of it and I haven't seen her since, apart from at Finlay's funeral. And I know all that makes me sound like a childish, needy cow."

"Don't be so hard on yourself, Soph," Steven said, seeing the obvious pain and the tears in her eyes. "Your parents getting divorced, that must have been tough. And then your mum moving away right after. It's a lot to get your head round. I don't think I'd cope very well in those circumstances either. Even though you're an adult they're still your parents. You're allowed to be childish in relation to them."

"Yeah, well, thanks for understanding but I'm not proud of how I reacted. And I guess if Finlay hadn't been killed we'd probably have talked and made up by now."

"So why the anger at her over your brother's death?"

"Because she didn't stop him joining up. Her father, my late grandad, he'd been in the Marines. Finlay idolised him and Mum encouraged that, encouraged Finlay in his dream to follow in Grandad's footsteps. She could have stopped him joining up but she didn't. He went with her blessing."

Steven was taken aback at the vehemence in Sophie's voice. Surely her brother's decision was just that – *his* decision. But he knew he shouldn't judge her, so he did his best keep his expression and his tone of voice neutral.

"And you haven't spoken to your mother since when? Since the funeral? Finlay's death is the main reason you don't talk?"

"Yes, more or less since the funeral, and yes, Finlay's the main reason. I was already hurt about the divorce, about her leaving, but Finlay dying, it was the last straw. She tries to keep in touch, sends me texts and she calls from time to time. But I can't ..." Sophie raised her hand and shook her head as if to indicate she couldn't go on.

Steven gave her a minute before going on to say, "What about your father? Did he support Finlay's decision to join up?"

"No, not really. He wanted him to go to university, follow him into the legal profession but that was never going to happen. So in the end Dad backed off."

"But you're close to him, your dad?"

"Yeah, always was a bit of a daddy's girl. He remarried after the divorce, married the woman he'd been having an affair with while he was still married to Mum, but for some reason I seem to have managed to forgive him for that. And I know that's not logical or fair when it comes to Mum." Sophie sighed. "Anyway, he still lives in Edinburgh, near to where I grew up as it happens, and I do get to see him from time to time. It's just Mum that I've shut out." Sophie's voice had become shaky as she referred to her mother and her expression showed a deep sadness.

Steven rubbed the back of her hand with his thumb. "Hey," he said raising his other hand to stroke her face. "Something I've learned going through what I went through, is it's not always easy for fairness and logic to prevail when emotions are involved. Maybe one day you and your mum can have a proper talk, clear the air, repair the damage, get close again."

"Yeah, maybe," Sophie spoke in a whisper and gave a slight shake of her head before she said, "Anyway, all I know about *your* parents is that they're retired and live here in Glasgow in the house you grew up in. Do you have a good relationship with both of them?"

"I do actually," Steven said, feeling suddenly grateful for that fact. "They're good people and they've always supported me. Mind you it wasn't always easy growing up, with both of them being high school teachers. It was good if I was stuck with homework but not so easy if I was ever trying to get away with stuff that differently employed parents wouldn't have picked up on."

"You mean you weren't the perfect child?" Sophie smiled after she'd pretended to be shocked.

It was good to see her smile and Steven continued to try to lighten her mood by telling her some of the escapades and scrapes he'd got into as a youngster. He knew he'd succeeded when she laughed till she cried at the tale of how he'd assumed a disguise involving a beard in order to skive off school, only to bump into his grandmother in the street. She'd recognised him instantly and marched him straight back to school and into the headteacher's office.

"That is so funny," Sophie said, wiping her eyes. "I'd love to have seen it." She looked properly relaxed again. In fact she looked downright bloody gorgeous.

Steven's gaze went from her smile to her beautiful eyes and then back to those full and inviting lips. "I … I want to—"

"So shut up and do it then," Sophie leant in and slipped her arms round his neck. "Kiss me, Steven."

He didn't need to be asked twice. At first it was a gentle sort of inquiring kiss but the intensity quickly ramped up. Kiss followed delicious kiss and he was lost. Lost in Sophie. His hands started in her hair, his fingers twisting in its long thick waves, then they moved to her jaw, down her neck before caressing their way down to her waist. And as he felt the lace of her dress under his fingertips, the urge to remove the dress and go much, much further in his exploration was almost overwhelming.

Eventually, when the need to catch their breath caused them to stop, he couldn't stop a low groan escaping. "God you don't know what you do to me, woman," he said as he leaned his forehead against hers.

"Oh, I think I have a pretty good idea." Sophie's grin was wicked. And that along with her swollen lips, tousled hair and the slightly breathless sound of her voice almost pushed him over the edge. He imagined throwing her over his shoulder and marching off to the bedroom.

Sophie laughed. "Easy, there, soldier. I know what you're thinking."

"You sure?"

"Oh yes, I'm sure and all I can say is good things come to those who wait. But now I really should be going."

Steven knew he was falling hard and fast. He also knew that he wouldn't be breaking their agreement to take things slow no matter how difficult it was going to be for him. But after Sophie left, he consoled himself with the progress they'd made so far. They were getting to know each other and the attraction was undoubtedly mutual.

It was the following weekend that they hit their first bump in the road when they returned to the topic of their parents.

Saturday dawned cold but bright and Steven made a snap decision. He'd already arranged to see Sophie that evening. She'd invited him round to hers for a movie night and a takeaway. But as he stood gazing out of his living room window while drinking his breakfast mug of tea he didn't want to wait until the evening to see her.

"This was a good idea," Sophie said an hour later as they walked hand-in-hand through the Botanical Gardens. She smiled up at him.

"Yeah, I have them occasionally," he replied. "I wasn't sure you'd be up for spending the whole day together but I thought it was worth a try."

"Definitely worth it. I was only too pleased to postpone the list of chores I should be getting on with and to spend some time outdoors instead. Especially on a lovely day and accompanied by a gorgeous guy."

Steven's heart did a bit of a flip as he looked at her. He stopped walking and pulled her to him before lowering his lips to hers.

"And then there was the possibility of that happening too," Sophie giggled after they'd kissed. "All in all it was an irresistible suggestion."

After their walk they headed over to the outdoor Christmas Market that Sophie noticed was on in a nearby park when she was on her way to the Botanics. They got hotdogs and coffee for lunch from one of the market's food wagons before Sophie insisted on exploring every stall, then revisiting several of them to make some Christmas purchases. So, it was late afternoon and getting decidedly chilly and dark when Steven suggested they go for a drink at a local pub.

They were lucky enough to get a table close to the pub's blazing coal fire and that along with the sparkling Christmas tree in the corner made it feel very cosy and comfortable.

"Cheers," Steven said before taking his first sip of beer. "Thanks for coming out with me today. It's been a fun sort of date."

"Cheers to you too," Sophie said, raising her wine glass. "Yeah, it has been fun. I'd forgotten that dates can be this relaxed." She looked thoughtful then a slight frown appeared before she took a gulp of wine.

"You okay?"

"Yeah, sorry. I was just thinking about my ex."

"Oh, right," Steven said unsure if this was a good or a bad thing.

"Rick, my ex, he would never have been up for a day like this. We, or rather he, didn't really do fun."

"His loss," Steven said. "Do you … that is are you … over him? You don't have any thoughts of getting back with him?"

"What? No! Not if he was the last man alive."

"Tell me about him."

So she did. Steven had been shocked to hear how Rick had sponged off her financially but when she got to how things had ended, to Rick's infidelity, Steven had gone from appalled to furious. How could her ex have treated her so badly? If Rick was to walk into the pub now …

"Hey," Sophie said. "Are *you* okay? You look upset."

"Not upset, angry. So angry. I want to punch Rick's lights out. How could he treat you like that?"

"Because he's a rat. A rat I'm so over. But enough about him. What about you? Any women in your life who you loved and lost?"

"Never anyone special. Not like—" he stopped himself before

he blurted out 'not like you'. "I've had girlfriends in the past and I've been out on a couple of dates since leaving the army, but there's been nothing serious."

They decided, having seen the pub's tempting Christmas menu, to stay and have dinner there. They shared more anecdotes both serious and funny and discovered a fair bit more about each other. By the end of the evening Steven couldn't quite believe all the topics they'd covered. They just never seemed to be stuck for stuff to talk about.

But there was one thing they hadn't discussed and that was where they'd be spending Christmas.

His mother had called him a few days earlier to remind him he still needed to let her know if he'd be joining her and his father for Christmas. And she added that of course he was welcome to bring a plus one. This was his mother's not so subtle way of asking him if he had a girlfriend yet. He wasn't sure he was quite ready to tell his parents about Sophie, but he did like the idea of her accompanying him.

With Steven's mother pressing him for a decision, he reckoned now, with him and Sophie so relaxed in each other's company, would be a good time to ask her. But he wasn't prepared for quite how strongly she felt about it.

Chapter Fifteen

Sophie

"It's really kind of your parents to invite me. But the answer's no," Sophie said. "I can't do it." She knew it sounded harsh but it was too soon, too full on to be meeting Steven's parents. "I'm really sorry," she added when she saw the look of disappointment on Steven's face.

"It's okay," he said. "I did think I might be too late asking you. So, you spending the day with your dad, or maybe even your mum?"

Sophie laughed but it was hollow and without mirth. "Dad and Carla are off on their annual festive cruise. He's not included me in his Christmas plans since he remarried. And no, I'm definitely not going to be spending Christmas with my mother."

"Oh, right," Steven said frowning. "So, you never spend Christmas with your family?"

"I did go up to Skye for the first three Christmases after she moved there, and the third time Finlay was on leave and was there too. It was actually good fun. But since he died … I didn't go last year and I've no intention of going this year either." Sophie paused to take a breath as she struggled to continue. "Anyway my mother has her friends and Grandma and the sheep to keep her company. She doesn't need me and I sure as hell don't need her."

Steven reached for her hand and squeezed it. "We could spend Christmas together, just you and me."

She was grateful that he didn't push her on how things were with her mother. She was also touched that he'd be willing to forego being with his own family to be with her. But she couldn't let him do that, tempting as his offer was. "No, you must go and be with your folks," she said. "I've turned down invites from both Paula and Lainey too."

"Really? You prefer to be on your own?"

"It's not necessarily a preference, it's just how things are. And please don't worry about me or feel guilty. I'll be fine. I'll be in my PJs all day binge eating and binge watching box sets. It's all good, really it is, so please, can we change the subject?"

Of course it wasn't all good. It was, simply something she had to get through. She couldn't face the family closeness and happy times that her friends or Steven would likely be enjoying. It would only rub in the fact that she couldn't have that with her own family. She also didn't want to put a dampener on anybody else's fun. Being on her own meant she could wallow as much as she liked. No need to pretend, no need for exhausting false jollity. In fact, the previous Christmas, it was her air of false jollity that had caused Rick to become exasperated. So exasperated that, at the last minute, Rick had broken his promise to be with her and had opted instead to spend the day with his parents and siblings.

So she resisted the Christmas Eve WhatsApp messages from both Paula and Lainey telling her it wasn't too late to change her mind about being on her own. Similarly, later the same day, she sent a persuasively protesting Steven away to his parents' house after they'd had dinner together. He accepted her continuing refusal to join him but promised to call round in a couple of days as soon as he got back from staying with his parents. She said she'd look forward to it.

In the end Christmas Day proved to be just about bearable. She stuck to her plan to spend the day in her pyjamas while watching Netflix, drinking wine, and grazing on the various savoury and sweet snacks and treats she'd filled the fridge and cupboards with.

Her father sent her a brief text message wishing her a Merry Christmas and she replied with the same message back, as well as thanking him for the generous gift voucher he'd sent her. A voucher she doubted she'd ever spend as it was for a shop she never went to.

Her mother on the other hand had sent her the prefect selection of items from her favourite makeup brand along with a bottle of the perfume she loved. She also phoned Sophie on Christmas morning. Sophie considered not answering but in the end she forced herself to take the call.

"Mum, hello."

"Hello, Sophie. Happy Christmas. How are you?"

"Happy Christmas to you too. I'm fine thank you."

"Really. You're well, you're … happy?"

"Like I said, I'm fine." She did her best to sound sincere.

"You're not on your own, are you?"

"No, not on my own. I've got friends coming round." Sophie felt a twinge of guilt at the lie. But it was just so much easier than getting into a discussion with her mother about why she preferred to be alone on this particular day. "Thank you for my presents," she said in a bid to change the subject. "They're lovely."

"You're welcome. Is it still your favourite cosmetic brand and do you still like that perfume?"

"Yes, I'm still using both when my budget can stretch to them." Her mother had certainly been very thoughtful and generous with her gifts. This brought on more guilt for Sophie, as did what she said next. "I'm sorry I didn't get you anything. I've just been so busy at work and—"

"No need to apologise. I know you're busy. I don't need anything. It's good just to talk to you."

The guilt factor kept on climbing. "So, how are you and Grandma?"

"I'm very well, busy on the croft and with my other work. Grandma's getting increasingly frail so I'm afraid she'll be spending today in bed, as she does most days now. But we plan to enjoy our day."

"Well, give her my love, won't you?"

"I will. Right I suppose I should let you go, get ready for your friends arriving. Merry Christmas, my darling."

"And to you. Bye."

Sophie sighed with relief when the call was over. She also pushed down the misery that she knew would overwhelm her if she let it. It didn't help that along with everything else there was the added pain of missing Steven.

It was then she decided to open the Christmas present he'd given her. It was a beautiful tree of life silver pendant and she had tears in her eyes when she read his message on the gift tag. It said, 'Life is precious as we both know. Live your best one sweetheart'" She was drying her eyes when her phone rang.

"Steven, hi," she said.

"Hi, Soph. Merry Christmas and thank you so much for my hoodie. It's prefect."

"I'm glad you like it. And … and thank you so much for my present. I love it."

"Good. I thought it was apt as well as being pretty."

"It's perfect."

"So, are you all right, on your own? I could come over. It's not too late."

"I'm fine, honestly. Let's just to stick to the plan. Go and be with your family. Don't worry about me."

"If you're sure."

"I am. Go." Sophie ended the call, hoping she sounded convincing.

Steven wasn't easily put off. After their call, he texted her a couple of times, checking she was okay.

She appreciated that he did but it was really a form of sweet torture and she had to ask him to stop. All she wanted was to be with him. It was then she realised that her need for him and her desire to be with him were actually stronger emotions than her grief and her other sadness. Acknowledging to herself that this was the case was like flicking a switch. Her friends were right. Steven was right. The time was right.

She needed to make some changes. It was indeed time to live her best life.

She was awakened at eight o'clock on Boxing Day morning by the door buzzer and her phone message alert both sounding at the same time. She considered not responding to either. The text could wait and she knew that her friends wouldn't be calling round for a visit this early. But when her phone then began to ring and the door buzzer sounded again – only this time whoever it was, was keeping their finger on the damn thing. She forced herself out of bed.

She answered her phone as she stood in the hallway pressing the door intercom button. "Yes?" she said grumpily and was greeted by a familiar voice through both.

"It's me. Let me in."

"Steven," she said, her heart racing and wondering what on earth was he doing here. He was supposed to be at his parents' house till the next day.

"Yep, it's me and don't even think about keeping me out."

Sophie buzzed him in immediately. It was only as she opened the door to her flat and heard his footsteps coming slowly up the stairs that she realised she was in her pyjamas, her hair was a mess and she was bursting for the loo. Knowing it would take him a minute or two to climb the two flights, and leaving the door ajar, she made a dash for the bathroom. She came back out into the hallway still in her pyjamas, but with her hair sort of brushed and feeling decidedly more comfortable, just as Steven came in through the door.

She gave a little gasp as she looked at him. God he was gorgeous – even in a beanie hat.

Steven returned her gaze before his eyes swept down her body and back up again. She was now even more acutely aware that she was wearing nothing but sleep shorts and a vest.

"What are you doing here?" she said as he took off his jacket.

At first he didn't reply. Instead he held up a finger as if asking her to wait a moment before turning to hang up his jacket, hat and scarf on one of the hall hooks. He then turned back to look at her and her breath caught in her throat at the intensity of his gaze, "This," he said walking towards her. "This is what I'm doing here."

The next thing she knew she was in his arms and he was kissing her, kissing her greedily and passionately. She responded by kissing him back just as passionately, inhaling the smell of his aftershave and the unique masculine scent of him. She shivered with pleasure as his hands slid down her bare arms, before moving down to her waist, slipping under the edge of her vest and then moving up her sides. Sophie let out a little moan at the feel of his hands on her skin. But it wasn't enough. She wanted him, all of him and she didn't want to wait a moment longer.

When she pulled back slightly, Steven immediately withdrew his hands from her waist and looked at her, concern in his eyes. "Sorry," he said. "I … I got a bit carried away there. I—"

"Don't be sorry," Sophie said, putting her hands on his shoulders. "It's just … it wasn't enough."

"Oh," Steven said, a small smile now appearing.

"Yes, oh," Sophie smiled back at him before giving him what she hoped was her best seductive look, accompanied by her best seductive tone. "So come on, soldier, it's high time you took me to bed."

Steven groaned a deep, sexy groan as she peeled off her vest. "Yes, ma'am," he said huskily before putting his hand in hers and letting her lead him to her bedroom.

They only made it to the doorway before Sophie pulled him in for more kisses. They staggered together towards the bed. "Too many clothes," Sophie said against his mouth as she pulled up his sweater. He quickly pulled it over his head, followed by his tee-shirt.

Sophie ran her hands over his bare chest and abdomen. His upper body was as impressive as she'd imagined – firm and contoured – and she loved the feel of his muscular tattooed arms as they pressed into her back. Steven eased her down onto the bed before pushing his jeans and boxers down to his knees. Then he sat down on the edge of the mattress with his back to her. "Just need to get these off," he said, glancing over his shoulder at her.

"Wait," she said pushing herself up and off the bed to kneel down in front of him. "Let me," she said as she pulled his jeans and underwear further down to below where his prosthetics joined his legs. She averted her eyes from the obvious sign of his arousal. All in good time, she told herself, before running her fingers along the join on his left leg then feathering kisses along it. She looked up as Steven, his head tipped back, let out a hiss.

"I need … you need … to stop that right now," Steven said in a strangled tone as he looked down at her.

"So show me," she whispered. "How do I get these off you?"

"Can't wait that long, baby," he said. "Just watch and learn for next time." His grin was the most wickedly sexy thing she'd ever seen.

She did as she was told and watched as he released both prosthetics and removed them along with his boxers and jeans.

She told him she was on the pill. She also told him that she'd had herself checked at the family planning clinic after Rick – just in case, as she put it, he'd left her with more than a whole lot of anger and hurt. He hadn't. She was good to go. He assured her that he was also clean but that he'd use a condom if she preferred.

"Seems there's no need for us to have any barriers between us," she said, pulling him to her.

As they explored each other's bodies, Sophie thought she'd never felt so alive. Steven was a considerate and attentive lover, putting her needs first and seeming to enjoy seeing the results, before giving himself up to the pleasure she gave him. Eventually they rolled apart and lay together sated and exhausted.

After a short while, Steven put his arm round her shoulder and pulled her to lie against him, her head on his chest.

"Wow," she said, looking up at him and smiling. "That was definitely the best sex ever."

Chapter Sixteen

Steven

Steven had fantasised plenty about having sex with Sophie. But he'd never imagined it would be as amazing as it was. He'd never experienced anything quite like it before. He loved how Sophie demonstrated her obvious desire for him and the way she acted and responded to him. He loved how she made him feel.

Christmas Day with his mum and dad had been as good as it always was with lots of good food and drink and plenty of laughter, but afterwards he'd lain awake for most of the night, unable to get Sophie out of his mind. He hated that she'd spent Christmas alone and he hated it even more when she told him to stop texting her – even if it was only for the rest of the day. He missed her so much he ached and all he knew when he got out of bed early on Boxing Day morning was that he had to see her.

So, as soon as he was dressed and had left a scribbled note for his parents saying not to worry but there was something he had to do, he'd driven straight to Sophie's.

He thought that at worst she'd speak to him through the intercom and assure him she was okay, and at best, she'd let him in, hopefully share more delicious kisses and she'd agree to spend the day with him. He hadn't dared to hope it would end up like this. But there he was, in her bed with her naked in his arms after having what, he had to agree, was the best sex ever.

"It certainly was," he said grinning at her as he agreed with her verdict.

"So, what brought you here?" Sophie asked as she stroked his chest before propping herself up on one elbow. "Not that I'm unhappy you turned up."

"I just had to see you. Couldn't sleep for thinking about you and next thing I know I'm driving over here."

"And what if I hadn't let you in?"

"At first, on my way here, I thought I'd be happy just to hear your voice and to at least be in the vicinity – but when I got here I realised that I wasn't going to take no for an answer. I had to *see* you, see that you were okay, and I'd break the door down if I had to."

Sophie giggled – a heavenly sound that did things to his body – things he would definitely be responding to before very much longer.

"How very caveman," she said, giggling some more. "And yes, you were very insistent – all that simultaneous and persistent buzzing and phoning."

"Like I said I was determined to see you, but I never thought we'd end up, you know …" he let out a gasp as Sophie began kissing a downward trail which started at his throat and was rapidly heading south.

"Doing this?" she said only pausing the kisses for a brief moment.

It was another hour before they even considered getting out of bed.

Before they got dressed, Sophie took a shower and then, with Sophie's help and the addition of a kitchen stool in the shower cubicle, Steven did too.

It was when they were seated at Sophie's small kitchen table having a brunch of bacon and egg rolls, that Sophie said, "So, do your parents know where you are? And won't they be cross with you for not being with them today as planned?"

"Ah, yes, about that," he said rubbing the back of his neck and feeling both sheepish and nervous. "I left a note saying I was out attending to something that couldn't wait. But Mum called me when you were drying your hair and she wasn't having any of it when I said I was with a friend who needed me."

"What did she say?"

"She said, and I quote, 'That's very good of you, son. So we'll expect to see you both here later and you can introduce us to the woman who had your head in the clouds all day yesterday.'"

"What? You've told her about us already? Before we'd even … you know …"

"No, that's just it. I didn't tell her. She guessed. That's my mum. I never could keep anything from her."

"Okay, so what did you say?"

Steven cleared his throat. "She … she asked, or rather she insisted, that we – you and me – join her and Dad for a leftovers buffet later followed by an evening of card games and cocktails. And I … I kind of said we'd be there."

Sophie gave another of her irresistible giggles. "Oh my God," she said. "That's so funny."

"What is?"

"You, a soldier who's been in the most terrifying situations, but who's scared to say no to his mum and is just as scared to tell me what he's agreed to."

"Ah, that's where you're wrong," Steven said shaking his head as he too laughed. "I'm way more scared of you than of my mother – and that's saying something."

"Okay, at ease, soldier. And I can't believe I'm saying this but I'll come with you."

"What? I can't believe you said it either. I really thought—"

"You really thought I'd get all defensive and cross again and refuse this invitation too?"

"Yeah, I did, as evidenced by my nervousness about asking you. But really you don't have to come. I can make excuses and stay here with you, if you like, that is."

"I know I don't have to come. But I actually want to."

He grinned at her "Well all I can say is I'm pleasantly surprised."

"It's taken me a while but meeting you and talking with Lainey and Paula, and Lizzie too, it's helped me to see I need to let myself be happy again. It has also helped me to realise that to do that I need to take risks, stop playing everything so safe." Sophie paused, frowning slightly as she took a breath.

Steven sensed there was more she wanted to say. "And?" he said gently.

"And it's not only taking a risk with you, it's everything else too. I need my life to be less cut off, to stop only going out for work or when my friends force me to. I need my life to stop being too much about grief and protecting myself and to be more about joy and taking chances."

He reached across the table for her hand before gently stroking the inside of her wrist with his thumb. "That's great, Soph. Realising all that, it's real progress."

"I know and, like I said, as well as my friends being there for me and cheering me on, a lot of my progress is down to you."

"Oh, how?"

"Getting to know you, hearing how you've been through so much, how you've overcome so much, it's made me think even more, not only about being in a relationship but about my life in general. You've helped me realise it's *me* who has to change things, I have to make an effort, stop hiding, make a new life, just like you've done. So I'm going to say yes to the stuff that will help me do that – starting today with accepting your mum's invitation."

"Okay," Steven said softly. "But this, whatever this is that we have, it works both ways. Getting my life back, it's still a work in progress but meeting you, getting to know you ..." he paused as he grinned at her and reached for her hand, "and then this morning, getting to know you even better ... and how you accept me as I am, accept me as the normal, regular guy I'm almost back to being."

Sophie squeezed his hand. "So, maybe it's like you said, we *are* helping to clear up each other's mess?"

"Yes, but for me at least, it's starting to be more than that." He looked into her eyes and she looked back at him with uncertainty and maybe even fear. Inwardly he cursed himself. He knew he shouldn't push it. She was making progress but he also knew she needed to take things slowly. It was amazing enough that they'd had sex. He really needed to rein himself in.

But when Sophie spoke, the momentary apprehension in her expression was gone and there was even a bit of a smirk on her lips. "Well that's as maybe, but right now there's still a mess." She nodded in the direction of the dishes and debris from their brunch. "And you need to help me clear this one up."

"Ma'am," he said, giving her a salute as he stood up and smiling with relief that he didn't seem to have upset her after all.

But the truth was he'd fallen for her in a big way. Sophie was way more than someone he fancied, way more than a friend with recent new benefits. The truth was he was falling in love with her.

Chapter Seventeen

Sophie

Sophie was thrown when Steven said that for him their relationship was beginning to be more than them being there for each other, more than them helping each other sort out their lives. Of course having sex with him was a big deal but she'd been ready for it – more than ready for it.

She meant what she said about the positive effects that meeting him had had on her. He was good for her as a friend and now as a lover too. She liked him a lot and he was already way better for her than Rick had ever been.

She certainly wanted to continue seeing him but she couldn't commit to any more than that.

So she knew she'd have to be careful, knew she'd have to remind Steven that she wasn't looking for a forever. There could be no moving in together, no long-term plans or commitments such as marriage or kids, no expectations beyond simply enjoying being a couple for as long as whatever was developing between them lasted.

She took comfort from the fact she succeeded in making light of his declaration. And he'd seemed relieved when she moved the conversation on in a light-hearted way. So it was likely that he hadn't intended to suggest anything too serious either.

Like she said to Steven, it was time to focus on enjoyment, on getting back to truly living, on saying yes to new experiences. So she started as she meant to go on and agreed to go with him to his parents' house.

The drive to Bearsden on the city's north-western fringe only took around fifteen minutes. As they pulled into the driveway of a substantial detached villa, the front door opened and a tall, smiling, silver-haired woman came out onto the step. She waved at them as they got out of the car. Sophie suddenly felt nervous.

"Hi, Mum" Steven said. He placed his hand gently on Sophie's lower back as they walked towards the house. "You'll be fine," he whispered.

"Hi, son," his mother replied while looking intently at Sophie. "And you must be Sophie," she said, opening her arms. "I'm Sue and it's so good to meet you." Before Sophie had a chance to reply she was enveloped in a hug.

Sue led then into a large living room. The first thing Sophie noticed was the huge Christmas tree filling the space in front of the bay window. Her gaze then travelled round the room. Two of the walls were lined with bookcases and framed photos and assorted ornaments sat on top of an old-fashioned sideboard. Three large sofas along with a worn comfy-looking brown leather armchair provided the seating. A wood burner glowed in the corner. The smell of the burning wood combined with the aroma from the tree filled the warm room with a wonderfully soothing scent and Sophie felt instantly at home.

"Hello," said a deep voice from behind her. She turned to see a tall man with short grey hair and a neatly trimmed beard smiling at them all. He was carrying a basket of logs.

"Hey, Dad," Steven said. "Here, let me take that," he said reaching for the basket. "Sophie, meet my dad, Bill."

"Hello there," said Steven's father. He handed the basket to Steven before reaching to shake Sophie's hand. "Welcome and Merry Christmas." The warm tone of his voice and the way he greeted her made her feel like she was already a friend of the family.

Sophie could also see where Steven got his good looks. As

well as having the same lovely eyes as his mother, he had his father's smile. "Merry Christmas to you too," she said.

"Right," said Sue. "Bill, you get everyone sorted with a drink and Steven can you help me set up the card table. Board game first, then food, followed by card games and cocktails. You know the drill."

Steven laughed and shook his head. "I do indeed and I knew there'd be no escape from the games." He turned to Sophie. "Sorry, I did warn you. I'm afraid there's no point in arguing. It's just a pity I decided to drive and can't even have some alcohol to take the edge off the torture."

"Why the warning and why are you apologising?" his mother said, winking at Sophie. "And of course there's no point arguing. Anyway, you know you love it." Sue tutted. "Torture indeed."

It was the most fun game of Monopoly that Sophie had ever played. She even managed to win despite some dubious deals struck by Steven and his dad to try to thwart her and Sue. She also felt relaxed and at home as they played and then talked together. Even when Sue said, "Our dear son has told us nothing about you, Sophie, and I'm sure he has his reasons, but is it okay to ask how you met and how long you've been friends?"

Sophie glanced at Steven. He rolled his eyes and mouthed 'sorry'. Sophie smiled at him.

"Of course it's okay," Sophie said. "We've known each other since the autumn. We first met through our work and then again at a party. We've been friends since then." Sophie went on to explain what her job was and how it had led to her going to Revive.

"I see," said Sue. "Steven has told us about the programme and it does sound like it could do Revive a lot of good. But he never mentioned meeting you and making a new friend." She raised an eyebrow at her son, her expression full of mischief and teasing.

Both Sue and Bill then went on to ask Sophie lots of questions about what it was like to be at the BBC and about her role there. Then, after they'd talked to Steven about how the making of the Revive programme was going, Sue said, "Right, time for food."

Steven's description of what they'd be eating as a 'leftovers buffet' didn't do the spread justice. There was a turkey platter, mince pies and Christmas cake, but there were also bitesize haggis bonbons, pork pies and sausage rolls, along with salads, dips, and homemade bread. It was all delicious. It was set out in the kitchen and they all sat round the large pine table to eat. It was while they were eating that Sue ventured to ask Sophie some more questions about herself.

Meanwhile Steven chatted with his dad but as he did so Sophie was aware of him occasionally glancing in her direction. It was clear from his expression that he was checking she was all right and she'd reply with a slight nod that she was. In fact far from feeling pressured by Sue's questions, Sophie found she was relaxed. She felt safe and she felt welcomed by Sue's interest in her, an interest that was perfectly judged so it didn't feel in any way intrusive. By the time they'd finished eating, Sophie had told Steven's mum a bit more about her job and about growing up in Edinburgh. She'd shared that her parents were divorced, that her mother lived on Skye and that her father still lived in the capital, but she didn't go into any more details on that particular topic. She explained more about her and Steven's mutual connection with Dean and confirmed that she and Steven had been on a few dates.

She even found herself telling Sue about what had happened to her brother. As she did so, Steven and his father stopped their conversation to listen too.

Sue squeezed Sophie's hand with tears in eyes when she'd finished and Bill said, "Ah, lass, I'm so sorry to hear about your loss." He put his hand on Steven's shoulder and added, "We're so grateful that our boy came home. We're very fortunate and don't take it for granted." He cleared his throat, obviously moved. Sophie could only nod as she wiped at her own tears.

"Right," said Sue. "I think a cup of tea is what's required now." She turned to Sophie as she stood up. "And thank you, darling, for sharing your sadness and loss with us. Have no doubt, Bill and me, we look on that as a privilege."

"Thank you," Sophie said, marvelling at just how amazing Steven's parents were. She could see how he'd turned out to be the amazing person he was.

The cups of tea were followed by the promised card games and cocktails. The cocktails were superb, both the alcoholic and the non-alcoholic variety. The games were great fun. It was also great fun for Sophie to hear Steven's parents' tales of Steven when he was growing up. Most of them were embarrassing for Steven of course but he took it in good part.

When it was time to leave, both Bill and Sue gave her a hug and thanked her for coming.

All in all, for Sophie, the visit to Steven's parents was a poignant reminder of what home and family could and should feel like. And she told Steven that on the journey home to her flat that evening.

"So, no regrets then?" Steven asked her, glancing over at her from the driver's seat. "I know Mum can be a bit full on."

"No, no regrets at all. Your mum and dad are lovely. And it made me remember the happy times I had with my own family before all the crap."

Steven reached over and squeezed her hand. "My folks liked you too and, who knows, maybe, in time, you can make up with your own mum and have happy family times of your own again."

"Maybe," Sophie said sighing and feeling far from convinced.

Both Sophie and Steven were on holiday from work between Christmas and New Year and they spent a lot of that time together sometimes at Sophie's, sometimes at Steven's. It was an easy and relaxing few days with lazy brunches, walks, sofa snuggles and lots of amazingly good sex.

They saw in the new year at a party at Paula's. Lainey was

there and so were Dean and his wife. She hadn't seen Paula or Lainey since before Christmas and although they'd kept in touch as usual via their WhatsApp group, it was good to meet up in person. However, though she'd been able to keep her text messages to her friends fairly non-committal, confirming only that she was continuing to see Steven, it quickly became obvious that meeting in person required full disclosure.

It wasn't long after she and Steven arrived that Sophie was beckoned by Paula to follow her out of the living room. Steven and Dean were deep in conversation about football so Sophie wasn't too upset at having to excuse herself. Paula led her to her bedroom where Lainey was waiting and it was immediately apparent why the three of them needed to be away from the other party guests. She'd walked into an inquisition.

"So, you and Steven?" Lainey said, with a wicked smile. "You look very … comfortable together. More comfortable than you've been admitting to in your texts. Would Paula and I be right in our suspicions that we haven't been given the whole truth?" Lainey and Paula shared a nod and a knowing look before turning back to Sophie.

"Yeah, Sophie," said Paula, her smile wicked then amused. "We need *all* the facts. So start talking."

Sophie couldn't help but smile wickedly back. "I don't suppose this could wait until after the party. Maybe next week we—"

"No, no, no," Lainey emphasised each no with a wave of her finger. "It's now and now only."

So, Sophie, accepting that only the whole truth was going to suffice, fully updated her friends on how things were going with Steven. She told them about the dates, about Boxing Day at his parents, and admitted that they'd slept together. She also told her friends that Steven and her had agreed to see how things went, to enjoy what they had while they had it and that neither of them were expecting anything long term.

"Well that's bloody brilliant," Lainey said before hugging her friend. Paula then joined in the hug and said, "Enjoy every minute you have with him for as long you want to."

"I will," said Sophie. "Now can we please get back to the party."

It was a cold and snowy Saturday morning at the end of the second week in January when her mother phoned to tell her that her grandmother had died. She'd been out at the cinema with Steven the previous evening and then they'd spent the night together at hers. They were in the kitchen having breakfast when her phone rang.

She was aware of Steven watching her as she took the call while seated opposite him at the table. He'd clearly figured out who was calling and what the call was about as he'd reached for her free hand as she talked.

As the rather brief conversation with her mother came to an end Sophie said, her voice trembling, "Thank you for letting me know and I'm … I'm so sorry. Grandma was one of a kind."

"Indeed she was," her mother replied. "I'm going to miss her."

"Yes, I will too," Sophie said, realising as she did so that she was also missing her mother. But right then she had no idea if or how she could fix that. She did, however add, "I hope the funeral goes okay. Take care of yourself."

"Thank you. I will. Love you, Sophie."

"Yes, bye, Mum."

Sophie flung her phone down on the table as the call ended. She covered her face with her hands as a mixture of a moan and a sob escaped from her mouth. "Not again," she spluttered as Steven pulled her to her feet and enveloped her in a hug.

For a few moments he hugged her and rubbed her back before leading her through to the living room where he gently pulled her down beside him on the couch. "Your grandma," he said softly rubbing at her tears with his thumb.

Sophie nodded as she accepted the tissues he'd grabbed from the box on the coffee table. "Yeah, she died last night at home with Mum by her side."

"I'm sorry," Steven said, hugging her again and kissing the

top of her head.

Nestling into Steven's side, Sophie said, "I knew Grandma was poorly and I know she was old but it's still a shock, you know?"

"Yeah, I do know," Steven said.

"And … and it's another loss on top of everything else." Sophie swallowed hard before blowing her nose. She moved away from Steven slightly and leaned forward, her elbows on her knees, her face resting on her clasped hands. She took a moment staring at the floor and trying to regain some control over her emotions. Steven, meanwhile, stroked her back and let her be.

When she was ready she sat up, took a breath, and went on, "The funeral is next week on Skye. Mum said if I wanted to go, that I'd be welcome to do so and could stay with her, but she … she also said that there's a weather warning of more snow in Scotland next week, especially from Perth northwards and so it was probably best I stay put. And she added that Grandma would have said that was the sensible thing to do."

"What do you want to do?" Steven said.

"I don't think I want to go," Sophie said, "but…"

"But?"

"But I'd just be using the bad weather as an excuse. It's not like I haven't driven in snow before and I haven't actually seen any weather warnings for next week. The truth is, I don't think I can face it … after Finlay … and with things being the way they are between Mum and me and everything. And I know that sounds pathetic."

"No, not pathetic at all," Steven said, slipping his arm round her shoulder. "It's understandable. It also seems like your mother guessed how you might feel and she and the weather forecast have given you an out. Maybe she's also aware that it would be easier on both of you if you stay away. I imagine she'll be wanting to focus on the loss of her mother while, like you, also still dealing with the loss of Finlay."

Sophie leant back against him. "You make it sound so

reasonable and simple."

"The bereavement itself isn't, but whether you attend the funeral or not definitely is. Do what works for you. If you want to go, then go, and I'll come with you if you'll let me. Or stay at home and remember your grandmother and say goodbye in your way. And if you want some company when you do that, I'll be here for you."

Sophie looked up at him as he spoke, looked into his beautiful eyes and saw nothing but warmth and concern in them. If only she could let herself believe …

"What are you thinking?" Steven asked, his voice still soft.

"I'm thinking I don't know what I did to deserve you. And I want to believe that it's okay if I don't go to the funeral because … because I don't think I can."

"Then don't go. It's definitely okay. And right back at you as far as the deserving thing goes."

Sophie smiled at him, already feeling a bit better. "Thank you," she said. "For listening and for understanding." She also realised as she spoke that despite her reservations about true love and long-term committed relationships, Steven was someone she could rely on to always make her feel better.

"Your mum also said that your grandmother would understand how you feel."

"Yes, I think she would. She was an amazing woman."

"So why don't I get us both a coffee and you can start remembering her right now by telling me all about her," Steven said.

"I'd like that," Sophie said.

"My grandmother's name was Miriam … Miriam Weitzmann," Sophie said. "She was Jewish, born in Germany in 1930. As you can probably guess she had a rough childhood but she was one of the lucky ones, if that's the right way of describing it, and she escaped Nazi Germany when she was only eight years old. She was one of the children sent to the UK on the Kindertransport. Her mother, father and older sister all died in the concentration camps."

"Oh no, that's awful," Steven said, clearly horrified. "So what happened when she arrived in the UK?"

"She was adopted by a Scottish couple, a couple who lived here in Glasgow. When she grew up she trained as a nurse. And it was one summer when she was on holiday in Skye with a friend that she met my grandad, Donald Macpherson, at a local ceilidh dance. Like I said before, he was a Royal Marine. He was home on leave at the family croft on the island. They were married for over fifty years until Grandad died four years ago. They had two children, my mum and my Uncle Jonathan."

"And were your mum and her brother brought up as Jewish?"

"No, actually they weren't. Grandad was presbyterian Church of Scotland through and through but he wouldn't have minded if Grandma had wanted their children to be raised as Jewish. But it was Grandma who was against it. She was one of the strongest most stoical people I have ever met but there was one thing she never came to terms with and that was what had happened to her family, simply because of their cultural and religious background. She equated being Jewish with being vulnerable and so she buried her heritage deep and became more Scottish than any of us."

Steven nodded. "Well if that's what worked for her, she was right to do so."

"Yeah, the only person who ever challenged her on it was Uncle Jonathan. He lives in Israel, has done for years, unlike Mum and Grandma, he fully embraced that part of his heritage."

"Interesting," said Steven. "And how was she with you – as a grandmother?"

"She was strict and she had high expectations. But she could also be great fun and she was always very loving towards me and Finlay, as she was to all the family, Mum, Uncle Jonathan and his wife and family too, even though he'd emigrated against her wishes. She was a very special woman. And in the end she had a good life."

Sophie noticed how calm she'd become as she talked about

her grandmother, and how that was down to Steven. She reached for him and pressed her lips to his. He too felt like someone very special.

It was a feeling that persisted for the rest of that day. It was there when she showed Steven photos of her grandmother and shared more stories about her. And it was still there later when they watched a couple of movie favourites from their childhoods and shared a delicious Indian takeaway. She knew she was going to have to be careful and guard her heart but she also knew she wasn't ready to walk away.

So as January progressed, Sophie was happy that she and Steven began to see each other more often. They no longer kept their meetups to the weekend only. They went out on dates but they also spent time together at each other's flats – sharing meals, relaxing while watching TV, and spending the night together. In fact they were spending so much time together that Steven made what he obviously saw as a sensible assumption but which Sophie saw as a possibly worrying signal.

It happened after work one Friday evening near the end of January. They hadn't seen each other for a couple of days and, as arranged, Steven would be coming to hers for dinner. Sophie felt the now customary butterflies as she anticipated his arrival and hoped he'd be staying over afterwards. When she opened the door to the flat to let him in she was puzzled to see he was carrying a folded up wheelchair.

Steven nodded at the wheelchair as he leant it against the hallway wall and took off his jacket. "I thought this would make showering here easier," he said. "And it means I can take the prosthetics off for rest periods when I'm hanging out here. It's the one I got when I first came out of hospital. It's a bit on the small side so I've since replaced it with the one I use at home now. But it'll do fine for when I'm here. So, where would you like me to put it?"

"Oh, I don't know. I …" Sophie felt twinges of anxiety. Was

this just the start? Was Steven planning on moving more stuff in, on moving himself in? Her sensible brain knew she was being ridiculous but her gut was another matter.

Steven picked up on her discomfort immediately. "I can take it back," he said. "The last thing I want to do is have you feel I'm encroaching on your space."

"No, no don't be daft," Sophie said. "I'm sorry. It's a good idea. I'm being an idiot, overthinking and—"

"Shh," Steven said, before preventing her saying anything else by kissing her, kissing her long and deep.

"What was that for?" she said breathlessly when he released her.

He gently pushed a lock of her hair behind her ear. "It was for you and it was to tell you to stop beating yourself up and to stop apologising for how you feel. I didn't intend to upset you and I should have asked first."

"Oh, right." Sophie ran her finger along her lips as she thought not only of the kiss, but also of how this man made her feel. He made her feel seen, valued, and respected.

"I promise you, there's no agenda," Steven said, looking into her eyes. "The chair's a practical piece of equipment that will make my life easier when I'm here. Think of them like the toothbrush I discovered, the one you sneaked into my bathroom cabinet – and the one I plan to sneak into yours." Then he grinned his sexy grin before kissing her again.

Chapter Eighteen

The next morning when Steven awoke he was glad it was Saturday and he didn't have to rush off to work. Instead he could spend a few moments enjoying looking at a still sleeping Sophie as she lay in his arms. It wasn't long before she too was awake. She smiled a lazy and incredibly sexy smile as she wriggled even closer to him.

"Hey there," he said softly, smiling back at her.

"Hey there, yourself," she said, before pressing her lips to his.

After they'd kissed, he cupped her face, stroking along her cheekbones with his thumbs and gazing into her eyes.

"What are you thinking?" she said.

"I'm thinking how lucky I am to be here with you, how lucky I am that you trust me and that you decided to give us a go."

Sophie smiled again. "Yeah, you are pretty lucky." She giggled but then looked serious. "But then so am I. I'm lucky that you understand me and why I can't commit to the forever, happy ever after stuff, and that you accept that's how it is."

"Of course I understand. I'm just happy to be with you now, to be enjoying how things are between us in the present." Steven meant what he said. He *was* happy to with her – at that moment and in all the other moments they'd had up till then. But the truth was he wanted more. He wanted lots of future moments, moments that *would* add up to happy ever after and forever. So he knew he'd have to be careful for both their sakes because he'd been kidding himself that he was falling for her. The truth was he'd already fallen for her. And he'd fallen hard.

His resolve to be careful was immediately tested when Sophie began running her hands down his chest and following them with a trail of kisses. Then all thoughts deserted him as he gave himself up to the delicious pleasure of making love with this amazing woman.

After he was showered and dressed Steven checked his phone. The two texts he'd been hoping for were there. His recent purchases were ready to be collected. He went over to Sophie who was still lazing in bed and after he'd kissed her he said, "I'm going out. Going to get us some breakfast."

Sophie yawned and stretched and looked so sexy and inviting it took all his self-control not to strip off and get back into bed with her. "Okay," she said. "Breakfast sounds good."

When he got back he left his other bits of shopping on the hall table and took the breakfast items through to the kitchen. Sophie was already in there.

Dressed, but with her hair still damp from the shower, she paused loading up the washing machine to greet him. "Hello, you," she said, coming over to him. "Mmm, something smells good." She put her arms around his neck and he pulled her in for a long deep kiss.

"Yeah," he murmured inhaling the scent of her shampoo as the kiss ended. "You smell divine."

"Not me, you idiot. Breakfast, the coffee."

"Oh, yeah, that," he said. "I got the bacon rolls at the place round the corner. And the coffee and croissants are from the bakery near the bus stop."

"Both good choices," Sophie said grinning at him. "So let's eat. I'm starving after all that exercise earlier."

"What? You've been out for a run?" Steven grinned back at her knowing perfectly well she hadn't.

* * *

When they'd finished, Sophie began to clear the table.

"No," Steven said, putting his hand on her arm. "That can wait. Please, can you sit down? I have something for you."

"Okay," Sophie said giving him a puzzled look.

He retrieved his other shopping from the hall. First he placed the pot plant on the table in front of Sophie who now looked even more puzzled. Pointing at the red rose blooms, he said, "It's called a Remembrance rose, apparently. The flower shop on the main road ordered it in specially when I told them what I was after. It can be grown in the pot or you can plant it in a garden. I thought you might like it as a way of remembering your grandma. You told me she liked gardening and I know you were upset not to be going to her funeral. So …" He gave a little shrug, hoping he hadn't messed up.

"Oh," Sophie put her fingers to her lips and blinked at him. "That's so—"

"And I got this too," he said, sliding a small velvet box across the table to her.

Sophie's eyebrows shot up. "Oh," she said again, only this time more loudly.

Steven suddenly realised what she was thinking might be in the box. "No, no," he said. "It's not … it's not that. Not what you think it is. It's just a …" He rubbed the back of his neck. "Just open it, for heaven's sake."

Sophie laughed as she shook her head. "Relax," she said. "I honestly wasn't thinking it was, you know, that diamond thing, well not for more than a split second anyway." She opened the little box and gasped as she removed the silver heart-shaped locket.

"I got the idea right after I thought of getting you something to mark your grandmother's passing. I thought … I thought maybe you'd also like a memento of your brother. Something you could wear and have close to you." He pointed to the tree of life necklace she was already wearing, the one he'd given her for Christmas. "I also thought you could maybe wear it on the same chain as that, if you wanted."

"Oh," Sophie said again, this time her eyes full of tears.

"It's engraved on the back."

Sophie flipped the heart over. "Forever Finlay," she whispered as she read what was etched there.

"And you could put his photo inside too if you wanted." Steven cleared his throat as his own emotional reaction mirrored Sophie's.

Sophie got up and Steven did too, coming round the table to meet her. "Thank you," she said before putting her arms round his neck and kissing him softly. Steven could taste her tears as he kissed her back.

"I'm sorry I made you cry," he said when the kiss ended. He placed his hands on either side of her face and wiped at her tears with his thumbs.

"Don't be sorry. They're good tears. I love the idea of wearing the heart together with the tree of life. These are such thoughtful gifts, Steven. No one has ever … I've never … I don't know what to say."

"You don't need to say anything. I'm just relieved you like them. I was so hoping you wouldn't be offended or think I was being presumptuous again."

"How could I be offended?" Sophie said as she grabbed a piece of paper towel from the worktop and wiped away her remaining tears. "It's such a lovely thing to have done. You're such a lovely person and I don't know what I've done to deserve you."

"Must have been something really bad," Steven said, stroking her face before pulling her to him again.

"So, I hear you're quite the natural in front of the camera," Sophie said with a teasing smile. It was a couple of weeks after he'd given her the plant and the locket, a couple of weeks when they'd both been exceptionally busy with work. Sophie was just back from a few work-related days away and they were once again at the Garam Palace for dinner. Steven had surprised himself with how much he'd missed her.

"Oh really, now how would you have heard that?" Steven pretended to look puzzled as he flicked his fingers against his chin.

"I have my sources," Sophie tapped the side of her nose. "I popped in at the office when I arrived back in Glasgow earlier and you were the talk of BBC Scotland."

"Aye right." Steven grinned. "I doubt that very much."

"Yeah well, okay, I bumped into a couple of the folk from the production team currently filming at Revive, and they seemed impressed by the good-looking manager of the centre and how he presented on camera."

Steven rolled his eyes as Sophie paused to take a mouthful of curry. He was then distracted by her appreciative moan as she enjoyed the taste. He squirmed in his seat. God, the effect this woman had on him. How he'd like to—

"Earth to Steven." Sophie was waving her hand in front of his face.

"What? Yeah, sorry. What did you say?"

"I asked how the filming's been for you?"

"Oh, it's been good, yeah. Joking apart, I was surprised how much I enjoyed being interviewed and then doing the guided tour thing. And the other folks involved, my colleagues, and the volunteers and users of Revive who were interviewed, they all seemed to enjoy the process too. I think I did the centre justice."

"I'm sure you did. You're so obviously extremely passionate about you're work, I'm sure that will come across."

"Passionate, eh?" Steven raised an eyebrow. "I hope your opinion on my levels of passion extends to areas beyond my job."

"Yeah, yeah." Sophie giggled and the sound just added to his torture. He really needed them to get out of the restaurant and home to his bedroom.

But with Sophie reading the dessert menu now she'd finished her main, he knew he'd have to be patient. So he hauled his mind back to the world of work in an effort to distract himself from the beautiful temptress sitting opposite. "Being involved in the making of the documentary and the potential positive effects it could have for the charity has been great. But I must admit my work passion is being tested at the moment and not just because the filming has caused a backlog in all the other stuff that needs my attention."

"Oh, that's a shame. So what else is putting pressure on you?"

"Two words. Spring Ball."

"What? Ball as in dance?"

"Yep." Steven sighed.

"And?"

"And, I have to organise it. Revive's trustees decided a Spring Ball would be a great idea as a fundraiser especially as it will happen not long after the documentary goes out. They plan to invite sponsors with deep pockets, as well as including the local community. All *I* have to do is make it happen, get a venue, a band, etc, etc."

"Aw, not exactly your comfort zone, I'm guessing."

"You guess correctly. I'll do it, of course I will, but it's got me wondering again."

"Wondering?"

"Yeah, I think I mentioned before that much as I enjoy the job at Revive and am grateful for it, I've never seen it as permanent."

"So you're wondering what? Whether to move on?"

"Yeah, maybe it's time."

"Have you any idea what you might move on to?"

"That's part of my problem. I'm not sure, a couple of things but they're vague and more pipe dreams than real possibilities. I'd like to get out of the city, move somewhere more rural, more peaceful." Part of him wanted to share his dreams with her, dreams which weren't quite as vague as he'd made out. But another part of him, the part that told him the time wasn't right, warned him not to. He took heed of the warning. Not yet. Maybe not ever.

He sighed. Being patient and remaining hopeful about the future of his relationship with Sophie was hard. But if things worked out the way he hoped they would then the wait would be worth it.

"I'm sure you'll work it out," Sophie said gently, presumably thinking his obvious consternation was solely due to his thoughts about his working life.

"Yeah, I hope so," he said, deciding it was time to change the subject. "But what about you? How's your work going?"

"It's good ..." She paused briefly, took a breath as she seemed to hesitate, but then went on, "it's crazy busy, even more than usual. I'm still finishing off the work for the programme about the scientists when I was given this latest one on the future of Scottish farming for the BBC Scotland's television series *Land Matters*. You know the one? It features Scotland's countryside and nature stuff."

"Yeah, I know it. Mum loves it and I've been known to watch the occasional episode too."

"Only the occasional episode?" Sophie laughed. "Well you're going to have to add the new series to your favourites list since I'll be part of it."

"Definitely." Steven smiled as he relaxed once more and just let himself enjoy the company of this beautiful, funny and fascinating woman. For however long it lasted, he was going to make the most of it.

Chapter Nineteen

Sophie

Sophie felt excited as she drove home from work. It was the middle of February, St Valentine's Day, and even though it was four months since Dean's party, the flutters of anticipation she got at the thought of seeing Steven showed no signs of lessening.

She'd insisted on cooking dinner for her and Steven at her place, and now, as she waited at a red light, she recalled the conversation they'd had about it a couple of weeks before.

"Doesn't seem very fair," Steven said. "Having you cook. Especially after work."

"You cook for me plenty. Seems perfectly fair that I return the favour occasionally."

"Yes, but not on St Valentine's Day. It's a day when I want to be spoiling you."

"A day for over-the-top prices at restaurants and florists, more like," Sophie said. "It's too commercialised."

"So beautiful, but so cynical." Steven laughed as Sophie let out a pretend gasp and playfully swatted at his arm with the back of her hand.

"I'll take the beautiful bit, but cynical, me? As if!" She smiled knowing he was just teasing but there was an element of truth in what he'd said. With what she'd been through, it was hard not to be cynical. Sure, Rick gave her flowers for Valentine's Day, albeit they were mostly rather bedraggled last-minute ones, and he'd taken her out for dinner, but she'd usually ended up paying at least for her share, if not the full bill. Like so much of what she'd come to realise since the split from Rick, it was just another empty and self-serving gesture on his part. But Steven wasn't Rick so she added, "*I* want to spoil *you*. So here's the deal. Let me cook for you and we can have a romantic night in at my place."

"Mmm, let me see." Steven's grin was mischievous and sexy as he tapped his chin. "I come to yours and I get fed and romantically spoiled. Sounds good, especially the romantic spoiling. We have a deal."

Sophie's recollection of the conversation made her smile as the lights changed to green and the queue of rush hour traffic began moving again. It was true. Steven was definitely not Rick.

Steven wasn't like any of the men she'd dated previously. His attentive and generous lovemaking made her feel worshipped in a way she'd never experienced before. But the effect he had on her was more than purely physical. His kindness, his patience and the way he listened, *really* listened, they were all helping her to heal. Steven was helping her find her way back to herself.

Steven was still on Sophie's mind after she arrived home and began preparing dinner. Recalling what he'd said about being ready to change his job, about wanting to move out of the city, caused the same feeling of dread as it had when he'd first told her. She knew it was irrational to be upset about it. She was the one who insisted their relationship wasn't going to last for ever. It was also hypocritical to want him to remain in Glasgow when she was considering a move to Bristol. She'd almost mentioned the possibility of her own move but something, she wasn't sure what, stopped her from doing so.

However, it wasn't something she was going to be able to keep from Steven for much longer. Not after the conversation she'd had with her boss earlier that day.

George had called her into his office and being George, he got straight to the point. "So, the Bristol senior researcher job I mentioned a while back, it's got the go ahead. Karen Phillips, the head of the Natural History Unit, she's been in touch. I'd said to her before that we had someone here who could be perfect for the job. She wanted to know a bit more so I told her a bit about you and your time here. She'll be emailing you inviting you to apply."

"Oh, right. That's good." Sophie's mind was in a whirl.

"Not only that. There's a vacancy coming up for a commissioning producer at the unit and Karen suggested you apply for that as well."

"What? Really?"

"Yes, really. I don't know why you're so surprised. You'd be ideal in either role but the producer one would be a fantastic promotion."

"I don't know what to say." Sophie struggled to take in what George had said. Her, a commissioning producer. Senior researcher at UK level was awesome enough, but to be in the position to come up with programme ideas, to bring those to fruition would be amazing.

"You don't have to say anything and much as I don't really want to lose you, you should get on and apply for both jobs and then make sure you get the producer one. You're more than good enough, Sophie and you've earned it. Now get out of here, you've got a CV to get together."

She sighed with frustration as she set the table. Why now? Why did two dream jobs, both of which would require her to move hundreds of miles away, have to come up now? Why couldn't it have been before, before she met Steven, before she'd got herself in way too deep with him?

Once in the shower she gave herself a talking to. Perhaps she and fate had actually got it right. Being with Steven was great, a lovely but temporary interlude. Perhaps, with his own talk of moving on, Steven had also come to accept that. She wouldn't mention Bristol this evening but she'd tell him soon. There was no need for a big drama, no need to feel sad or regretful. A whole new life could be waiting for her. She would embrace it if it happened and perhaps Steven and her could even remain friends.

That's what she told herself as she put on the little black off-the-shoulder dress she'd recently treated herself to. She applied her makeup and perfume and slid a sparkly clasp into her hair. She also put her heart and tree-of-life pendant back on. She only ever took it off when she was having a shower. Then after slipping her feet into a pair of black high-heels and a final check in the mirror she was good to go, determined to give Steven the most romantic night of his life.

She checked on the main course cooking in the oven and then lit the candles she'd placed on the kitchen table and all around the living room. Steven was due to arrive in about half an hour.

As she wondered what to do in the meantime the door buzzer sounded making her jump and setting her heartrate climbing. He was early. "Come on up," she said into the intercom not even checking that it was Steven. Who else would it be?

She opened the door to the flat and waited. Hearing the rapid speed of the footsteps coming up the stairs should have alerted her. Her visitor wasn't Steven.

Sophie's gut twisted, her heart hammering even more now but no longer for positive reasons. "Rick! What are *you* doing here?"

"Now, what sort of greeting's that, babe?" Rick smiled his slick smile as he strode up to her, his arms outstretched. "I was in the area. It's Valentine's. I thought I'd call in to see how you're doing."

Sophie took a step back, her hands raised in front of her. "Woah," she said. "You can't just turn up like this. We're … I'm—"

"Look, I need to talk to you. I can see you're dressed to go out with the girls but can you just let me in, hear what I've got to say, in private." Rick nodded at the doors to the other flats on the landing. "You never know, it could be worth your while."

"I doubt that very much," Sophie said scowling.

"Please just give me ten minutes then I'll be on my way, if that's what you want. Or, you know you could cancel the girls and we could—"

"Enough!" Sophie shouted, Rick's suggestive tone and expression brought her close to losing her temper. She desperately wanted to tell him to piss off but she suspected he'd just keep bugging her until she gave in. Better to get it over with. "Right, ten minutes, then you're gone." She stood aside and waved him in.

Once they were in the living room, Rick headed over to the sofa.

"Don't bother sitting down," Sophie said, her jaw beginning to ache from the pain of gritting her teeth. "Just say whatever it is you've come to say."

"Aw, don't be like that, babe. Haven't you missed me even a little bit?" He gave her his trademark cheeky grin.

"No, I haven't." Sophie looked at him, at his tousled dark hair and those deep brown eyes with the mischievous twinkle she remembered so well. Old memories of the good times they'd shared began to bubble up. She shoved them down. Of course she'd missed him. At first, the extent of her missing him had been almost unbearable. But she wasn't going to tell him that. The suddenness of the breakup, the betrayal, the sheer lack of guilt and ingratitude on his part, they'd all but broken her. There was no way she was giving him the smallest crumb of comfort or affirmation. "So spit it out," she said.

"Me and Lisa, we've split up."

Sophie fought down the urge to punch the air and kept her expression neutral as Rick looked at her, obviously waiting for a reaction. When he didn't get one he continued, "It was never going to work, her and me. She didn't get me, not like you do. She didn't like that I'm all about the music, that making money's not important to me. She said she wasn't prepared to subsidise my life."

Sophie felt a sneaking admiration for Lisa. She'd done what

Sophie should have done. Sophie couldn't understand how she'd been so blind. But still she said nothing.

"And the thing is," Rick went on, "I realise now I never should have left you. We worked so well together. You supported me. I supported you. It was good. And you must be lonely just like me. My stuff's all in the van. I could bring it up now. You could still go out with the girls but you'd have me to come home to. Or maybe you could cancel and we could have a proper Valentine's night in, get to know each other again."

Sophie gasped. She tried to speak but didn't know where to start.

Rick came towards her, took hold of her hand. "So what do you say, babe? Can I move back in?"

She pulled her hand free. "What do I say? I say absolutely no way. No way are we getting back together."

Rick gave a scoffing laugh. "Aw, come on. You don't want to end up a lonely old spinster, do you? Not when you can have this." He lifted his arms and flapped his hands to indicate his body. "Why would you not?"

Sophie continued her struggle to keep calm as she looked pointedly at her watch. "There isn't time for me to list all the reasons why I would never get back with you. All I'm prepared to say is I've moved on and it looks like I'll soon be leaving Glasgow."

"Moved on? Leaving Glasgow?"

The door buzzer sounded before Sophie could reply. "Ah, that will be my Valentine's dinner guest," she said before going to the intercom.

When she returned to the living room, Rick said, "Dinner guest?"

"Yes, I'm in a new relationship. Not only that, but I could also be getting a new job in Bristol." Rick's expression was priceless. "But even if neither of these things had happened, there's still no way I'd be getting back with you. And now it's time for you to go." She stood aside and gestured for him to leave before following him to the front door.

Rick turned to her as he stood on the threshold. "Sophie, please just say you'll think about it. I still love you, you know, and I get that you're angry but I think deep down you still feel the spark." He moved closer and before she had time to realise what was happening she was in the tight grip of his arms and he was kissing her. She fought against his hold, tried to turn her head away, but it was no use. When he finally ended the kiss, he still kept a tight hold on her as he said, "See, there's no point fighting it, babe. There's no way Mr New Guy can kiss you like I do. Just let me know when you've stopped resisting. I'll even come live with you in Bristol so that's not a problem."

"Sophie? What the hell's going on?" The sound of Steven's voice was enough to make Rick release his grip on her as he turned to see who was there. Sophie took her chance and shoved him away from her. Her stomach churned as she looked at Steven standing at the top of the stairs, a horrified expression on his face.

"Mind your own business, buddy," Rick said, before turning back to Sophie. "This him? Your new guy?"

Sophie swallowed, her mind reeling. How much had Steven seen? What was he thinking? "Yes, it is," she said. "This is—"

"Not interested, babe," Rick said, pulling her towards him again and snaking his arm round her shoulders so that now they were both facing Steven who was walking towards them. "And what's with the stop gap's weird walk?"

Sophie winced not daring to look at Steven. "Let go of me," Sophie said, her initial shock giving way to anger as she twisted and pushed to get free of Rick's grip.

"Yeah, let go of her," Steven growled. He was up close now but all his attention was on Rick.

"No way. This is my girl. And you, you're history." Rick's stance and tone oozed a smug possessiveness.

Steven prodded Rick in the chest. "Says who?"

Rick let go of Sophie and forcefully shoved Steven back.

Sophie gasped as Steven struggled to keep his balance. "Yeah, that's right. I'm Rick, the love of her life, and I'm back."

Steven grunted, and as he steadied his stance, his fists curled. Sophie stepped forward to go to him. "Rick, no! Steven, I'm sorry, I—"

Rick grabbed her arm. "I got this." He pushed in front of her. "So, Steven," he sneered, "you need to walk away now. I say walk, but it's more like limp from what I'm seeing. You hurt yourself, have you? Maybe it's not just your walking that's limp." Rick smirked before giving Steven another shove. Steven staggered again but maintained his balance.

"Is that right?" Steven looked and sounded furious.

For a moment the two men stood facing each other. At first Sophie was mesmerised watching them, but then her own, already building anger kicked up a notch. What about her? What about what she wanted? Rick wasn't asking but Steven wasn't paying her any attention either. Instead they were focussed only on each other.

She pushed herself between them. "Right, that's enough. Rick, I can speak for myself and it's you who needs to go. I've already told you, I'm not interested in getting back together with you. You had your chance with me, you blew it. We're over. I don't love you. And after today I don't even like or respect you. I want nothing more to do with you. Leave me alone."

Rick shrugged and it was as if he hadn't heard anything she'd just said. "Have your fun with Mr Limp Along. Then when you change your mind and need a real man, get in touch. And remember, I'm more than happy to move to Bristol with you."

With that he turned his back and disappeared down the stairs.

Steven didn't move and when Sophie looked at him he was clearly still furious, but now his fury seemed to be aimed at her.

Chapter Twenty

His emotions were in turmoil, a broiling mix of anger, deep hurt and utter dismay. For a moment, Sophie held his gaze. She looked shaken and confused. She also looked stunningly beautiful. A part of him wanted to hug her but another part of him said not to. Right now he had to protect himself. He had to know exactly what was going on. So, when she turned to head into the flat, he followed her.

"What the hell just happened?" he bit out as soon as they stood facing each other in the living room.

"I … I'm sorry. I didn't know he was … I didn't know Rick was coming. And what he called you, how he treated you with such disrespect, I'm so sorry for that."

"I've been called worse and I don't give a fuck what that prick thinks of me." Yes, it hurt to be the target of ignorant abuse. Of course it did. But he'd survived far worse than ignorant name calling. That he could deal with. "What I am having trouble with is that he was here at all."

Sophie sighed out a long breath and closed her eyes for a moment. "Look, take your jacket off, sit down. I'll get us a drink and we can talk. I can explain what happened."

"No, I don't think so. I don't need an explanation."

"But you—"

"No, let me speak." Steven was doing his best not to shout,

to howl with anger at what he'd just witnessed. There was a lot he needed to say but Sophie's gasp of outrage and her own now obvious anger made him pause.

"Let you speak! That's rich. You didn't want to speak to me out there on the landing. You couldn't even look at me. You were much more interested in going toe to toe with my ex."

"Yes, I was, because from what I heard and saw it looked like you two were friendly again and it didn't seem like he was your *ex* anymore."

"What? You can't be serious! You heard me telling him to go, telling him we weren't getting back together."

"Yeah, after you noticed I was there. But before that I saw you, Sophie. I saw you kissing him, heard him tell you … tell you he'd move to Bristol with you."

Sophie shook her head and sighed as her anger seemed to be dissipate. "I can explain."

Steven suddenly felt beaten. The adrenaline that had flooded his system when he saw Sophie in Rick's arms was subsiding. The horror remained though, along with the desolation. He sighed heavily before sinking down onto the sofa.

"He turned up out of the blue," Sophie said, as she sat down at the opposite end of the sofa. "Typical Rick, no warning, took it for granted I'd be here and that I'd want to see him. The woman he left me for has dumped him. He's struggling financially. He assumed he could just come back to me and my bank account and we'd take up where we left off. Long story short, he hasn't changed. But I have."

"He seemed pretty sure you'd come round to the idea of getting back with him."

"No way. That's not going to happen. And if he doesn't stay away I'll be getting the police and a lawyer involved." Sophie looked stricken. "As I said, I'm truly sorry that you were confronted like that, shown such utter disrespect. The kiss you saw, it was totally against my will. You have to believe me, Steven. It was completely one-sided on his part. He's a totally deluded narcissist." She reached over and put her hand on his. Again he resisted the urge to hold her close. There was more that needed to be said.

He removed his hand from under hers and leaned away. "Okay, I believe you. I do. And if that's all there was to it, I'd be willing to apologise to you to. But the bit about you moving, about you going to Bristol? What was that? And how come he knows about it and I don't? Please tell me you made that up to put him off."

Sophie flinched, her discomfort obvious. "I … it's not …" She wrung her hands as she looked at him, her expression was both embarrassed and guilty. He'd rather have had the pain of a punch from Rick than the emotional pain he felt now.

"So it's true then," he said. "You *are* moving away. But you didn't think you should tell me?"

Sophie let out a half sigh, half sob. "Yes, it's true, or rather it could be. I *might* be moving south to take up a new post at the BBC. I was going to tell you when the time was right, when there's more to tell. So far all I've done is apply, it might not come to anything. And although I didn't make it up, I *did* only tell Rick in order to put him off."

Steven ran his hand through his hair as hurt and anger warred inside him. "I told you I was thinking of moving out of Glasgow. I prepared you for that even though I probably won't be far from the city, even though we could probably still see each other. I did you the courtesy of letting you know what I was thinking. It's just a shame you couldn't show me the same respect, especially as your move could have much more significant consequences for us." He struggled not to shout, to keep hold of his temper.

He forced himself to acknowledge that she'd never promised to be with him forever. She'd been upfront about not being ready for a serious relationship. But now he could see that even when they'd talked about all of that stuff, it was already too late for him. He'd already been hoping for more. He was already in love with her. "And if it does happen, when … when would you be leaving?"

"I don't know exactly, two- or three-months' time maybe."

"And you're happy to walk away, to walk away from us, from what we have."

"Not happy, but it … it's not about us. It's about me, about my future after … after—"

"After you dump me." Steven swallowed down the bile that was threatening to choke him.

"No, no it's not … I don't want to dump you … it's complicated, it's—"

"No, actually, it's not. It's not complicated at all. It's simple. Even if you don't get this job it's clear you want to move on. So let's not prolong my agony. Let's call time on us now." Panic threatened to overwhelm him. He had to get away. He stood up. "I'll see myself out. And Sophie, I hope if you get the job that it makes you happy, and if you don't, I hope you find happiness elsewhere. You deserve it. You're an amazing, beautiful woman and I'll never forget you."

Chapter Twenty One

Sophie

Disbelief, anger and guilt threatened to overwhelm Sophie as she sat on the sofa, rocking back and forth, her arms folded tight against her chest. How could the romantic evening she'd planned, and looked forward to so much have gone so terribly wrong?

She was angry at Rick, angry at how life kept dealing her these low, painful blows, but most of all she was angry at herself.

Her anger was made even worse by a large dose of guilt. She should have told Steven that she was considering leaving Glasgow as soon as she'd known it was a possibility. He seemed to believe what she told him about Rick turning up, so she was fairly certain he'd have accepted her apology for the shock and hurt Rick had caused him – if only she'd been open and honest about the possibility of her leaving Glasgow. She was an idiot to think she needed to wait for the right moment. By doing so she'd allowed the news to come out at precisely the wrong moment and in a very cruel way. She was just as guilty as Rick was of causing Steven to be hurt.

In the end though, all her other emotions were swamped by just one. When she finally crawled into bed on that disastrous wreck of an evening, she was enveloped in a deep and terrible sadness. It was a tearful, long and sleepless night.

Next morning the first thing she did was check her phone. Steven hadn't made contact.

She called him. The call went to voicemail.

She texted him, keeping it brief.

I'm so sorry. I don't want us to end. Call me. Please.

He didn't call. He didn't text. Somehow she got through the rest of the week. Somehow she got through the next one too. And still not a word from Steven.

She did, however, hear from the BBC's Natural History Unit. She got an email inviting her to attend interviews for the post of senior researcher and the commissioning producer role on the same day in April. She confirmed she'd attend both, but right then she couldn't get excited at the thought of either job.

Her present job though was a godsend. It took her mind off Steven. During the two weeks after Valentine's Day, she travelled all round Scotland meeting with farmers and gradually compiling a folder of ideas and recommendations for the Land Matters farming feature.

But during her non-working hours she struggled. She missed Steven terribly. The end had come so suddenly she couldn't get her head round it. She constantly checked her phone in case he reached out. He didn't. And all the while she beat herself up for not telling him about Bristol.

By the Friday evening of that second week, she was desperate. The guilt and the longing were wearing her out. She needed to do something. She considered contacting Lainey and Paula, telling them what had happened, getting some of their sage advice. She thought about calling Lizzie. But in the end she decided this was something she had to sort out for herself. She couldn't leave things as they were. She liked Steven a lot and missed him terribly. If it was truly over between them it would be hard, but she'd deal with it. It wasn't as if she'd been under any illusions that at some point it would end but she didn't want it to be like this. She wanted them to part as friends. She needed to put an end to her anguish. She needed to speak to Steven. And there was no time like the present.

She grabbed her coat and bag and was about to head out when the door buzzer went. It was most likely one those random people who wanted access to the flat dwellers in order to sell them something they neither needed nor wanted. She sighed as she pressed the intercom. Why now? "Yes," she barked.

"Hi, it's me, Steven. Can I come up?"

"Steven? What are you doing—? I mean, yes, yes, come on up." She buzzed him in and flung the door to the flat wide open. Her heart hammered and those bloody butterflies in her tummy were back as she waited for him. Then there he was, tall, muscular and oh so sexy, walking across the landing towards her. She feasted her eyes.

"Oh," he said. "You're going out. Sorry. I should—"

"No, or rather, yes, I was going out. I was coming to see you."

"You … you were?" Steven smiled tentatively and ran his hand through his hair. Hair that he was now wearing a bit longer. Hair that Sophie wanted to run her own hands through as she stood there staring. And that was just for starters. "So, can I come in?"

Sophie smiled, as she stood back. "Yes, yes of course. Sorry I was just—"

Her words were cut off mid-sentence as Steven crushed his lips to hers. With his hands on her shoulders he walked them both inside, shoved the door shut and pushed her back against the hallway wall. The kiss deepened as Steven entwined his fingers in her hair and she linked her hands behind his neck. She let out a little moan of pleasure and tipped her head back as he, in turn, growled and trailed kisses down her neck.

It was Steven who broke away first. He was as breathless as she was. He grinned the sexiest grin before unzipping his jacket and saying, "Maybe we should take our coats off."

"Why stop at our coats?" she said, heart racing as she shrugged out of hers.

"Glad to see you're on my wavelength," Steven said before pulling her in for another kiss, his eyes full of desire.

Leaving a trail of discarded clothing from the front door to the bedroom, and pausing only for Steven to remove his prosthetics, they fell onto the bed entangled in each other's arms. Steven kissed her, caressed her, teased her and satisfied her. And she did the same for him. They made love passionately, tenderly and several times over. Their bodies had no difficulties in communicating just how much they felt for and had missed each other. Any talking would have to wait.

Chapter Twenty Two

Steven

Sunlight was peeping through a gap in the bedroom curtains when Steven awoke the next morning. Sophie was still sleeping, curled into his side, her hand on his chest. He kept still, savouring her warmth and closeness.

The last two weeks had been grim. He'd known almost straight away he'd made a terrible mistake storming off like he had. He'd messed up big time. As the days passed the need to see Sophie grew until it was stronger than his fear there was no way back. He had to try, even though he wasn't at all sure she'd want to see him – and he couldn't have blamed her if that was the case.

At most he hoped not to have the door slammed in his face, to be able to apologise, to state his case for forgiveness. Then when she'd opened the door to him, told him she was on her way to see him, and invited him in, he'd lost all reason. All he could think about was how much he needed to kiss her, to do more than kiss her.

So it would be fair to say that, so far, things had gone better than he'd dared to expect. So far.

He kissed the top of her head and she stirred. Her eyes opened and she looked up at him and smiled.

"Morning, beautiful." He grinned back at her.

She propped herself up, her hand still on his chest and kissed him gently on the mouth. "Morning, handsome."

"Is it a good sign that you're still wearing the pendant?" he said as it brushed against his chest.

"It might be." She gave a little laugh before her expression became serious. "The truth is, whatever happens between us, I think I'll always wear it. It already means a lot to me. There's what the heart and the tree stand for, of course, but even more than that, it's the fact that a very kind and thoroughly good guy gave me it."

"Right," Steven's throat had gone dry as tears appeared in his eyes. Whatever he'd been hoping for when he'd turned up at hers, he hadn't dared hope for this.

"Oh, Steven," Sophie said, stroking his face. "What are we going to do?"

"We're going to fix this," he said. He took hold of her hand and kissed her palm. "And, I don't know about you, but I won't be able to concentrate if we're lying here naked while we do so."

"Hmm, there's that." Sophie gave him that sexy grin of hers. "Plus *I* don't know about *you*, but I won't be able to concentrate if I don't get something to eat. All that exercise last night has left me starving."

"Okay, so here's the battle plan," Steven said, loving the new lightness he felt. "Shower, breakfast, talk."

They were both so hungry that there was no awkward conversation while they sat at the kitchen table and wolfed down the bacon and egg rolls Steven had made for them while Sophie was in the shower. But when they finished eating, Sophie refilled their coffee mugs and said, "Let's take our coffees through and get comfortable."

Sophie sat on the armchair, nursing her mug, her legs curled underneath her. Steven took a seat on the sofa.

"So, you were really about to come and see me when I turned up last night?" he said.

"I was. It's been a miserable couple of weeks. I missed you so much. I hated that you didn't want to talk to me. Then last night

I decided enough was enough. I couldn't leave things the way they were even if… even if it meant having you tell me it was really all over between us."

"I overreacted," Steven said.

"I messed up," said Sophie.

"I'm sorry," they both said together.

"So what did you come here to say to me?" Sophie asked.

"I came to apologise for being a dick. Rick wound me up that day and it was a shock hearing you were maybe leaving Glasgow, but I shouldn't have stormed off like that and I certainly shouldn't have let it eat away at me for the past two weeks. But as the days went on I preferred the torture of limbo to knowing for sure you wanted to end things."

"So what changed? Why did you turn up yesterday?"

"In a word, Dean. He knew there was something up when we met for a pint a couple of days ago. I told him what had happened. Long story short it was him who pointed out I'd been a dick and that I needed to get over my hissy fit and apologise. He couldn't see a problem with you wanting to move on with your career and, if we were serious about each other, he said we'd find a workaround if and when the time comes."

"Right," Sophie said. She looked thoughtful for a moment. Steven wished he could see what was going on in her mind.

"I really am sorry, Soph. I hope you can forgive me, that we can get back to how we were before."

"I'd like that," Sophie said smiling. "There's nothing to forgive, apart from you being a dick and throwing a hissy fit, that is." Her smile turned into a laugh. Steven loved that it did, loved the sound of it. "But I need to apologise too. I should have told you about Bristol. I was an idiot for putting it off. The last thing I would have wanted was for you to hear it from Rick of all people."

"Okay, so I'm a dick and you're an idiot. A match made in heaven, I'd say." Steven grinned at her. "But seriously, tell me about Bristol."

Sophie sighed. She paused before she said anything, as if weighing it all up. Then she sat up, straightened her shoulders and went for it. "I was invited to apply for two jobs in the BBC's Natural History Unit. One is a senior researcher's post and the other, the one I'm really excited about, is for the post of commissioning producer. I've got interviews for both in April."

"I hope it goes well for you, I really do, and that you get offered at least one of them. But I'd be lying if I said I wouldn't be gutted on my own behalf. He managed a weak smile as he ran his hand through his hair, his emotions nearly getting the better of him again. "Truth is, I've become quite fond of you."

"Oh, Steven." Sophie came over and sat beside him on the sofa. She leaned into him and he put his arm round her. "I'm quite fond of you too. And I know we agreed we aren't in a forever, happy ever after relationship, that we said we'd enjoy it while it lasted, but I'm not ready to give it up, to give you up."

"Jesus, Soph, am I glad to hear that," Steven looked into her beautiful eyes, before placing his hands either side of her face and kissing her.

It was Sophie who broke away first. "Okay, soldier," she said laughing, "that was an awesome kiss, but we need to stay focussed on our talk."

"Yes, ma'am," he said, laughing too. "So, here's what I suggest. For now we continue as we were but with the proviso of no more secrets." He waved his finger as he said those last three words. "If something is going on in either of our lives that will affect the other person, we spill."

"I promise," Sophie said. "And yes, we go on as before."

"Good. Let's enjoy the present, what we have now. And like I said recently, I'm thinking of leaving the city too. Although I was imagining it would be to live and work in a rural setting in Scotland, within an hour or two's travel time from Glasgow, maybe I could look at the Bristol area if and when the time comes."

"Oh, I don't … you'd do that? Really?"

"Yes, really, if it's what we both wanted. But like I say, that's for the future. Who knows what that holds?"

"Okay." Sophie squeezed his hand.

It didn't take them long to get back to how things had been between them. In fact, Steven thought their relationship was even stronger after they'd faced up to and dealt with their first real challenge, something he confirmed to Dean when he spoke to him on the phone. It was just a few days after he and Sophie had sorted things out when Dean checked in with him.

"Yeah, Soph and me are good. We're not worrying about the future, just enjoying what we've got now."

"I'm glad to hear it," Dean said. "So we still on for a curry on Friday night?"

"Absolutely. We're both looking forward to seeing you and Emma."

After he'd hung up Steven punched the air. Sophie and him really were sorted. And even though he knew it was against the rules they'd agreed on, he let himself dream that the present would lead to a future where they remained together.

It was good to be back at the Garam Palace. Steven noticed Sophie looked rather pale and tired when she arrived at the restaurant, but she seemed to be enjoying their evening out with Dean and Emma as much as he was. It was while they were waiting for their main courses that Sophie excused herself and made a dash for the toilets. When she came back, she looked even paler than before.

"I'm so sorry," she said, as she stood by the table, "but I'm going to have to go. I'm not feeling very well, bit of an upset tummy."

Steven stood up as Dean and Emma commiserated with her. "No, no," she said. "You stay. I'll call a taxi and go wait by the door. I could do with some air."

"You're not going home on your own," Steven said. "Sorry folks," he added, turning to Dean and Emma who assured him he should indeed go with Sophie.

She didn't put up any resistance and they only just made it back to his before she had to run to the bathroom.

Steven felt helpless as he heard her retching. All he could think to do was to be with her and hold her hair out of the way as she was sick. The skin on the back of her neck felt clammy and he could feel her body shaking. Eventually she collapsed against him and seemed unable to move. Steven propped her against the bath and then ran a face flannel under the hot tap.

"Thank you," she whispered as he gently wiped her face and neck.

"Do you think you can stand now?" Steven straightened up and held his hand out to her.

She nodded and he helped her up.

After he got her into bed and, having fetched her a glass of water and placed a plastic 'just in case' bucket on the floor beside her, he sat with her, stroking her hair, hoping she'd give in to sleep.

She resisted at first. "I'm so sorry," she said. "That was so embarrassing. I should go home. You don't have to look after me."

"I know I don't have to," he said. "But I want to. And besides, you can hardly stand up never mind make the journey home."

"But I threw up. Looks like I've got the bug that's going around. What if I give it to you?"

"I'm willing to take that chance," he said, kissing her on the forehead.

Weirdly, it had been as he cleaned up in the bathroom afterwards that he knew for certain he was in love with her and that she really was the woman he wanted to spend the rest of his life with.

By the end of the weekend Sophie was feeling a lot better and they arranged to meet at hers for dinner on the Tuesday evening after work. Steven insisted he'd cook and Sophie was having a soak in the bath while he got on with the food preparations. He'd just put the wine he'd bought into the fridge to chill when Sophie's phone which she'd left lying on the kitchen table began to ring. He glanced at it and seeing who the caller was, he decided to pick up.

"Hello, Sophie's mum," he said.

"Oh, hello is Sophie there? It's her —"

"Mum, yes, you came up on caller display. I'll give her a shout."

Taking the phone with him he found Sophie in the bedroom getting dressed. "It's your mum," he said, waving the phone at her.

"What? And you answered it?" Sophie frowned.

"Yeah, well, I saw it was her and I didn't think you'd spoken in a while so I just thought …" his words trailed off. He stood, his hand still raised clutching the phone, hoping he hadn't spoiled the plans he had for the evening.

Sophie sighed. "I really wish you hadn't," she said. "But it's done now. Tell her I'll be ready in a minute."

"Will do," he said. As he walked back along the hallway to the kitchen he spoke again to Sophie's mother. "Sophie's on her way," he said. "She's just out of the bath but she won't be long. I'm Steven by the way."

"Oh right, I'm Rachel. You're a friend of Sophie's?"

"Yes I am. Has she not— oh, here she is now. Nice talking to you, Rachel."

Steven looked at Sophie as she stood in the kitchen doorway. Her hair was down, she was dressed in dark blue jeans and a long-sleeved pale blue tee-shirt and she looked so beautiful. However, she also looked cross. "Really?" she said, frowning deeply. "Rachel? You and my mum on first name terms?"

"Just being friendly," he said. "I introduced myself and so did she." He smiled a hopeful smile. It wasn't returned. Sophie shook her head before snatching the phone from him.

A little while later Sophie was very quiet as they ate the hot-smoked salmon linguine he'd made for them. Other than assuring him it was delicious when he asked if the food was okay and giving monosyllabic replies to his questions about how her day had been, she didn't say anything. In the end with her so obviously lost in thought, he let her be.

However, by the time he served up dessert he decided he had to broach the subject, if only to clear the air before he made his suggestion. "So do you want to talk about it?" Steven said as he placed the bowl of her favourite vanilla and salted caramel ice cream in front of her.

"Talk about what?" Sophie said, looking at him as if she'd forgotten he was there.

"About your conversation with your mother."

She pursed her lips and gave a little shrug. "Not much to talk about really," she said. "My mother has started grief counselling." Sophie's expression was fierce. "Apparently this is helping her get over the death of my brother." She reached for her dessert spoon but didn't begin eating. Instead she twisted the spoon round and round in her hands. "And she wants to come and see me in May. She'll be coming to Glasgow to get her flight to Israel. She's going to stay with her brother and his family for three months."

"This will be her first time in Israel?" Steven asked. "First time she's visited your uncle?"

"Yep, like I said before, Grandma wanted nothing to do with the place and Dad was never keen on her going. He didn't like the idea of her travelling alone – especially to the Middle East." Steven was about to say that surely that was her mother's decision to make. But he didn't get the chance. "Anyhow she doesn't have to take Grandma's feelings into consideration anymore, and she said she's told Dad and thinks he's okay with it. Not that she cares what he thinks. She said it's something she needs to do and now feels like the right time. So she's going."

"I think that's amazing," Steven said without thinking. "Good on her for following her heart."

"Hmm," was all Sophie said, clearly not liking that Steven was impressed.

He decided to move the conversation on. "And did you say she could come here to see you?"

"Yeah." Sophie sighed. "I suppose if she's going to be away for so long I should at least touch base with her. So, yes she'll be coming for a visit."

"Right," Steven said. He nodded in the direction of her bowl of dessert. "Ice cream's melting," he said.

Sophie pushed the bowl away and stood up. "You know what, I don't really feel like it," she said, scowling. "Thanks for cooking. But having to take that call, it kind of killed the mood. I'm going to get an early night." Her whole body looked tense and her voice sounded strained. "Don't bother clearing up. I'll do it tomorrow. See yourself out." And with that she was gone.

Standing alone in the kitchen, Steven let out a long breath as he heard Sophie close the bedroom door behind her. Without consciously deciding to disobey Sophie's instructions he began clearing up the kitchen.

It was unfortunate that the phone call had come when it did, but his earlier annoyance with himself for answering it was gone. He'd done it with the best of intentions, thinking it would be a good thing if Sophie and her mother talked. Yes, he would apologise to Sophie but he would also explain that he hadn't meant to cause her any upset. He decided to finish tidying up, go home, and call her in the morning.

It was as he was about to set the dishwasher off that he heard a sound behind him. He turned and there was Sophie standing in the kitchen doorway, in her pyjamas, arms folded, shaking her head and frowning.

"Sorry," he said. "I was—"

"You were disobeying a direct order, soldier," Sophie said, shaking her head again, the corner of her mouth twitching.

"Yeah, I didn't mean to. But it's done now and I was just about to head home. Sorry if I disturbed you."

Sophie put her hand over her mouth but her eyes gave her away. She was smiling. Then she laughed. "So you cleared up by accident?"

Steven laughed too, partly with amusement but mostly with relief. "Seems like it," he said.

"Oh, Steven," she walked towards him, her arms outstretched. "It's me who's sorry," she said as he pulled her against him. After a few moments she lifted her head from his chest and looked up at him. "I'm sorry I got so cross and upset after Mum's call and I'm sorry I took it out on you. You didn't deserve that." She laid her head on his chest again and he dropped a kiss on her hair.

"It's okay," he said. "I should have let the damn thing ring. I shouldn't have assumed. I'd no idea it would upset you that much."

"I told you I was a mess," she said, her voice a whisper. She put her hands on his shoulders and reached up to brush her lips against his before adding, "Now, are you coming to bed or what?"

He didn't need to be asked twice.

Chapter Twenty Three

It was Friday evening, just a few days after the phone call from her mother, and Sophie was with Lainey and Paula on a long overdue girls night out. They were in Bella Bodega, a tapas and cocktail bar in the city centre. Lainey and Paula had already shared their latest news as they all enjoyed their selection of small plates including olives, ham, cheese, meatballs, prawns, lamb kebabs, bread and various salads. Now it was Sophie's turn to update her friends on what was going on with her.

"And when I say what's the latest with you," Paula said, "I mean with you and Steven. Rickgate and all the crap afterwards, are they well and truly behind you? We need to know."

"Yeah, seconded," Paula said.

Sophie took a deep breath. Steven. He was never far from her thoughts. "Yes," she said. "Rickgate, Bristolgate and Vomitgate are all behind us." She took a sip of her mojito, before going on to tell them about the aftermath of his answering her mum's phone call and how good he'd been when she'd been snarky.

"He's one of the good guys," Paula said.

"Hang on to him, Soph. He's the one," Lainey said.

"Yeah, he's definitely one of the good guys," Sophie said, horrified to find tears in her eyes. "He's sensitive, caring and kind ..." She reached for her glass, taking not so much a sip as a gulp of her cocktail. "But ..."

"But what?" Lainey said, frowning. "And, oh no!" She leaned in towards Sophie. "Why are you crying?"

"What's wrong?" Paula said, reaching across the table to place her hand on Sophie's.

"It's nothing. Well, not nothing exactly." Sophie wiped her tears with the back of her hand. She sighed. "It's just … I'm scared. I think I've got in too deep and I don't *want* my relationship with Steven to end, but I kind of know that it will. It's got to, hasn't it?"

"So, let me get this straight," Lainey said. "He's prepared to go with you if you go to live in Bristol. He didn't take it personally when you were upset over your mother's phone call. He was even prepared, to be with you when you were throwing up. But you don't think he's a keeper?"

"Oh, I think he's a keeper for somebody, just not for me. I know that sounds pathetic but—"

"But you don't believe you can be truly happy, do you?" Paula's voice and expression were so full of compassion that Sophie felt her tears start again.

She shook her head. "No, I suppose I don't."

"Well you better believe it, sweetheart. If anyone deserves happiness it's you," Lainey said, as she moved closer to Sophie on the bench seat they were sharing and put her arm round Sophie's shoulder. "Of course there are no guarantees in life, but you've got to give yourself a chance, give you *and Steven* a chance. It's like we've said before, you need to relax and enjoy what you have with him *now* and not go second-guessing the future. Don't rule anything out or let your doubts spoil things between you."

Sophie smiled a rueful smile as she looked from Lainey to Paula. "Talking of deserving, I don't know what I did to deserve two such amazing friends but I'm so bloody grateful to have both of you in my corner. Thank you. And yeah, you're right, I do need to relax and enjoy being with Steven." She paused and took a deep breath. "So that's what I'm going to do."

"Yes!" Lainey said, grinning, before lightly punching Sophie on the arm.

"Here's to friendship and being happy," Paula said raising her glass.

"Yes, indeed," Sophie said clinking glasses with the other two. She could do this. She could enjoy what she had with Steven and she could even dare to hope.

The final fortnight of March was busy for Sophie and Steven. Sophie was researching a programme about Scotland's rivers that would be presented by a famous Scottish crime writer as he walked each river from source to sea. So she was away from home a lot as she travelled the country from the north to the south, from the Spey to the Tweed. And Steven was deep into the planning and organising for the Spring Ball at Revive which would be happening in early April.

When they did get together though things between them were better than they'd ever been.

"I like this new relaxed version of you," Steven said one evening as they lay stretched out together on his sofa. Sophie was nestled into his side and he kissed the top of her head before she turned to look up at him.

"Mmm, I like it too," she said before kissing him on the mouth. She meant it. Yet again the advice given to her by her two amazing friends had been spot on. She was enjoying going with the flow. She was enjoying being in a relationship with such a wonderful guy. Bristol might happen, it might not. Steven and her might remain as a couple, they might not. But for now she was making the most of what she had there and then.

"So, everything all organised for the ball? Can't believe it's only a week away." She swung herself up to a sitting position and grabbed her glass of wine from the coffee table.

"Yeah, just a few last minute details to sort but I think we're all set." Steven also sat up and reached for his beer. "I just hope it all goes well on the night and we raise lots of funds for the centre."

"It's going to be great," Sophie said. "With you as commanding officer, how could it not be?" She grinned at him.

"I appreciate your faith in me." Steven grinned back. "And I'm so glad you're going to be there with me."

"Nowhere else I'd rather be. Besides, it gave me the perfect excuse to buy a new frock."

The ball was a great success. The venue, the band, the buffet, everything was perfect. Sophie and Steven were sharing a table with Steven's parents, and Dean and his wife. Paula and Martin and Lainey and her date, Ed, were also close by at a neighbouring table. So the company and the chat was good too.

"You've done a brilliant job, soldier," Sophie said to Steven when the band were taking a break. She was helping Steven get prepared to draw the raffle and announce the winners of the impressive prize donations. "And I don't just mean the raffle prizes – and just so you know I'd like to win the spa day."

Steven grinned at her. "I think there might be claims of a fix if that happens."

"Pfft, that won't stop me accepting my win," she said, grinning back. "But seriously this evening, all of it, it's incredible. Everyone's enjoying it and you must have raised a good sum."

"Thanks, I'll take incredible," Steven said. "And yes we've raised an awesome amount, been worth all the stress. Mind you," he said slipping his arms around her and pulling her to him, "it would have been worth it just to see you in this dress." He ran his hands down the silky bodice, before kissing her.

"Glad you like it," she said giggling as she indicated the long green, lowcut dress she'd spent a record amount on and which even she had to agree suited her perfectly.

"I'm going to like it even more when I'm removing it later," he whispered in her ear.

A couple of weeks after the ball both Sophie and Steven were preparing for a few days away from home. Steven was going to visit his aunt and uncle and cousin, Aidan, at their farm in the

Scottish Borders and Sophie was heading off to Bristol for her interviews.

"So, you raring to go? Ready to knock 'em out at the interviews?" Steven said.

"I'm not sure why," Sophie said, when they were having a drink together at a pub near Steven's flat on the evening before they both went off on their respective journeys, "but I don't feel as excited as I thought I would at the prospect of either of these possible new jobs."

"It's probably just you brain's way of not letting your expectations get out of hand, protecting you from disappointment," Steven said. "Not that I think you're going to be disappointed. I reckon you'll be snapped up for both and the higher-ups will have to fight it out to claim you."

"Hmm, maybe." She wasn't convinced. Something had definitely changed regarding how she felt about both the posts she was going for. Something was trying to push her to pursue something else entirely. She just hadn't figured out what it was yet. "Anyway, how about you? You looking forward to your few days away?"

"Yeah, it'll be good to see my aunt and uncle. It's been too long since I visited. And Aidan has promised to talk me through the kinds of jobs I could consider if I do decide to base myself in a rural setting. He's even going to let me help with the sheep and cows on the farm – something I haven't done since I was a teenager."

"Sounds like you're going to have a great time," Sophie said.

"I think I will but it would be even better if you were coming with me. It's such a pity my leave and your interviews ended up coinciding."

"I know, can't be helped," Sophie said, thinking she would actually prefer to be going with him. There was something definitely weird going on in her mind but she was baffled as to what it was.

It was only when she was actually offered both jobs following her interviews, that she realised why she didn't want either role after all. She'd always dreamt of leading a team, and as for the producer role she hadn't even dared to dream she'd ever get that. But something in her had changed recently.

She didn't want to be desk-based and now she was faced with that prospect she realised just how much she loved the excitement of the hands-on, in-person research process. She'd miss travelling to new places, meeting new people and she'd miss the adrenalin rush of excitement as she uncovered facts, ideas and angles that could lead to great programmes.

She had a sort of epiphany on the train home. Maybe she should be considering going freelance, be her own boss, maybe set up a small company of her own. She even started jotting down some ideas about how that might work.

Sophie was surprised by her new thoughts on her career but she was also excited by the possibility of change. She opened up her laptop and as the train headed north she sketched out some ideas. She couldn't wait to share them with Steven. Maybe instead of him following her to Bristol, she could go with him to wherever he was considering and base herself and her business outside the city. She smiled as she looked out the widow of the carriage and allowed herself to dream.

It was a couple of days after she got back from Bristol when, for the second morning in a row, she had to make a dash for the toilet as soon as she got up. When she was finished throwing up, she got in the shower and it was as she stood under the soothingly hot water that the realisation of the likely significance of what had just happened hit her.

Looking back over the last couple weeks she could see she should probably have been more aware that something was up with her. She'd had vague feelings of nausea on and off during that time but they were short-lived and she put them down to being tired or not taking the time to eat properly. But now that the nausea had evolved into early morning throwing up she realised what she needed to do. She needed to rule out the obvious possibility of what might be causing her symptoms.

As soon as she was dressed she headed out to the supermarket. When she returned she did what she had to do.

Even though she kind of knew the pregnancy test would be positive it was still a shock when she saw the two vertical lines on the test stick. Such was her reluctance to believe it, she called into work to say she'd be a bit late then went back to the supermarket and bought another test.

The result was the same. She was definitely pregnant.

So much for her dreams.

Chapter Twenty Four

It was the weekend following Steven's visit to his cousin's farm and Sophie's trip to Bristol. They hadn't had a chance to meet up since they'd both got back a couple of days earlier so they'd arranged to spend the whole weekend together at his place. Sophie arrived at the flat straight from work on the Friday evening.

From the moment she arrived, she appeared tense and preoccupied. "Dinner's ready," he said, ushering her into the kitchen as soon as she'd hung up her jacket.

But instead of her usual curiosity and enthusiasm about what he'd made for them she just sat down at the table without a word and watched him as he served up the chicken casserole.

"I hope you like it," he said as he laid her plate in front of her.

She gave him a small smile and a small nod of acknowledgement.

"So, the interviews went well," he said as they began to eat. "You sounded positive when we spoke afterwards."

"Yeah, both of them went well," she said.

"Good," he said. "And I had an interesting few days on the farm with Aidan. He said to come again soon and to bring you with me."

"Did he?" Sophie's voice was weak and her tone flat.

After a few more moments of watching her pushing the food around her plate without actually eating any of it, he said, "You okay?"

"I'm fine," she said, a touch defensively, before sighing. "Sorry, I'm just tired. It's been … it's been quite a week."

"I'm sure it has," he said gently. He smiled at her but she didn't return it. "Yeah, well, eat up and then we can relax together with a movie."

She hardly ate anything and said even less and in the end she pushed her plate away. "I'm sorry," she said. "Seem to be too tired to eat or speak."

"Doesn't matter," he said. "I'm just glad to be with you." He decided not to take it personally when she didn't return the sentiment. She obviously didn't want to share what was bothering her, and he wasn't going to push her to talk until she'd had a good night's sleep. He consoled himself by putting her unease down to the impending visit from her mother. That and the fact she was clearly exhausted was more than enough for him to cut her some slack. So he wasn't overly concerned when halfway through the movie he'd picked out for them to watch she announced she was having an early night and went off to bed without him.

On the Saturday morning, she got up before him and when she returned to his bedroom from the bathroom she looked a little pale. She also said she didn't want any breakfast which wasn't like her. After they both showered and dressed she said she fancied going for a walk.

"Good idea," Steven said. "Get some colour back in your cheeks."

"Yeah," she said smiling, but the smile didn't quite reach her eyes. The tension was back but then she seemed to gather herself. She stood a little straighter and looked as if she'd come to a decision. "Do you want to come with me?" she asked.

"Actually, I think I'll stay here. I really should change the bed and get some laundry done. Why don't you go, I'll catch up with the domestic stuff and then I'll make us both brunch when you get back."

For a moment she looked uncertain, disappointed even. But then once again she seemed to make a decision. "Okay," she said.

"But there's something I really need to discuss with you. So we'll do that first. When I get back, yeah?"

"Absolutely," he said. He couldn't be sure of course but he bet she'd had a job offer and wasn't sure how to tell him. He gave a little shrug as he contemplated moving south. If it meant being with Sophie that's what he'd do.

It was almost an hour later when she returned. He'd finished his chores and was about to pour himself a coffee when she let herself in. He loved the fact they had keys to each other's flats and it really felt like maybe the next move could be them living together – wherever that might be.

"Hi," he said, smiling when she came into the kitchen. He was pleased to see she was no longer looking pale but she still appeared nervous. He held up the coffee pot. "Want one?" he asked.

"Em, no," Sophie said as she walked towards the sink. "I think I'll just grab a glass of water and then can we talk?" Her voice was a bit shaky when she spoke and her hand seemed to tremble as she turned on the tap. She was definitely nervous.

"Of course," he said. "Let's go through."

Steven sat down on the sofa and sipped his coffee as he looked at Sophie. She laid her glass of water on the coffee table but remained standing, twisting her hands as she looked back at him.

"What is you want to say, Soph?" he said softly. "No need to be nervous."

Sophie laughed but it was a small, strained sound completely lacking in mirth. She took a deep breath. "I don't really know how to say this, how to tell you…" she sighed and looked briefly at the ceiling before going on. "I'm pregnant."

Steven managed to stop himself choking on the sip of coffee he'd just taken. "What?" he stuttered. "Sorry." He shook his head, he hadn't seen that coming. "You're pregnant?" His mind was racing. He thought back to first thing, when she'd come out of the bathroom looking so pale. Was that morning sickness? And her being so preoccupied lately, now it made sense. Okay, so it was unexpected. But it was all right. Actually it was more than all right, it was good, great in fact. Raising a child, their child, it could mean they'd remain as a couple long term, live together as a family—. He stopped the stream of thoughts and reined himself in as he became aware Sophie was speaking again.

"Yes, pregnant," she said. "I've missed two periods now. I hadn't realised as I tend to be a bit irregular but eventually it dawned on me it had been while since my last one. So yesterday I did a test, in fact I did two, and yes, definitely pregnant."

"But how?" he said gently. "How could it happen?"

"It was the tummy bug, I think. Remember back at the start of March?"

Steven nodded.

"I probably threw up one pill and then the next day, when I stayed in bed to recover, I forgot to take that day's pill. Then next day when I felt so much better, we … we—"

"We had morning sex, unprotected morning sex?"

"Yes," Sophie said, wringing her hands again.

Steven got up, hating see her so distressed. "It's okay, Soph, we can do this," he said, extending his arms towards her. "We can have a baby, raise a child together in any way you want, separately, together, whatever." He meant what he said. They were having a baby and it felt right. But as he attempted to hug her she raised her hands in front of her, warding him off.

"No," she said. "Please, don't. There's more I need to say. Please just—"

"Okay, okay," he said, still speaking softly as he backed away. "But at least come and sit."

However, before either of them could move Sophie said, "I can't keep it. The baby. I've thought about it and it's for the best. I'm going to have an abortion." Sophie's voice had become quieter and quieter as she spoke and she was now looking down at the floor. "I'm sorry," she whispered still not looking at him.

Steven could take no more. He shoved aside the twist in the

gut disappointment he felt at her decision. All he knew was he loved her whatever, and he had to close the distance between them. This time when he went to take her in his arms she didn't resist. Instead she collapsed against him as she let out a huge sob. He held her tightly as she cried, stroking her hair as he too spoke in a whisper, repeating over and over, "It's okay."

After a while as he sensed her stilling, he moved back slightly and tilted her chin with his finger so he could see her face. He rubbed at her tears before saying, "I'll be with you whatever you do. But know this, if part of your decision not to go through with the pregnancy is because you don't think I'd want the baby, then please disregard that. I'd love to have a child with you."

Sophie let out a little gasp, her eyes large with surprise or was it shock. She shook her head and looked away.

"Soph," he said, gently turning her head so she was looking at him again. He cupped her face in his hands. "Don't look so worried. What I'm saying is, this is your decision but I'll support you either way. We're in this together, like I said. And I want us to be together, to really be together in all aspects of our lives. In fact what would you say to us moving in together? Obviously I'd prefer it to be here at my place with it being ground floor and adapted but if you'd rather—"

"No!" Sophie's voice was back to full force as she pulled away from him and the hand-wringing was back. "No, Steven," she said. "I need space, some time on my own. I need you to let me go. I've been offered the producer job in Bristol. Maybe this is fate's way of telling us now's the time."

"The time for what exactly?" Steven struggled to keep calm as a mixture of frustration and apprehension coursed through him.

"Time for us to call it a day. Seems to me our relationship has run its course."

Chapter Twenty Five

Sophie

Devastated didn't begin to cover the look on Steven's face as she stumbled away from him. He called after her as she dashed into the hallway, his voice full of anguish as he begged her not to go. But she knew she mustn't hesitate, mustn't give in to her own anguish. She had to go. So she grabbed her jacket and the bag she'd packed the night before, the bag containing most of the stuff that had gradually found its way from her flat to his, and she fled.

She was so angry with herself. She should never have let things get this far with her and Steven. She should have ended it weeks ago. She shouldn't have waited for a crisis to rip her world apart once again.

Would she never learn? Her estrangement from her mother, the loss of her brother, the disaster that was Rick, she'd been through enough. She had nothing left to give.

By the time she got home, she had two missed calls from Steven followed by a couple of text messages. The texts were brief but heartfelt.

The first one said,

Talk to me Soph. I need to know you're ok. Please don't shut me out xxx

And the second one was a stab to her heart,

We're in this together, the pregnancy, our lives, everything. So worried about you. Please call me xxx

She couldn't take any more. She couldn't face talking to him right then. She switched off her phone, before collapsing on the sofa.

She was exhausted. Having started the day by puking her guts up, followed by a walk she could scarcely remember taking, and then not being able to face breakfast hadn't exactly helped her physical wellbeing. However, her physical exhaustion was nothing compared to how wrung out she felt mentally and emotionally.

Even though she couldn't imagine a better father for a child than Steven, the reasons behind her decision not to have children remained. So the time had come when she needed to let him go, to let him find someone who had their life – or more precisely their head – sorted out. He deserved much more than she could offer. No ifs, no buts. It was the right thing to do, as was ending the pregnancy.

After seeing the test result she knew that her dream of going freelance was just that, a dream. It was going to have to wait until she'd recovered and regrouped. So, she decided instead that she would accept the producer's job in Bristol despite her earlier qualms. Instead of fearing the changes it would bring to how she spent her working days, she needed to embrace them. A fresh start in a new place hundreds of miles away was exactly what she needed.

But telling herself she was doing the right thing didn't make her feel any better. Feeling utterly defeated, she curled up on the sofa and cried until she fell asleep.

It was only when the door buzzer sounded loud and persistent, that she jumped awake. She sat up in a panic before making her way to the intercom. "Yes," she said as she held down the communication button. "Thank God," came the reply. "You're alive. Buzz me in right now." Paula's voice was a mix of concern and pissed off.

As soon as Sophie opened the door to her flat, her friend came into the hall and grabbed her by the shoulders. She looked Sophie up and down before staring her in the face. "What the hell's been going on?"

"What do you mean?" Sophie said.

"I got an anxious call from Steven, after he'd begged my brother for my number. He said you walked out on him, that you were very upset, and that you weren't answering your phone. He said he didn't think you'd let him in so could I come and check on you. Then all the way here I try phoning and texting you, and I get no response either."

"Right," said Sophie. "You'd better come in."

"So what's going on?" Paula said once they'd both sat down on the sofa. "You and Steven fallen out?"

Before Sophie could reply the flat buzzer sounded again. "That'll be Lainey," Paula said. "I called her to see if she'd heard from you and when I told her about Steven's call she said she was coming over too."

Paula was right as to the identity of this latest caller, and soon Lainey had joined them in the living room.

"So, spill," said Paula.

Sophie knew there was no way she could avoid telling her friends what had happened. And so with Paula and Lainey sitting either side of her, and with the support of lots of hand holding and back rubbing as she spoke through her tears, she told them about the pregnancy and that she wouldn't be going through with it.

"Oh Sophie," Paula said as she hugged her. "I don't know what to say other than I love you and I'll support you through this any way I can."

"Ditto," said Lainey as she took over the hugging. "I'll go with you to the clinic when you go for the termination if you want. Unless Steven's going with you, of course."

"No, he's not going to the clinic. I didn't ask him to come and I didn't exactly give him the chance to offer. I've told him it's over ... we're over." Sophie almost choked on the sob that followed her words.

Her friends glanced at each other before turning back to her. She knew they must be wondering why she'd ended things with Steven. But right then she couldn't face saying anything more about it.

And being the amazing friends they were, they seemed to sense her reluctance and they didn't push her on it.

Sophie was not only grateful for that, but she was also filled with love for her two wonderful friends. "Thank you," she said, as she wiped her eyes and her stomach let out the loudest rumble.

Paula smiled. "Well, I think I know what my first job's going to be," she said as got to her feet. "When was the last time you ate?"

"Em, that would have been yesterday evening," she said. "Steven ... Steven was going to cook me brunch this morning but then I told him about ..."

"Right, so let me see what I can find in your fridge and I'll rustle us all up something edible."

With Paula in the kitchen, Lainey moved closer to Sophie and took her hand in both of hers. "You're going to get through this," she said. "And like Paula, I'll be with you all the way, whatever you need."

"That's good of you," Sophie said. "But I don't want to take up your time, to be a nuisance. You've got—"

"I've got a friend in need of support. I'll make time," Lainey said. "Now, have you got an appointment fixed up?"

"Only with my GP. I'm seeing her on Monday to confirm everything and the appointment for the termination will be set up then."

"And you're really sure that's what you want? Steven isn't putting you under any pressure or anything, is he?"

"What? No! As soon as I told him he said that we could have

the baby and could bring it up together in any way I wanted. He actually said he'd love to have a baby with me."

Lainey raised her eyebrows. "Wow," she said.

"Yeah, I know," Sophie said, a mixture of sorrow and yearning gripping her as she spoke. "So, no, he didn't put any sort of pressure on me. It's all me. The need to terminate, it's all me."

"Okay. Well let me know when you have the clinic date."

"I will. It will be after my mother's visit. I need to get that out of the way first." Sophie sighed a soul deep sigh as Lainey gave her another hug.

"Lunch is served," Paula's voice reached them from the kitchen.

Sophie wolfed down the bacon, eggs, mushrooms and fried bread that Paula had cooked. "Thanks so much," she said, already feeling a bit better and smiling at Paula when she'd finished. "I needed that." Both her friends were still eating.

"I can see that," Paula said, grinning back. "And you're welcome."

"But I feel guilty, you being here," Sophie said. "Shouldn't you be spending your Saturday with Martin and Molly?"

"It's no problem," Paula said. "Martin's seeing to lunch for him and Molly and then he's getting some daddy time at the park with her. It's all good."

Sophie turned to Lainey. "And you too. It's your time off, you—"

"You're saving me from cleaning my flat. Besides my chores can wait. Being here for you can't."

After their brunch together Sophie told Lainey and Paula she was tired and that she thought she'd go for a nap. She assured them she was fine, promised to call them if she needed anything, and finally persuaded them to go home and get on with their weekends.

She napped for a couple of hours and felt better for it, or at least she did physically. Her emotions remained all over the place. When she switched her phone back on there was a message from her mother telling her she was looking forward to seeing her in a week's time. Sophie's heart sank as she read it. She texted back to her mother asking to meet at the Botanics or a café. At least that way they'd keep things calm and polite, keep to small talk and she could leave when she'd had enough. She'd thought she could face a heart to heart when she initially agreed to seeing her mother but now it just felt like too much on top of everything else. Her mother wasn't having it though, probably guessed it was an avoidance tactic on Sophie's part, and she insisted that she'd come to the flat so they could 'have a proper talk'.

As well as the message from her mother there were several from Steven, ones from much earlier along with a couple of new ones. All continuing to ask if she was okay, all begging her to get in touch. She didn't reply to any of them and switched her phone back off.

It remained switched off until mid-morning the next day when she had to do the promised check-in with Lainey and Paula via their group chat. She assured them she'd slept reasonably well and that after the morning sickness had passed she'd made herself some tea and toast before having a shower. She also told them she was heading out for a walk.

It was as she walked that she realised she was already missing Steven. She wanted to see him, to be held by him, to be told by him that everything would be all right. But much as she yearned for him, she knew it was too late. She'd burned her bridges. There could be no going back.

However, so strong was her longing that when he called her just after she got back to the flat, she took the call.

"Soph! Thank God. Are you okay?"

"Yes, I am, I think."

"You think?"

"Actually I'm not. I'm far from okay."

"You're not in pain or anything? Do you need a doctor?"

"No, no nothing like that. It's my head, it's all over the place."
"I'm coming over. Don't even think about shutting me out."

Chapter Twenty Six

It had hurt like hell watching Sophie walk away after she told him about the pregnancy. It felt like it had when he'd found out just how bad his injuries were. He was emotionally overwhelmed. There was shock, disbelief, sorrow and anger too.

Sophie was pregnant. That was hard enough to get his head round. The fact she didn't want the baby, he'd need to process that too. But he meant it when he said he'd support her whatever she wanted to do. And as if that wasn't enough, she also wanted to end things between them. There was no way he could let that happen.

He'd been frantic when he hadn't been able to contact her after she walked out. He needed to know she was okay. He had to talk to her.

In the end he'd called Dean. He got straight to the point.

"I need Paula's number," he said. "Need it now."

"And hello to you too," Dean said, laughing.

Steven grunted. "No time for pointless chat."

"Okay. Can I ask why?" Dean sounded more serious now.

"Need her to contact Sophie. Check she's all right."

"And you can't do this yourself because?"

"She wants to be left alone and she's not taking my calls or answering my texts."

"Oh no, you've not messed up, have you? Got her blocking you again?"

"In a way, yes I have messed up. It's complicated. Please Dean, Paula's number."

"Okay, okay, I'll text it to you now."

As soon as he got Dean's text, Steven called Paula and practically demanded she drop everything and check on Sophie. Unlike her brother, Paula didn't ask questions. She simply accepted that Steven couldn't contact Sophie, that he was concerned about her, and said she'd go and check on her.

After what felt like an eternity but probably wasn't, he got a message from Paula saying that she was with Sophie, that she was okay, and that Sophie'd explained what had happened.

Not long after that Dean arrived at Steven's flat.

"What?" Steven said when he opened the door.

"You know what. So let me in."

"I don't suppose 'no' is an option," Steven said.

"Damn right it isn't."

Steven stood aside to let him in.

"So, you going to tell me what's going on?" Dean said as they both took a seat in the living room.

"I don't suppose 'no' is an option to that request either," Steven said, not sure he was ready to share.

"You bet it isn't. I've got my sister and my wife nipping my head about coming here and checking on you. And besides that I care about you, even if you are a rude grumpy idiot. So spill."

So Steven told him.

Dean listened to it all without interrupting.

"So there you have it," Steven said when he'd finished. "She's pregnant, she doesn't want the baby and she doesn't want me. And I don't know what to think or feel or do. All I do know is … is I love her." Steven sat back in the armchair and ran his hand through his hair as he sighed.

"Jeez, man," Dean said, "that's a lot to take in."

"Yeah, tell me about it."

"Don't think there's any right or wrong way to feel. You've had a shock, you need to let things settle."

"Easier said than done."

Dean nodded. "And you've heard back from Paula? Sophie's okay, yeah?"

"Yeah, she's okay. Paula and Lainey are both with her."

"Good, that's good. It can't be easy for you, staying away."

"Understatement."

"But it seems to me you've done the right thing."

"I don't know," Steven said. "Can't help wondering if I should have gone after her, insisted she let me be with her."

"No, no, I reckon you've handled it right. You listened to her, you offered her assurance and reassurance, said you're on her side no matter what, respected her wishes."

"Maybe. But I don't think I can stay away from her for long. It took both of us to create the pregnancy. It should be both of us dealing with it together."

"I agree. And I'm guessing if you give her a bit of time, she'll see it that way too. She thinks she doesn't need you, that she can end things just like that, but I'd be willing to bet that's shock talking."

"I wish I had your confidence. I'm so scared this really is the end of us," Steven said.

"My advice," Dean said, "Let the dust settle. Call her tomorrow. Reassure her again that you're there for her. Tell her how you feel. Do whatever it takes to hold on to this woman you love and be prepared to be patient."

Steven managed a wry smile. "Never had you figured as a relationship guru."

"Married man and want to remain so. Picked up a few pointers along the way. Now, what do you say we head to the pub, grab some lunch and a couple of beers?"

"You're on," Steven said.

Steven took his friend's advice and, in spite of his impatience, he waited until the Sunday morning before phoning Sophie.

"Thanks for seeing me," he said when she opened the door to

him. She looked pale but so beautiful and he just wanted to hold her. "The last twenty-four hours, it's … it's been killing me not to be with you."

For a moment they stood there looking at each other. And then she was in his arms.

"I'm sorry," she said looking up at him. "Sorry I walked away, sorry I told you I didn't want to see you anymore."

"Shh," he said before kissing her, hesitantly at first then more deeply when she didn't push him away. Eventually he pulled back, took her by the hand and led her through to the living room. "Come and sit," he said, gently pulling her towards the sofa.

When they were seated he moved to face her and took her hands in his. "I get it, Soph. You, us, being pregnant, it's been a shock. It's a big thing. And it's right you should take the lead."

Sophie gave a little nod and then looked down at the floor.

"Hey," he said, reaching under her chin and tilting her head to look at him. He hated that she looked so sad.

"I'm sorry," Sophie said again. "I've really ruined things this time, haven't I?"

"What? No! No, you haven't. This is down to both of us."

"But I don't want … I can't have a baby. We weren't …" she paused.

"We weren't what?" he asked.

"We weren't properly together, we didn't live together, hadn't made any formal commitment to each other and—"

"But we could—"

"No, hear me out," she said. "We'd not made any formal commitment as a couple and that's the way I wanted it. I told you I wasn't ready to do that again. I don't know if I ever will be. And this last couple of days, finding out I'm pregnant but not able to go through with it, it's reminded me that my fear of commitment isn't fair on you."

"Surely I should decide what's fair on me?"

"Yes, of course. But the commitment thing, it's about me too.

I'm so done with being hurt, with losing people. I just … I just think that all this with the pregnancy is a sign I'm pushing my luck."

"You're not going to lose me," Steven said. And he meant it. He'd never willingly let her go.

"You don't know that. You can't promise me that."

Steven remembered Dean's words about sharing his fears and about being patient. "I think I can promise you that. But I can also promise you that I'm not going to put you under any pressure. I'm just afraid you're going to let the pregnancy drive us apart. And … and it doesn't have to. Yes, in the future we could decide our relationship has come to a natural end." He paused to run his finger gently down her cheek. "But I reckon it's got a way to run yet. We can get through this, whether you keep the baby or not, we can still be together for a good while longer."

Sophie got to her feet and began pacing, her expression anguished.

"Please, Soph," he said, his voice full of longing, "don't push me away."

She stopped pacing and turned to face him. "Okay, but if we are going to stay together for a bit longer, here's something I have to make absolutely clear. Something you have to know and take fully on board."

"Tell me."

"Before I met you, I'd already decided I didn't want to have children. It was partly because of how I feel about the whole relationships thing but it was also because my mum and dad had to get married because of me. My mother got pregnant when they were both still at university and their parents more or less forced them to get married. And their marriage was a disaster. Me being born, it wasn't exactly a positive for either of them. And I won't risk putting that sort of burden on any child of mine, now or in the future. So I *will* be seeking a termination and I'll understand if that's a deal breaker, if you want to walk away. Really I will."

"Come here," Steven said, as he stood up. He pulled her into his arms. "I'm not going anywhere – except maybe to Bristol – but that's a conversation for another day." At first Sophie was tense but then she relaxed against him and they remained in their embrace for a few moments before he spoke again. "For now, I'll come with you to the clinic when you go for the termination. Until then and immediately afterwards, I'll be with you whenever you want me to be, but I'll also give you all the space you need. All I ask is that you let me check in with you, and don't shut me out.

"And we're not your parents," he continued. "We're us. We don't need to make any big commitments or grand plans but I want to be with you through this difficult time. And then after it's over, when we're both ready, we can talk again. But for now let's just take it one small step at a time."

"Baby steps, right?"

Steven saw a hint of a smile and couldn't help smiling back. "Exactly that, Soph. Exactly that."

"Why don't you hate me? God knows I hate myself at the moment."

"I could never hate you, Sophie," he said. "And you shouldn't either."

Chapter Twenty Seven

Sophie

Sophie's emotions were all over the place as the new week started. She woke up on the Monday morning after a restless night during which her thoughts about the pregnancy, the termination, and about Steven had run round and round in her head, completely out of control. And on top of all that there was her mother's impending visit.

She was so tired she contemplated pulling the duvet over her head and staying in bed all day. For one thing, not getting up might mean the morning sickness wouldn't be triggered, and for another, maybe she would fall into a deep sleep and awaken later to find her wreck of a life was just a bad dream.

Eventually her sensible brain kicked in. She sat up slowly, hoping to keep the nausea at bay. It didn't work and she made a run for the bathroom. However, in spite of the bad night and the throwing up, she was pleasantly surprised to find that after a shower and a breakfast of toast and tea, she felt quite a lot better and ready to face the day.

She had her appointment at the GP's surgery to go to first thing before heading into work, and as she prepared to leave the flat she paused for a moment. She took some deep breaths to calm herself and as she did so, she recalled what Steven had said about taking things one step at a time. He was right. And before her mind flooded with thoughts about Steven, she took his advice and focussed only on getting to the doctor.

The appointment went smoothly and she left the medical centre with her pregnancy confirmed, her desire for a termination listened to, discussed and accepted, and a referral made to the Glasgow clinic that would carry out a pre-assessment in two days' time followed by a surgical termination early the following week.

She held it together emotionally during and after the appointment but it wasn't easy and she found herself wishing she'd accepted Steven's offer to come with her. However, her job was an effective distraction for the rest of the day and it wasn't until Steven called round after work as they'd arranged, that she let her feelings out.

"It was hard," she said as they sat together on the sofa. "Talking about being pregnant and then admitting I didn't want …" She didn't get any further before the tears began to fall.

Steven pulled her in for a hug. "It's okay, sweetheart," he said, stroking her hair. "It will all be okay." She let herself relax against his chest, enjoyed the strength she felt in his arms, was soothed by the smell of him and the sound of his deep but gentle voice.

"I should have let you come with me," she said, looking up at him. "It was your voice I heard in my head, telling me it would be all right."

Steven looked at her with incredible tenderness before kissing her. Then he'd said, "So would you like me to come to the pre-assessment with you?"

"Yes," Sophie said. "I'd like that very much."

Steven arrived at her flat early on the Wednesday morning and she knew as soon as she saw him that it had been the right decision to have him accompany her to the clinic. This became even more obvious as the appointment progressed and he offered her his quiet and steady support. He held her hand as she answered all the questions, as she had the ultrasound that showed she was just over nine weeks pregnant, and as the procedure for the surgical termination to be carried out on the following Monday was explained to her.

Both of them had taken the morning off work, Sophie telling her boss only that she had a hospital appointment, and Steven taking time owed to him for some weekend working he'd recently done. So Steven took her back to his place when they left the clinic. And on the way there, Sophie answered the text messages from Lainey and Paula telling her they were thinking about her and hoping the appointment had gone well.

"You look exhausted," he said as he handed her a mug of herbal tea as she'd gone right off anything caffeinated since getting pregnant. He sat down beside her on his big comfy black leather sofa. "The staff at the clinic were great but I could see it was tough for you. You did very well," he added before taking a sip of his coffee.

"Yeah, it was pretty tough, but all necessary," Sophie said. "It was good that you were there. It made it all a bit more bearable. Thank you for coming." Her voice trembled as she spoke but she held it together as she had all morning.

Steven cleared his throat. He looked quite emotional as he spoke. "There was nowhere else I could or should have been. I just wish I could do more."

"You being with me as we do this, it's more than enough," Sophie said. "And it's good we've been offered counselling if either of us need it after … you know…" The more they talked about the termination and the more real it became, the harder it seemed to be for her to say the word.

Steven nodded and squeezed her hand, seemingly unable to speak at all.

It was a couple of days later, on the Friday evening, before Sophie saw Steven again. She met him, as arranged, at Lorenzo's Trattoria. He'd insisted on taking her out so he could check how she was before her mother was due to visit the following morning.

Lainey had called her that afternoon to see if she wanted some company later and when Sophie had told her she already had plans and what they were, Lainey said, "Ah right." And she said it in a way that was loaded with meaning. But before Sophie could change the subject, Lainey added, "I wasn't going to say anything, with all that you're going through, but …"

"But?" Sophie said, realising it would be pointless to try to deflect the conversation from where she guessed it was heading.

"It's just, I think it's great you've changed your mind about keeping your distance from Steven, letting him go with you to the clinic and to carrying on seeing him. Don't know why you don't move in together. That guy loves you, you know. It's so obvious. And I reckon you love him too."

"Oh, I don't know about that. He's a good man and right now I'm so glad of his support. But as for love and moving in together that's not … it's not…" Sophie sighed. "Anyway can we talk about something else?"

And Lainey, being the good friend that she always was, took the hint, and they chatted about some less sensitive topics before they said their goodbyes.

Later, in spite of what Sophie had said to Lainey about her feelings for Steven, when she met him at the restaurant she couldn't ignore the excitement that bubbled up when she saw him. She was also grateful to him as he kept the conversation light for the most part and even had her laughing when he told her about some of his childhood adventures during holidays on his uncle's farm in Argyll.

"So rounding up the chickens led you to falling face down in a cow pat," Sophie said.

"Yep, and believe me when I say I can still taste it. And my dad has the photo to prove it," Steven said pretending to frown.

"So that farm is the one on the other side of your family, is it?"

"Yeah, the one I just visited in the Borders is Mum's side. Her sister married a farmer. But the Argyll one where the cowpat catastrophe happened was my grandparents' place and my dad's older brother took over the running of it when they retired.

It was that farm we went to for a lot of our holidays." Steven sounded wistful as he spoke.

"So you like farm life, do you?"

"Oh, I like it, even fantasise about maybe doing it as a job. Probably don't know enough about it though. And it was one thing helping Aidan out on my recent visit but I don't know if these would be up to it full time," he pointed at his legs. "But I'd love to give it a go."

"I bet my mother would enjoy showing you round her croft but …" Sophie shrugged. "I don't suppose that's ever going to happen."

"Hey," Steven said, reaching for her hand across the table. "You never know, if tomorrow's visit goes well, things might improve between you, then—"

"Then what? We're suddenly back to having a nice, close and normal mother-daughter relationship? I somehow don't think that's ever going to happen either."

"Okay, so tomorrow will probably just be a baby step but it could lead to more."

Sophie had to smile. "You and your baby steps," she said.

"Great believer in them," Steven grinned. "It's how I learned to walk again after all. I went from believing I'd be in a wheelchair for the rest of my life to this agile fellow you see now."

As she laughed once more, Sophie thought yet again just how amazing this man was.

The night out with Steven proved to be the perfect diversion for Sophie before her mother's arrival. After they'd finished eating, Steven saw her home. When they got to her door she found she didn't want to let him go just yet. "You could come in," she said. "I'm going to have a peppermint tea, but there's beer or coffee if you prefer."

"I'd like that," he said. "I'll even make the tea," he added smiling his irresistible smile.

It somehow felt so right having Steven there that when they'd finished their tea and he stood up to go, Sophie said almost without thinking, "Stay, please. I don't want to be on my own."

"Oh," Steven said, his surprise obvious as he rubbed the back of his neck. "Yes, of course I can stay. If that's what you want. I can sleep here on the sofa."

"You could but I'd prefer it if you came to bed with me. I kind of need to be held."

Before she could even take another breath she was been pulled to her feet and was in his arms. Steven kissed her gently and then said, "Whatever you need, I can do."

After the most restful night she'd had since before finding out she was pregnant, Sophie woke to find Steven already awake and looking at her. He'd been as good as his word and once they'd got to bed the night before he'd enveloped her in his arms and gently soothed her to sleep. "Morning, sleepyhead," he said before kissing her softly. "You okay?"

"Yes, I think I am," she said smiling at him.

"Good, I'll fix us some breakfast and then head out. Leave you to get ready for your mum."

A wave of the now customary nausea hit her when she got up, but she hadn't actually been sick.

And the poached eggs on toast that Steven made them both for breakfast along with more peppermint tea seemed to settle her stomach.

Her nerves, however, didn't settle and she paced the living room unable to focus on anything as she waited for her visitor to arrive.

At ten-thirty on the dot the intercom buzzed. Rachel Campbell had arrived. Sophie tried to greet her mother with a smile but didn't think she quite succeeded. She showed her mother into the living room and went to make them both a hot drink.

"Here you go," Sophie said, placing a mug on the coffee table in front of her mother who was perched on the edge of the sofa.

"Thanks," said her mum. She then took a sip or two of her tea before adding, "Your flat seems very nice."

After a bit more awkward small talk about the flat and Sophie's work, her mother put her mug down on the coffee table and said, "Sophie, I want us to talk – to really talk. This has gone on long enough. You're all I've got, I miss you. I want and I need to be close to you, like we used to be."

Sophie felt anger flooding through her. "Oh really?" she said. "Like we used to be? When was that? Ah, yes, that would be before you divorced Dad. Before you supported Finlay's decision to join up. Before you wrecked our lives." Again the small voice inside her whispered that she wasn't being entirely fair. Sophie also registered that her mother didn't appear shocked by what she'd just said. Not surprising really as Sophie had made these accusations before.

Her mother's voice was calm as she replied, restating all the things Sophie already knew. "I had to leave your father, Sophie. There was nothing to stay for. He'd met someone else and I'd had enough of being in a difficult marriage. And look how happy he is now, how happy he is with Carla. He was never like that with me."

Seeing her mother's sad expression didn't do anything to calm to Sophie down. In fact it had the opposite effect. The quiet voice of Sophie's conscience, the one that had been urging her to be honest with herself and fair to her mother, was now completely drowned out by the force of her angry grief.

"You could have tried harder," Sophie said. "If you'd wanted to. But you couldn't wait to get back to your precious Skye. Did you even try to forgive Dad when he told you about Carla? He made one mistake, one mistake and you didn't even try to fight for him." Sophie suspected the 'one mistake' thing was untrue. But she somehow couldn't bear any of this mess to be her father's fault because that would mean he too had let her down.

"No, no, that's not how it was," her mother said. "There was nothing left, not for me. You and Fin were grown up. I didn't have to stay. I *couldn't* stay."

"It suited you, didn't it, that Finlay left when he did, cleared the way for you to go too. No wonder you couldn't wait to see the back of him."

Her mother looked stunned and she paused before she answered. Sophie justified the obviously ghastly effect that her words had inflicted by telling herself it was her mother who had wanted them to talk. So that's what she was doing.

"That's not fair," Rachel said. "Come on, Sophie, you know it isn't. Finlay left home two years before I did. I'd no plan to leave your father at that time. It's ridiculous to suggest I sent Finlay away for my own convenience. Yes, I gave him my blessing. I was very proud of him. But don't you think I'd do *anything* to turn back the clock and persuade him not to go."

Sophie shrugged, feeling suddenly defensive. Her mother moved as if she was going to reach out and touch her, but then she sat back and clasped her hands together.

"We need to put this behind us," she said softly. "I miss you, Sophie. Can't you forgive me? I didn't plan for things to turn out this way."

"Okay, I know you didn't plan it, but…" Sophie felt another surge of emotion. She got to her feet and began pacing. "But you could have stopped it all from happening." She was crying now, angry tears that she swiped at with her fist. "I'll never forgive you," she shouted before turning her back on her mother. She stiffened as she felt Rachel's hands on her shoulders.

"Please, look at me," her mother said. But Sophie couldn't.

Her mother continued anyway. "Dad's happy and you have the same strong relationship you always had with him. Our divorce hasn't changed that. Losing Fin was terrible for all of us. It nearly broke me. I can't bear to lose you too. If you had a child you'd know … you'd know—"

"Shut up!" Sophie shouted, the mention of her having a child triggering an overwhelming fury. "Shut the fuck up!" She spun round so fast that her shoulder caught her mother under her chin like a punch. She staggered backwards with her hand on her jaw. Then Sophie heard a horrid empty mocking laugh. It took her a second or two to realise it was coming from her. "*That's* never going to happen," she said.

"What isn't?" her mother mumbled.

"Me having a child," Sophie said, surprised to find herself speaking calmly. "It's not going to happen. I've made up my mind on that."

Her mother went to speak again but Sophie put up her hand to stop her. "It's all right," Sophie said. "I know what you're thinking. You think I'll change my mind, that I'll get pregnant and be happy about it, but I won't. How could I be happy about bringing a baby into the world knowing I couldn't protect it from…" Sophie paused, raised her arms in a helpless gesture, before continuing, "from all this shit, its parents hating each other, then growing up only to be killed in some pointless act."

Her mother crumpled before collapsing back down on the armchair. "Stop it," she said. "Please just stop. I need a minute and then I'll go. Do you think I could have a glass of water?"

Sophie began to feel the beginnings of remorse as she went to the kitchen to get her mother some water. The adrenaline that had coursed through her body moments ago was disappearing. Yes, she wanted her mother to know how she felt, even if that hurt her feelings, but she certainly hadn't meant to physically injure her. When she handed her mother the glass, Sophie said, "Is your face okay? There's a bit of a bruise. I didn't mean to bump you like that."

"It's fine," her mother replied. "It hurt at first and I got a fright."

"Right," Sophie said quietly, noticing how pale her mother looked. She took a few sips of water and then reached for her jacket and bag. She stood up. "I'm sorry," she said. "Sorry you still feel so angry, sorry I came. But you're my daughter and I love you. I always will, no matter what you may think of me. I hope in time you'll get over everything."

This was the moment, Sophie would realise later, when she should have left it at that. She should have told her mother she hoped so too, told her that she too was sorry, and that they'd keep in touch and work out their differences. It was also the moment she should have calmly and compassionately told her mother about the pregnancy. But she said and did none of these things. Instead she retorted, "Like you have, you mean? All over Fin and now gallivanting halfway across the world."

Her mother put on her jacket as she replied. "I need to make this trip," she said. "And I'll never be over Fin. You lost your brother, Sophie, but he was my son. You can't possibly understand what it feels like to lose a child – and heaven forbid you ever have to."

Sophie flinched at her mother's words and her retaliation was out of her mouth before she could stop it. "That's where you're wrong. I'm nearly ten weeks pregnant and I'm terminating the pregnancy on Monday. It wasn't planned, and besides the reasons I mentioned earlier for not having a child, unlike you did with me, I won't be giving birth to an unwanted baby. So yes, I do, or at least I will, know what it's like to lose a child."

At that her mother had fled. She looked utterly stricken and Sophie now felt utterly terrible.

It could only have been a minute or two later that Steven arrived back just as he'd promised he would. "I think I may have met your mother on the stairs just now," he called through from the hallway as he hung up his jacket. "She pushed past me like she couldn't get away fast enough," he added as he came into the living room. "I hope that wasn't …" he stopped when he saw she was curled up on the sofa, sobbing. "Sophie! What is it? What's wrong?" he said as he sat down beside her.

"Oh, Steven," Sophie said reaching for him. He pulled her up so he could put his arms round her and hold her close.

"I'm here, Soph. I've got you. It's okay. Let it out, let it all out."

Sophie gradually calmed down, soothed by the feeling of Steven's strong arms around her, the scent of his skin and the reassuring sound of his voice.

When Steven eventually relaxed his hold on her, he passed her the box of tissues from the coffee table, "Glass of water, tea?"

"Both please," Sophie said, her voice hoarse as she realised how dry her mouth was.

By the time Steven returned from the kitchen with both her drinks and a mug of tea for himself, Sophie was already feeling better. And she acknowledged that was in no small part due to Steven's presence.

"Thank you," she said after drinking almost all the water in one go. "Thank you for being here."

"I said I'd come back," Steven said.

"I know, but you didn't have to and I appreciate it."

"It didn't go well, then, with your mum?"

"You could say that." Sophie sighed.

"Tell me," Steven said softly as he moved closer and put his arm round her.

So she told him about Rachel's visit, leaving nothing out, even the stuff she wasn't proud of and Steven did what she now knew was his usual thing. He listened.

When she finished, he squeezed her hand. "Sounds like you were honest, even if you were—"

"Brutal? A bitch?" Sophie said.

"Hey," Steven said as he stroked her cheek. "Don't be so hard on yourself. You said what you needed to say. You didn't waste the visit talking only in polite platitudes. You let your mum see how you're truly feeling. And yes, okay, you could argue you could have handled it better, especially when telling her about the pregnancy, but there was no easy way to say any of the things you did."

"Hmm, maybe. But I haven't exactly mended any fences. And hitting her in the face even though it was accidental, she must think I'm a right cow and she'd be right." Sophie rocked forward and hugged herself before looking at Steven again. "I've really messed up," she said. "What if that's the last I hear from her? Maybe she'll not want to have any more to do with me."

"I doubt that very much," Steven said. "It sounds to me like your mum loves you unconditionally and I'd be willing to bet that even though it must have been hard for her to listen to you, she'll be relieved that you actually opened up to her. And besides that, maybe now you've let all the poison out you can make a start on healing, both yourself and your relationship with your mum."

"I suppose …" Sophie said. Her voice trailed off as she thought about what Steven had just said. He was right, talking about it all, all her feelings of loss, unworthiness and anger had actually helped. It was as if telling her mother exactly how she was feeling, including about the pregnancy, had opened a valve and released the toxic pressure that had been building up inside her for some time. "I know I've got a way to go with my mother," she said, "and it's going to take time but you're right, we've made a start. And …" She paused again as she looked into Steven's eyes and, as always, saw nothing but understanding and kindness there.

"And, what?" he said.

"And I owe you a big thank you for helping me through. You told me seeing my mum would help, that it was a small step … a baby step," she smiled at him at the mention yet again of his baby step approach to things. "You were here for me before and after, and you've listened and not judged. It means a lot, Steven."

"Come here," Steven said, holding his arms out to her and as she once again nestled in his embrace, she began to wish … to wish if only things had been different, if only *she* could have been different.

Chapter Twenty Eight

As Steven held Sophie in his arms trying to offer her some comfort in the aftermath of her mother's visit, his own feelings were in turmoil. He loved her so much.

He was touched by how grateful she was to him and he took it as a good sign that she'd been so open with him. It was also encouraging that she wanted him with her at the clinic.

But what if she only needed him in the short term, to get over the stress of her mother's visit and to see her through the termination of the pregnancy? And that was another thing, the thought of the abortion was killing him. It wasn't what he wanted and although he believed it had to be Sophie's decision, he reckoned he was going to need the post-termination counselling he'd been offered.

However, that was for another day. Right now he had to continue taking things at Sophie's pace. It was the only way he could see that their relationship would have any chance of the long term future he hoped for. The 'baby steps' phrase really was becoming his mantra.

After they'd eaten the lunch he made, Sophie said she was going for a nap, and since he knew she had Paula and Lainey coming round later to have dinner and a girls' night in, he reluctantly said he'd get away.

As she watched him putting on his jacket, Sophie said, "I'm

sorry I told Mum about the pregnancy and the plan to terminate it. I know we'd agreed that apart from Dean, Paula and Lainey we weren't going to say anything to anyone else at the moment. And I'm really not proud of the way I did it …" Sophie twisted her hands together as she looked down at the floor.

"Hey," Steven said, reaching to gently tip her chin up so she had to look at him. "It's okay. It sounds like it was a heat of the moment thing and it was a necessary part of your honest conversation."

"Thank you," Sophie said.

"For what?"

"For understanding – and I don't just mean about me telling my mother. I mean understanding about all of it, the pregnancy, everything." She let out a sigh. "And I need to ask for your understanding about one more thing." She looked at him apprehensively.

He stroked her cheek with his thumb. "First of all you don't need to thank me. As far as the pregnancy goes and how we handle it all, we're in it together. So ask away."

"I think I should let my father know that I'm pregnant and about the termination. Now that my mother knows, I don't—"

"You don't want him to hear about it from her. You want to be the one to tell him."

"Yes, but I also know it's not fair to you as you haven't told your parents."

"It's fine, Soph. Let your dad know and we can leave what and when to tell my parents until after Monday."

"If you're sure."

"I'm sure." Steven pulled her to him for a kiss – a kiss she fully participated in. He smiled at her as he reluctantly ended their embrace. "Now go and rest and then enjoy your evening with the girls later." He meant what he said. She looked pale and exhausted and in need of a rest, and he knew that spending time with her two best friends would be good for her, even though he really didn't want to leave.

If only they could be a proper couple, living together, sharing a life. Then he could stay while she napped, make himself scarce when her friends came round, and then be back with her in their shared bed for the night. But that was all just wishful thinking, for now at least. So he gave her one last hug then turned to leave.

But before he could open the front door, he felt Sophie's hand on his arm. "Steven, wait," she said.

"What is it?" he asked, turning again to look at her.

"Tomorrow," she said, "could you, that is, would you, like to spend the day with me? I could come to yours, whatever you prefer. It's just I don't want to be alone the day before we go to the clinic."

He had to clear his throat as all his earlier emotions made themselves felt. "Of course," he said. "I'll be here first thing. And I'll bring breakfast."

Steven was as good as his word and arrived at Sophie's on the dot of nine o'clock on the Sunday morning. On the way he'd stopped off to buy a selection of muffins, bagels and croissants.

When Sophie opened the bakery bag, she said, "There's enough in here to feed the whole tenement block." She laughed as she looked at him and he loved that she did.

They ended up having a reasonably pleasant day, walking in the Botanics and then having a lazy afternoon listening to music and reading the newspapers they'd bought while they were out. It was in fact just the sort of Sunday Steven had imagined they would have if things hadn't taken the turn they had, the sort he longed to have, the sort that couples who lived together probably took for granted. He tried not to overthink it, to enjoy it for what it was, but he was aware that although, for the most part, Sophie seemed to be enjoying it too, she was at times a bit distant, preoccupied and lost in her own thoughts.

Sophie had continued to look a bit out of it as they'd eaten an early dinner of takeaway pizza, giving only monosyllabic answers as he'd tried to keep a conversation going while they ate. Eventually he gave up trying to chat and let her be, deciding she was probably exhausted, what with her mother's visit and now the anticipation of the next day's appointment. So when they'd finished eating, Steven said he'd head home.

"So," he said before reaching for his jacket from the hook in the hall. "I'll pick you up tomorrow morning in good time for getting to the clinic. I hope you sleep well." He stroked her cheek before resting his hand on the back of her neck and planting a kiss on her forehead. Then as he withdrew his hand Sophie caught hold of it.

"Please," she said gazing up at him, her expression troubled and tears in her eyes. "Please, don't go yet. I need to talk to you. I've been thinking and there's something I need to say."

"Okay," Steven said, dreading that this was it. This was what had been preoccupying her. Was she going to end their relationship? They'd go to the clinic, abort the pregnancy, and then that would be it.

"Come back and sit down," Sophie said. And while he took a seat on the sofa, Sophie began pacing. "I can't do this," she said. "I thought it was what I wanted, but … but it really isn't." She stopped pacing and turned to face him, wringing her hands, her brow furrowed with anxiety.

"Right," Steven said, "I don't know what to say—"

Before Steven could finish the door buzzer sounded. "You expecting someone?" he said.

Sophie shook her head, looking puzzled as she went out to the hall. Steven couldn't stop himself from following her.

"Hello," Sophie said as she held down the intercom button.

"Sophie," a male voice replied. "It's Dad. I need to see you."

"Dad! What are you doing here?"

"Let me in and I'll tell you."

Sophie pressed the main door release button and opened the door into the flat before turning to Steven. "Sorry," she said.

"I should go," Steven said. "Let you and your dad talk."

"No, please, Steven, don't go. I really need to talk to you. Dad visits me here very rarely and never uninvited. I guess he's here because of my phone call but I'll tell him now is not a good time and to keep it brief."

Steven hesitated. Putting off hearing that Sophie had decided to end their relationship was tempting. He could go home and have some more time pretending they had a future. But it was only delaying the inevitable and besides that she was looking at him with so much pleading in her eyes he couldn't refuse her. "Okay, I'll stay," he said. "I'll go into the kitchen, do the washing up, give you both some privacy."

"Thank you," Sophie said softly before a much louder voice boomed in greeting.

"Good evening," said the tall, silver-haired, and somewhat imposing man approaching the front door. His smile was warm as he stretched his arms out towards his daughter.

"Hi, Dad," Sophie said as she moved into his embrace. Sophie's father glanced over her shoulder as they hugged and he noticed Steven.

"Oh, sorry," her father said. "I didn't mean to interrupt." His tone implied he wasn't sorry at all.

"No, it's fine. Come in." Sophie ushered her dad inside. "Dad, this is Steven Jackson. Steven, this is my father, Peter Campbell."

Steven and Peter shook hands. Steven couldn't help but be aware of the intense scrutiny of Peter's gaze as they did so. A gaze he returned in equal measure.

"Pleased to meet you," said Steven.

"Likewise," said Peter raising an eyebrow. He turned to Sophie. "So this is—"

"Yes, it is," Sophie said, indicating to her father to go through to the living room. She then glanced at Steven and gave a slight nod of her head as if to suggest Steven make himself scarce.

"Right," said Steven, clearing his throat as he looked from Peter to Sophie, "I'll just … I'll be in the kitchen."

Steven closed the kitchen door behind him. He tried to distract himself by tidying, but it didn't take long to put a couple of plates and glasses into the dishwasher and to bin the pizza boxes. He sat down at the table and continued his attempts at distraction by scrolling through social media on his phone and then trying to watch a podcast. But he couldn't concentrate.

Peter Campbell was obviously a force to be reckoned with and he most definitely had an imposing presence. Steven was fairly sure Sophie had been right that her phone call to her father the previous day that had prompted him to visit. A call that Sophie had described as short and to the point. He hoped her father wasn't giving her a hard time. But then again Peter was more than likely just checking on his daughter's welfare. Something he couldn't blame the guy for doing.

Steven's thoughts returned to the break-up conversation that Peter's arrival had interrupted. Contemplating the remainder of that conversation made him feel sick.

It seemed like ages before Sophie appeared in the kitchen. Steven immediately got up from the table and went to her. She looked tired but didn't appear to be upset. "You okay?" he said, cupping her face.

"Yes, I'm fine," she said, leaning into his hand and giving him a small smile. "Dad's just about to leave but he wanted to speak to you before he goes."

"Right," Steven said, his heart sinking. He felt fairly sure he wouldn't exactly be popular with Peter Campbell. But compared to what he was going to have to listen to from Sophie, anything her father had to say would be nowhere as difficult to hear.

"Come on then," Sophie said, surprising him by slipping her hand into his and leading the way through to the living room.

Peter was looking out of the bay window to the dark street below and he turned to them as they came into the room. "Ah, Steven," he said, causing Steven even more surprise, by smiling what seemed to be a genuine smile. "Sorry, for interrupting your evening—"

"Oh, no, that's quite—"

"Let me finish," Peter raised a finger to quieten Steven. "I don't usually barge in on my daughter. I know she's a grown-up and more than capable of taking care of herself but I'm her father. And as such I love her dearly and want to offer her support in any way I can. So when she called me yesterday evening to tell me about the pregnancy, I did my best to be supportive. But earlier on today as I thought about what she would be going through, I had this irresistible urge to see her, to tell her face-to-face that I love her and to offer to go with her tomorrow, if she wanted me to."

"I see," Steven said with a sigh, thinking he would no longer be needed to go to the clinic with Sophie.

"But it seems I'm not required," Peter said. "And I have to say, from what my daughter has told me about you this evening, that I'm happy to stand aside. Seems to me she's met her perfect match."

"Oh, right." Steven hadn't been expecting that. Sophie squeezed his hand. He hadn't expected that either.

"It was good to meet you, Steven," Peter said. "But now I must go."

"I'll see you out," Sophie said, smiling at her father.

"He likes you," Sophie said, still smiling when she returned to the living room and sat down beside Steven on the sofa.

"Seems so," Steven said, trying and failing to smile back. Then, when Sophie tried to take hold of his hand again, he pulled away.

She frowned at him. "What's wrong?" she said.

"What's wrong?" Steven said. "What do you think's wrong? It hardly matters what your father thinks of me, and what's with all the hand holding and smiles? That's just not fair. You don't get to be all affectionate, not after what you said before your dad arrived. Not after you've told me it's now really over between us." Steven's voice cracked as he said those last few words and he ran his hand through his hair.

Sophie looked shocked. "I never said that."

"You did," Steven glared at her. "You said you couldn't do this—

"What? No that's not—"

"I should go," Steven said. "Like I was saying before your dad arrived, I don't really know what to say about it – other than I'm so, so sorry that we … that things haven't worked out. I've never known anyone like you Sophie and it's … it's going to take me a while to get over you. Of course I'll still accompany you tomorrow, if that's what you want, but then—"

"No, no, Steven, I'm so sorry that's what you thought. You've misunderstood." Sophie looked stricken. "I wasn't talking about us, about our relationship. I was talking about the baby. I can't … I can't go through with the termination. I want to keep it. I want to keep our baby."

"I … I … what, why, when did you …?" Steven felt like his brain was crashing.

"I'm going to have the baby. I've been thinking about it non-stop since we were at the clinic, my mind going round and round in circles. Didn't sleep much last night. I realised I didn't want the termination. I want the baby. And today the feeling that it's the right thing to do got even stronger. I didn't tell my dad about my change of mind as I wanted to tell you first, but talking things through with him, talking about tomorrow's appointment, it just confirmed for me that I couldn't go through with ending the pregnancy."

"Okay," Steven said, running his hand across his head, still trying to process Sophie's announcement. "Sorry," he said. "It's all a bit of a shock, just need it to sink in."

"Yes, I can imagine. I'm sorry to have messed you about like this. And I know you originally said that you wanted to be involved in bringing up the baby, but I'd completely understand if after all this you've changed your mind too."

"No, no," Steven said. "If it's really what you want then I'm all in, totally, one hundred percent. And as I also said before,

I'd want to be involved whether … whether we were together or not." He leant against the back of the sofa and took a breath. He felt tears building and swallowed hard.

"Steven? Are you okay?" He felt Sophie's hand on his arm. "Oh," she said as he looked at her. "You're … you're crying." She moved her hand to his face and rubbed at the treacherous tears which had escaped. He tilted his head to lean into her hand and for a moment they paused and looked into each other's eyes. In Sophie's he saw concern, tenderness and maybe … maybe a look of something that seemed like love. It was everything he needed to see.

"We're having a baby," he whispered, putting his arms round her.

"Yes, it seems we are," Sophie smiled as she spoke.

Before he knew it, he'd pulled her to him and was kissing her. Kissing her hard and passionately and she responded with just as much enthusiasm. He loved this woman, loved her so much, wanted her so much, that he'd do whatever it took to make things right between them, to get her to fully trust him, and to commit to a life together.

It was Sophie who broke away first. She pulled back slightly and said breathily, "Bed."

There was no mistaking what she meant especially as she stood up and almost ran towards the bedroom. He was only too happy to follow her.

By the time he'd got undressed, Sophie was already lying back naked on the bed, watching him with an unmistakeable look of lust in her eyes. He kissed her on the mouth before moving down to her neck, then tracing his tongue along her collarbone and on down to her breasts. He loved the little moans of pleasure she gave as he continued to trail caresses and kisses down her body.

He only paused to say, "You're sure about this?" as she arched her back. "It won't hurt the baby, will it?"

"Yes I'm sure and no, it won't hurt the baby. So, please—" She gasped as he took her at her word.

Later, as they lay entangled in each other's arms, exhausted and satisfied, Steven shook his head and smiled to himself as he drifted off to sleep. As if it wasn't incredible enough that he was spending the night with Sophie, they were also going to have a baby together. He was going to be a dad.

The baby steps they'd spoken of so often before, took on a whole new meaning.

They both agreed they had a lot to discuss, to sort out and to agree on, not least how they were going to go about raising their child. But first, they had to let the fact of the pregnancy fully sink in. The only decision they made immediately was that apart from Lainey, Paula and Dean who already knew, they wouldn't tell anyone else about the baby until after the twelve-week scan.

The only exception to that was the agreement they'd reached about telling Sophie's father. So on the evening after his surprise visit, when he called her to find out how she was after the termination Sophie told him she hadn't gone through with it. He was delighted to hear the news and he understood why she hadn't told him when he visited, agreeing it had to be Steven who was the first to know. He also agreed not to mention the pregnancy to anyone else for the time being, including Sophie's mother. He assured Sophie that he understood why she wanted to tell her mum the news in person.

For Steven, it all felt a bit unreal at first and as if he was in limbo. He liked that after telling him of her change of heart about the baby, Sophie was no longer asking him to stay away. But apart from asking him to spend that Sunday night with her, she wasn't actively pursuing contact with him either. She wasn't exactly ignoring him but it was down to him to message or call her.

It was the beginning of June, three weeks on from the fateful weekend, when Steven decided enough was enough. He'd only seen Sophie a few times in the intervening period and it had mostly been at his instigation.

As well as that, when they did meet, Sophie had gone back to seeming distracted in the same way she'd been in the days leading up to her changing her mind about the baby. They hadn't properly discussed her reasons for her change of heart and neither had they discussed their feelings for one another and how they were going to make it all work.

It had once again been a conversation with Dean that helped Steven reach a decision. It was a Thursday evening and they'd met after work for a pint and a catch up at Dean's suggestion.

"So, enough about me," Dean said after he'd told Steven how things were going with him. "How's Sophie and the baby? And how are things between you and her?"

"Your first question is the easier one to answer," Steven said. "Sophie and the baby are well. We went for the twelve week scan last week and all is as it should be."

"Good," said Dean. "And you said *we* went for the scan. Can I take that as a good sign as regards your relationship?"

"Yes and no," Steven said. "We see each other when Sophie's up for it, but it's usually me who initiates it. We haven't discussed any arrangements for how we'll live after the baby is born. I'm not even sure exactly why she had the change of heart about the termination. And besides all of that, we haven't slept together in a couple of weeks. Any time I suggest or hint at it, she always has some plausible excuse not to and I don't question it because I don't …" Steven let out an exasperated groan and shook his head.

"Because you don't want to put pressure on her, push too hard," Dean said.

Steven took a swig of his beer then sighed. "Yep, that's about right. That and I'm a coward."

"I don't think anyone could accuse you of cowardice – and I don't just mean because of your exemplary military service. I mean the way you've handled this whole thing, the relationship, the pregnancy, everything. You've taken responsibility, you've supported Sophie one hundred percent, and you've given her time and space to process."

"Yeah, that's as maybe, and don't get me wrong, I'm doing all of that willingly, but it feels like …" Steven shrugged still unsure of how to express his frustrations.

"It seems to me maybe you feel like Sophie isn't showing you the same level of understanding, isn't showing any awareness of how you must be feeling?" Dean came to his rescue again.

"Yeah, I suppose."

"And could it be she doesn't show any awareness because you haven't told her how you feel, what you need from her?"

Steven shook his head again but this time a small smile broke through. "God, Dr Dean does it again. Bloody smartass."

Dean laughed. "Yeah, I am, aren't I?"

"So, what do you prescribe, Doc?"

"Well, it seems to me that you've made progress already. After all Sophie has gone from not wanting to see you, to letting you back in."

"Yes, but—"

"Hang on," Dean gestured at Steven to let him continue, "You recognise that Sophie's on emotional overload at the moment and you're making allowances for that. But you also need to take care of yourself too. And to do that you have to get over your fear of the worst case scenarios because hiding from them could be the very thing that lets one of those scenarios happen."

"Right … so?"

"So you need to tell her how *you're* feeling, what *your* fears and worries are, how *you* feel about her, about the baby and its future – everything. Open up to her, man."

"I love her, Dean. I love her like I've never loved anyone. I want us to be together forever. I want us to bring up our child together and to be a family."

"Great, so never mind telling me all that, go and tell her."

Chapter Twenty Nine

Sophie

Sophie knew she wasn't being fair to Steven. He was a great guy, supportive, caring and sexy, and he'd been nothing but kind and attentive since finding out about the pregnancy. He certainly didn't deserve the mixed messages she'd been giving him lately. Yes, she was scared of commitment, scared of loss, and so she was holding back. But it had been nearly three weeks since she'd told him she'd changed her mind about the termination and since then she'd been less than communicative.

Sophie also knew she hadn't been fair to her mother and that she had to sort things out there too.

However, on both counts she felt stuck about how to proceed, uncertain how to move forward, uncertain about what to say, and uncertain about opening herself up to the possibility of getting or causing hurt.

There were two things she was certain of however, she definitely wanted her baby and, if she needed help figuring out the rest, Paula and Lainey would be there for her.

"Cheers and thanks for coming at such short notice," Sophie said, raising her glass of soda water in a toast to her two friends who in return raised their own glasses of red wine. It was a Thursday evening and following her earlier, short-notice request both Paula and Lainey had agreed to come to hers for dinner and a chat.

"It was about time for a meet up," Lainey said. "I know we said we'd leave it to you to say when, but Paula and me, we were about to come round here and break your door down if you didn't come out of hiding soon."

"Yeah," said Paula. "Texts and calls are all very well but we needed to see you face to face, put our minds at rest that you really are doing okay. You are, aren't you?"

"Yes and no," Sophie said. "That's why I needed to see my two wise besties. I'm so confused about my mum, Steven, everything. I really need to talk. So thanks again for coming when I called."

"No worries," Lainey said smiling as she pointed to the homemade spaghetti bolognese that Sophie had served up. "This certainly beats the leftover takeaway pizza I was planning on having for dinner."

"Yeah, too right," said Paula also grinning. "I was glad to leave Molly's dinner, bed and bath time to Martin and have my own dinner made for me."

"Cool, so let's eat and we can talk later," Sophie said, smiling too as she realised she already felt better just for having her friends there, two friends who had just made it sound like she was doing them a favour and not the other way round.

"So, let's have it," Lainey said after they'd finished eating and had moved through to the living room. "What's been going through that head of yours since you decided you were keeping the baby and why has it taken you the best part of three weeks to let us see you? And why are you talking to us and not Steven?"

"And," said Paula, jumping in before Sophie could respond, "delighted as we were to get your text about your change of heart, because we know you'll be a fantastic mother, what made you change your mind?"

Sophie couldn't help laughing. "Right, well that was a lot of questions." She paused as she took a deep breath. "But first of all I need to say I really appreciate that you've both been so patient with me, not pressuring me to talk, just letting me know you've been thinking about me and that you care. It's means a lot."

"It's what you wanted," said Paula. "So that's what we did."

Sophie nodded. "I'll start with the positives, then. As regards the pregnancy, all is well. Like I said in my texts to you after the twelve-week scan, everything is as it should be. I want this baby. And, if I'm honest, I have done since I found out I was pregnant. But it took the disaster of Mum's visit and a chat with my dad to make me be honest with myself and I realised I was allowing guilt and fear to drive my life, to drive my decisions and to prevent me dealing with my feelings about the baby, about Steven, about everything."

"And you said Steven is being supportive?" Lainey asked.

"Yes, he's been fantastic. Like you two, he's giving me space to try to sort out my thoughts, but I know I'm not being fair to him. And I can see he's desperate to talk."

"So why not let him? You two have a lot to sort out," Paula said.

"Steven's definitely one of the good guys," said Lainey. "And he loves you. Anyone can see that. I'd also put money on you loving him—"

Sophie couldn't help interrupting "Oh, I don't know about—"

But Lainey, too, had no qualms about interrupting as she raised a hand to stop Sophie objecting. "And quite apart from being baffled as to why you're not cuddled up with him this evening," she went on, "I don't get why you're not making wedding arrangements. It's so obvious you love each other. But however daft you're being about admitting that, you do have a lot to sort out. So stop procrastinating and set up some proper quality time together. And whatever you do, Sophie, you need to kick all that guilt and fear you mentioned right out of your life."

"Seconded," said Paula. "So, task number one in your homework is talk to Steven and to do it with a positive attitude, calmly, clearly, and from the heart."

"Right," said Sophie, wondering if it really could be that simple.

"And what about your mum?" Paula continued. "How are

you feeling about things between you and her now that the dust has settled a bit?"

"That's the other thing that's got me going round in circles. I need and I want to apologise to her. I want us to work on fixing our relationship."

"But?" Paula said.

"But I don't know where to start with that either."

"Simple," said Lainey. "It's just like with Steven, really, although not quite so urgent. You need to talk. Again it has to be from the heart, from the love you feel for your mum, no blame or anger getting in the way. But you can take homework task number two more slowly and focus on it after you've sorted things out with your man."

And that was it. Suddenly Sophie was laughing, laughing like she hadn't in quite some time. Sometimes all a person needed was good friends, good friends who you could trust with your life. It was time she did more than work, sleep and eat. It was time to live. "Who's for ice cream?" she said.

After Paula and Lainey left at around nine-thirty, and without allowing herself any second guessing, Sophie sent Steven a message.

I'm done being a self-obsessed, mixed-up pain in your arse. Time to talk properly – if you can face it xxx

Steven replied immediately.

Yes! I can definitely face it. In fact I was about to suggest we have a talk even if you are a pain in my arse :-) Come to mine on Saturday morning. I'll fix us some brunch xxx

Great! See you about 10 xxx

"That was amazing," Sophie said sitting back and pushing her plate away. "My jeans were already straining to stay fastened. There's no way they're not going to pop now."

Steven grinned at her. "I don't think it's just the food that's causing the strain. But yeah, you can't beat a full Scottish."

"Oh Lord, it's only going to get worse, isn't it," Sophie grinned back at him. "It's time for stretchy lycra and elastic panels."

"Yeah," Steven said softly as he reached for her hand across the table. He rubbed the back of her hand with his thumb. "We really are having a baby." His voice was full of emotion and he cleared his throat. "Right," he said, "You go and get a comfy seat. I'll clear up and join you."

Sophie didn't argue, sensing he needed a little bit of time to get his feelings under control.

"I'm sorry," she said when he joined her on the sofa a little while later. "Sorry for the mixed signals, saying I wanted an abortion, then saying I didn't. Demanding to have sex with you then keeping my distance. It all got a bit messy for a while there. But I shouldn't have shut you out and I really do appreciate that you didn't give up on me."

"I could never give up on you, Sophie. But I do have a couple of questions, if that's okay?"

"Of course. Fire away."

"Why did you change your mind about the baby?"

Sophie told him what she'd told Lainey and Paula. "And that's it," she said as she finished, "it was the fear, the anxiety that's been ruling my life for far too long. It was stopping me from properly living. It was telling me there was no way I could have a child. But, as I've said, I never really wanted to get rid of it. I would never have gone through with the termination. I'm sure of that." Steven nodded and squeezed her hand. She could see him swallowing hard, seemingly unable to speak.

She squeezed his hand back before continuing, "Mum's visit, the things I said, and they were terrible things, it was like you said. Saying out loud all the stuff that's been tormenting me lessened its hold over me. Then afterwards when you were so supportive, it meant I could acknowledge what I wanted to do before I even got to the clinic door."

"And now, it still feels like the right decision?" Steven looked concerned.

"More than ever. I want my … I want *our* baby. And I can't imagine a better father for it."

Steven gave a wry smile. "I'm glad you think so but how do you see my role in the baby's life?"

"I want to co-parent with you, no doubts about that."

"That's good. I want that too, and I know how I'd like us to do that."

"I wish I did. I mean I haven't even begun to think through the logistics of it all. How do you see it going?"

Steven let out a deep sigh and ran his fingers through his hair as he frowned, as if deciding something. He moved closer to her on the sofa and reached for her hand. "I love you, Soph."

Sophie let out a little gasp. "Oh," was all she could say.

He ran his free hand down her cheek. "It's okay," he said, obviously seeing the slight panic his declaration had caused. "Don't say it back, not until you mean it. But I have to tell you how I feel. I want us to be together. I want us to live together as a family. And I want to marry you."

Chapter Thirty

"Oh," Sophie said again, putting her hand over her mouth, looking even more panicky now. Steven swallowed down his disappointment. It wasn't as if he hadn't suspected beforehand that she wouldn't be ready for either the L word or the M word, but he'd promised himself and Dean that he'd be honest and tell Sophie exactly how he was feeling.

"I don't … I can't …" Sophie shook her head, clearly flustered.

"It's fine, Soph," Steven said. "You don't have to say or do anything. But I had to say it. I had to tell you how I feel. I need to be honest with you."

Sophie gave a small nod. "Thank you," she said. "Thank you for loving me and wanting to marry me. That's a crazy big thing. But I'm not …" Sophie closed her eyes and sighed.

Steven rubbed her arm. "Hey," he said. "You've got enough to deal with at the moment. I know that. It's like I've said all along, I'm happy to take my lead from you, to do what you're comfortable with. I'm just glad you don't want to end things but please don't stay in a relationship with me just because of the baby. We can come to an agreement about raising our child, even if we're not together."

"No, no it's not that. I'm not staying in a relationship with you because of the baby. I'm staying in this relationship because I don't want to give you up, to give up on us, even though I know you deserve better than me."

"Don't!" Steven said, his voice harsher and louder than he'd intended. Sophie jumped and pulled her hand away from his. "Sorry," he said. "I didn't mean to shout but I hate it when you do yourself down like that. Remember we agreed to be each other's emotionally-messed-up-but-recovering buddies. Yes, you've got issues you need to work through and, as you're aware, I know what that's like. You've already made great progress. You're an amazing person, Sophie – way more than *I* deserve."

Sophie was looking down at her tightly clasped hands. "But—"

"No buts." Steven put his hands on Sophie's shoulders and waited until her eyes met his. "You're going to work through your issues, your fear of loss, your anger, your grief, and I'm going to be there for you. I'm going to wait until you've done that and we can take it – take us – from there."

Sophie nodded. She still looked sad and troubled, and Steven wished there was more he could do. Then he had an idea. "Actually," he said, "I could give you the contact details of Dr Blakemore, the counsellor I saw, the one who helped me with the PTSD. She's really good and she's based here in the west end of Glasgow. Maybe you could arrange to get some help from her."

"Okay," Sophie said, surprising him with her lack of hesitation. "Yes, I think I'd like that."

"Good," Steven said. "It will give you a bit of a structure and a timescale for getting your equilibrium back, finding some sort of peace."

"I like the sound of that." Her voice had lost its earlier fragile tone and a small smile had now appeared on Sophie's face.

"And in the meantime we prepare for the baby as we are now. We see each other even if it's just to talk. We can sleep together or not, but we keep communicating. Yes?"

"Yes," Sophie was now smiling properly. Steven couldn't resist pulling her in for a hug and his heart was comforted when she relaxed against him.

Then they both laughed when Sophie looked up at him and they said together, "Baby steps."

Sophie snuggled into him for a few moments more before she said, "You mentioned you had a couple of questions. So far you've only asked me about why I changed my mind about the baby. What was your other one?"

"Ah, yes, it's related to what we've just been talking about. It's about you getting your equilibrium back."

"Right."

"Yeah, I was wondering about things between you and your mum."

Sophie gave a little laugh. "What?" Steven said. "Why's that funny?"

"Have you been talking to Paula and Lainey? Me fixing things with Mum – that was the second of the homework tasks they set me."

Steven wasn't sure he followed. "No, not been talking to your pals. And homework? What's that all about? And what was the first task?"

"Ah, right, well I walked into that," Sophie grinned before going on to tell him about her recent conversation with her friends.

Steven also grinned as he listened. "Well," he said when she was finished. "I can tell Paula and Lainey that you did well on the first task. You've talked to me and you've certainly done so calmly, positively and from the heart. And as for the second task, I agree with your wise advisers that you *can* fix things and you should work up to doing that. Maybe you could set yourself a target for the autumn, go and see her when she's back from Israel and do your calm and positive talking thing with her then."

"Yeah, that sounds like a plan."

"And, maybe by the autumn you'll be clearer about things between us and … you know …" Steven hesitated, not wanting to put pressure on her, but also trying to be optimistic about their future as a couple.

Sophie stroked his face and her smile was tender now. "I know," she said softly. "Maybe by the autumn I'll see that we really do deserve each other." And then she kissed him on the lips.

"Exactly," said Steven before returning her kiss.

As summer progressed, they continued to see each other and to get to know each other even better. They did a lot of talking – including discussions about their parenting ideas, hopes and fears. And yes, they had a lot of sex too. They often stayed over at each other's flats and they socialised with each other's friends.

However, one of the best things about that summer from Steven's point of view was seeing the positive changes in Sophie. She attended weekly sessions with the therapist Steven had told her about and those combined with the pregnancy and, Steven hoped, the lack of pressure from him regarding their relationship, all seemed to be helping her be more at ease with herself and life in general.

They attended the ante-natal appointments together and were grateful that everything was fine with the baby. They declined the offer to be told the sex of their baby and gradually shared the news of the pregnancy with family, friends and colleagues.

Steven's parents had been thrilled at the news and had done a fairly good job of trying to hide their bemusement at the fact that Steven and Sophie had no plans to move in together, far less get married.

They told his mum and dad after a Sunday lunch they'd been invited to at his parents' house. Steven had held Sophie's hand as he broke the news knowing that she was nervous. He didn't mention that a termination had been a possibility, simply saying, "So, yes, we didn't plan it, but we are very happy about it." His parents had hugged them both after Steven's announcement and his mum had had a bit of a cry which she assured them were happy tears. Steven had then also added, "And, no, before you ask, we've no plans to cohabit at the moment but we will be co-parenting."

"That's grand," his father said, glancing at Steven's mum who nodded as if she'd received some sort of message from him. "You do what's right for you and things will work out right for your wee one."

"Thanks, Dad," Steven said, suppressing a laugh as he realised that his dad's glance at his mum had probably carried the message 'no, we won't interfere or comment on the fact they're not getting married'.

"Yes, absolutely." Steven's mum smiled at him and Sophie. "Whatever works for you and our … our grandchild." His mother let out a little squeal of delight before wrapping Sophie in another hug. Steven felt as if his heart was going to burst as he watched them.

"Your parents are great," Sophie said when they were in Steven's car on their way home. "Non-judgemental and kind and so enthusiastic."

"Hmm, yes, you're right of course," Steven said. "But I think it took a lot of self-control, especially on Mum's part not to ask a whole lot of questions."

"Well that just makes them even more great," Sophie said.

Steven smiled. "Yeah, I suppose it does. And while we're on the subject of parents," he said glancing sideways at her, "when are you going to tell your mum?"

"I want to tell her in person. I don't want it to be via text or a stilted phone call."

"Well then," Steven said, "you should probably start planning that trip to Skye."

Sophie nodded. "Yeah, I'm going to call Mum next month once she's back from the Middle East. I'll suggest I go up and stay with her – maybe during the last couple of weeks in September as I already have some approved holiday time from work then."

Having decided to wait until her mother was home, Sophie also decided to let her father know what she was planning. There followed a series of calls with him during which, Sophie told

Steven, they'd properly opened up to each other. It seemed her dad had put her straight on a few things, declaring he was far from deserving to be on the pedestal Sophie had placed him on. He'd surprised her by standing up for her mother. And he'd further surprised her when he offered to drive Sophie to Skye, saying she shouldn't drive so far in her condition and, besides that, he wanted to spend some time with her.

"I agree with your dad that you probably shouldn't drive all that way alone," Steven said, when Sophie told him about the latest conversation she'd had with her father. It was a Saturday afternoon near the end of July and they were spending the weekend together at Sophie's. They were chatting while cuddled up together on the sofa after lunch. "Of course I'd like to be the one to drive you but I get that your dad wants to be with you."

"Yeah," Sophie said. "It's been ages since we've seen each other. He's always so busy and, on most of the occasions that I have seen him since the divorce, Carla's been there too. I'm actually amazed she's allowing him to drive me." Sophie laughed.

"That's a lovely sound, you know," Steven said. "A lovely sight too."

"What is?"

"You laughing and looking so relaxed." He reached over and gently rubbed Sophie's baby bump. "It seems pregnancy suits you."

"Oh it's more than the pregnancy," Sophie said, moving closer to him and putting her arms around his waist.

"Yeah, it seems to me like the therapy is helping you too. Even though you've only had a few sessions so far, you already seem so much more at ease, more comfortable in your own skin. It's good to see." Steven swallowed hard as her body pressed against his and she looked up into his eyes. She was so beautiful.

"You're right the therapy is helping but it's more than that too," Sophie said, before brushing her lips against his.

"So, what else has helped?" Steven said, now feeling breathless.

"You, Steven, you. You've been amazing. Your patience, your

support, your ... your love. It's seen me through. I feel free. For the first time in a long time I feel free and I feel comfortable with who I am. I no longer feel like a messy screwup." She ran her finger down his face and along his jaw as she looked into his eyes. "And I've realised something else too, something that deep down I've known for some time."

"Oh, and what's that?"

"I ... I love you Steven. I love you so, so much." And then she kissed him.

Chapter Thirty One

Sophie

"You love me?" Steven said in a whisper, when Sophie released him from one of the most passionate kisses she'd ever experienced.

He was holding her close and when she looked up into his eyes she saw they were filled with tears. "I do," she replied. "You are the most remarkable, adorable and sexy man I've ever met. I've never felt like this about anybody before and I love you with all my heart."

Steven pressed the heel of his hand to his eyes to stem the flow of his tears. "Sorry," he said, "but you've turned me into a blubbering mess."

Sophie smiled softly at him. "I thought you'd be happy that I love you."

He grinned back at her – an incredibly sexy grin that flooded Sophie with desire.

"Oh, believe me, I'm happy," Steven said. "In fact I'm going to take you to bed right now – in the middle of the afternoon – and I'm going to show you just how happy I am."

Sophie giggled as he took her by the hand and led her to her bedroom. "And there it is again. That sound right there," Steven said glancing over his shoulder at her. "Sexiest sound ever."

Sophie hadn't exactly planned to make her declaration of love for Steven on that Saturday afternoon. It just suddenly felt like the right moment. She'd meant what she said about feeling better, about feeling more like her old self. And she also meant it when she told him that much of her new sense of wellbeing was down to him and his love for her.

It was true that the pregnancy was also playing a part in her new sense of wellbeing. Being past the halfway mark meant the morning sickness had passed, and her bump was pleasantly obvious but not yet cumbersome – so she was feeling good physically. As well as that, she was excited at the thought of becoming a mother. She already felt so much love for her baby – and it was a love that she didn't question and that filled her with hope. In fact lots of people had commented on how well she looked – using words like radiant and blossoming and glowing.

And as the weekly therapy sessions with Dr Blakemore, or Nora, as she'd insisted on being called, continued during August, it felt like a fog was lifting and she could see her way ahead. But more than that, she could see the place where she was now. And that was a place where fear, guilt and anger were no longer holding her back. She could allow herself to feel the good as well as the bad.

But it was Steven's unconditional love, his unwavering support, and his endless patience that had had the biggest effect on her. He was willing to let her take the lead in their relationship, to go at her pace – so unlike Rick whose ego had got in the way of everything. Then there was how calm and caring he was about the pregnancy. It wasn't surprising she'd fallen in love with him – and not only that – she now even found herself thinking that maybe she could trust her heart to him in a fully committed, living together, long-term relationship.

However, as the weeks passed she became increasingly impatient to embark on the final and vital part of her healing process – and that was making her peace with her mother. For the last four months, while her mother had been away, there was little communication between them. There had been a few minimal texts – when her mother asked how she was and Sophie assured her she was fine. There had also been a couple of calls from her mother which Sophie had let go to voicemail and then not responded to. Neither of them had mentioned the pregnancy or the planned termination.

So, at the end of August, as soon as her mother had returned home to Skye, Sophie called her.

"Sophie?" Her mother's surprise was evident as she took the call.

"Hi, Mum. How are you?"

"I'm well, thank you."

"Good … that's good."

"And how are you?"

"I'm good, thanks. Actually, I'm thinking of coming to visit … coming to see you … in Skye … if that's okay."

Her mother didn't reply.

"Mum, did you hear me? I'd like to come up and stay for a couple of weeks, around the middle of September if that's okay?"

"Yes, sorry, yes, I heard you. Of course it's okay. I was just surprised. You've not been here for such a long time. Why now? Not that it's a problem."

"I need to talk to you, Mum. And I want to do it face to face."

"Oh, right, okay. That's good. It will be lovely to see you."

"So, how was your time in Israel? Did you enjoy it?

"Good, yes, it was amazing. I'm so glad I went."

"You can tell me all about it when I come up."

"Yes, I will. I'd love to. When were you thinking of coming?"

"I was planning to arrive on the fifteenth. It's a Saturday. If that works for you?"

"Yes, of course. Right, good. See you then."

Her mother's voice had sounded shaky and Sophie couldn't blame her for that. She was obviously shocked to hear from her, which was understandable. But despite them both keeping the talking to a minimum, there had been a detectable warmth in her mother's voice and Sophie believed that despite its brevity their conversation had been another small step – *baby step*, she reminded herself – in the progress she was making in sorting out her personal life.

The two weeks leading up to her trip north passed reasonably quickly.

Work was busy as she strove to finish the two big pieces of research that had to be completed and handed over before she took her fortnight's leave. Her colleagues had got over their initial surprise that she was pregnant with most of them managing to restrain their curiosity about the fact she was in a relationship they'd heard nothing about. And they'd all proved supportive when she clearly couldn't keep up her usual superhuman work rate. In fact a couple of them admitted it was a relief that she'd slowed down to their pace. Even her boss, George, had got over the double whammy of surprises she'd sprung on him when she not only turned down both the promotions she'd been offered, but then also went on to announce that she was having a baby. He'd also surprised her by taking it in his stride when she told him she was considering going freelance at some point.

She also had her six-month ante natal appointment which she attended with Steven and which confirmed that everything was as it should be and their baby was developing normally.

Another highlight during those two weeks was that the TV programme about the Revive Centre aired one evening. She and Steven watched it at her place together with Lainey, Paula and her husband, and Dean and his wife. As she listened to everyone's approving comments, Sophie felt not only very proud of Steven, but proud of the part she'd played in getting the programme made. She got an extra kick out of the fact that not only had Steven thought it was brilliant but he'd been amazing on screen as he'd talked about all the work carried out at the centre. It was also gratifying to hear that, following the transmission, Revive had received lots of enquiries from possible donors and from prospective users of the centre.

Despite the time going quickly and how busy she was, Sophie found she was impatient to get away – even though she knew leaving Steven behind was going to be hard. The two of them had become even closer since Sophie's declaration of love and although she knew that going to see her mum was something she had to do alone, a part of her wished he was coming with her. However, Steven had made it a bit easier for her by saying he'd come up at the end of her time on Skye and drive her home.

The journey up to Skye proved to be pleasant. Sophie had to admit it was much more comfortable being able to sit back in her father's spacious luxury car and either doze or listen to music than it would have been, being somewhat cramped in her own much smaller car, and having to concentrate on driving for the six-hour journey.

Her heart had lifted when they crossed the bridge that connected the Isle of Skye to the mainland and she took in the stunning beauty of the island. She was reminded of happy holidays at her grandparents' croft at Burnside in the small township of Dunhalla – the place her mother now lived. It had been far too long since she'd visited.

Even after they'd crossed the bridge it was another couple of hours before they arrived in Dunhalla at the top end of the island's northern peninsula of Waternish.

Her father walked ahead of her when they got out of the car at her mother's cottage and Sophie heard her mother's voice before she saw her.

"Peter!" she called out, her voice full of surprise. "Hallo … I didn't … that is I wasn't—"

"Expecting me," said Sophie's dad. "I know. Don't panic. There's a good reason for me being here. I insisted on driving our daughter."

"Oh," her mother said, craning her neck to see Sophie.

"Yes," Peter continued, "It's a tiring journey at the best of times, but more so when ..." Peter moved aside so Rachel could see her daughter – her very obviously pregnant daughter.

"Hello, Mum," Sophie said smiling.

Her mother gasped, her hands over her mouth, and tears in her eyes as she looked at Sophie. "Oh Sophie, Sophie," she said, before coming forward to hug her. They stood there simultaneously crying and laughing, oblivious to Peter who was unloading Sophie's luggage from the car. It was only when he joined them and cleared his throat loudly that her mother said, "Sorry, come in, both of you, come in."

Once they were inside Peter insisted on making them all some tea and ordered Sophie and her mother through to the living room telling them they needed to talk.

Sophie followed her mother and sat down on the sofa beside her. Deciding there was no time like the present, she turned to face her mother and said, "I'm sorry, Mum. I've been a bitch and I'm so sorry."

Her mother took one of Sophie's hands in both of hers. For a moment she didn't speak but just looked at Sophie as both of them cried once more. Sophie saw only love in her mother's eyes and her shame made her look away.

But her mother wasn't put off and she put a hand under Sophie's chin and tipped her face up so she had to look at her. "I love you, Sophie, and I'm so glad you're here. I've missed you so much."

"Oh, Mum," Sophie said as a sob shuddered through her. Then she was in her mother's arms being rocked and soothed by her until she was calm again.

"May I?" her mother said after she released Sophie from the hug. She nodded in the direction of Sophie's bump.

Sophie took her mother's hand and placed it on her belly. "I didn't want to tell you on the phone. I hope you understand. I wanted it ... *needed* it to be face to face, but I'm sorry for prolonging the agony for you ... as well as everything else."

Her mother shook her head and her expression seemed to suggest none of that mattered now. "When is it due?" she asked.

"The sixth of December. I'm twenty-eight weeks."

Her mother's smile was full on. "I can't believe it," she said as she withdrew her hand and sat back. "What made you change your mind?"

"Lots of things. I realised as the termination got nearer that I wasn't going to be able to go through with it. I never really wanted to end the pregnancy, not deep down. I phoned Dad the day before the termination appointment. He drove through to Glasgow that evening."

"Did he?" Her mother's surprise was obvious.

"Yeah, and talking to him, it helped me see that I was acting out of anger, anger at myself, at life, and that those feelings were misplaced. And when I told him what I'd said to you when you visited the day before, he helped me see I was being completely unfair. All that stuff I said to you, it was ridiculous, unforgiveable."

"No, not unforgiveable, never that," her mother said.

"I was so angry at Fin dying, Mum. Blaming you, it stopped me falling apart. It was like if I didn't have someone to blame then his death was completely senseless, and down to him, to his decision to go."

"I see," her mother said. She paused for a moment before she added, "And the stuff you said about you not being a wanted child, about the guilt you feel that Dad and I weren't happy—"

"I told her to let go of any such feelings," Sophie's father said. He'd come back into the room carrying a tray, followed by Bonnie, her mother's collie sheepdog, who'd apparently been keeping an eye on him. Her father laid the tray on the coffee table before passing Sophie and Rachel a mug each. He took his own mug and sat in one of the armchairs before continuing. "I told her how much you wanted her," he said looking at Rachel. "I told her it was me who considered not going ahead with the pregnancy. I told her how amazing you'd been, coping with our parents and all the pressure we were under to get married, how you carried on with your studies and made a home for us. And I told her how very loved she was and is by both of us."

"Oh," her mother said, clearly so surprised by her ex-husband's defence of her that words failed her.

"I also told her," Sophie's father went on, "that I don't want the pressure of being a hero. I told her I don't deserve to be seen in that light and filled her in on the full facts about just how hopeless a husband I was. And I informed her that you were always the strong one, the truly loving and unselfish one."

"Oh," her mother said again.

"Yes, Rachel," her father said. "You were, are, amazingly strong. You stuck around for the children, even when you knew what I was up to. You kept the family together. And then later, you set Finlay free to follow his dream. You gave him your blessing and I … I didn't."

Her mother nodded. Sophie was lost for words. She had been so unfair and so cruel to her mother.

She put her mug down on the table and turned to her mother. "I've been such an idiot," she said. "I never really doubted I was loved. I think … I think, after Finlay, I think I went a bit mad. The anger was overwhelming. But I shouldn't have taken it out on you. Can you really forgive me?"

Her mother leant towards her, pushed a stray lock of hair back from Sophie's face and stroked her cheek. "There is nothing to forgive. You're my daughter. I love you no matter what. All that matters is that you're here now. So stop apologising and let's just enjoy our time together."

At her mother's insistence Sophie's father stayed the night at Burnside cottage rather than going to a hotel in the island's main town of Portree before his drive home the next day. So the three of them had spent a strange, but from Sophie's point of view, a rather wonderful evening together. It was a time when their emotions were heightened as they reminisced, remembered Finlay, and laughed and cried together. And Sophie felt it was better than any therapy.

It was the next morning, just before her father left, that Sophie heard the tail end of a conversation her parents were having when she was about to join them in the kitchen. Her mother had just confirmed that she planned to live on Skye long-term and had gone on to say, "And I've made a new friend. He's … he's you know—"

"Oh my God, Mum's got a boyfriend!" Sophie blurted out from the doorway.

"Why is that so amazing?" Her mother turned to look at Sophie. "But before you get carried away, no, I haven't got a boyfriend. But I have made a new friend, he's a neighbour, Jack. He's a retired policeman from Edinburgh and he's bought Dun Halla Cottage, just up the road."

"Jack," Sophie said as she nodded and smiled at her father.

"Jack," he said as he smiled back at Sophie. "Mum's new *friend.*"

Her mother ordered them to change the subject but she was definitely blushing as she did so.

During their time together Sophie and her mother hardly stopped talking. They had a lot to catch up on but they were also cautious and gentle with each other to begin with.

On their first afternoon her mother told Sophie about her trip to Israel and Sophie had enjoyed hearing about her Uncle Jonathan and his family and their life in Israel. They also talked a bit about the plight of the Palestinians, as her mother saw it, and about the politics of the situation. Sophie loved hearing her mother's passionate views and seeing her look so alive and enthusiastic.

She also took Sophie into her study to show her a proof copy of her latest children's book. Her mum was a talented artist and writer and her drawings and the accompanying story in *Seamus the Sheep* were funny and clever. "This is brilliant, Mum," she said when she finished looking through it. "My baby's very lucky having such a talented grandma."

Her mother smiled. "I love the sound of that," she said. "Grandma – can't wait."

"Have you ever thought of doing any sort of writing for teens or adults – graphic novels are really popular at the moment?"

"Hmm, funny you should say that," her mother replied. "I recently had a discussion with Lana, my literary agent, about a book I'd like to do which wouldn't be for children – not a graphic novel – more graphic non-fiction."

"Oh?"

"Yeah, it's an idea I had while I was in Israel. I'd like to do a book about my time there. I'd want it to be informative about the realities of the country but without it being preachy or overtly political. The themes would be displacement, exile and loss – both metaphorical and actual – and how even in the most difficult of circumstances it's possible to flourish and grow stronger. I'd use my sketches and photos from my visit and intersperse them with personal reflections. Lana liked the idea and told me to put together a proposal."

"Wow, Mum, that sounds great," Sophie said, genuinely excited by her mother's ideas. "It's the sort of thing I could see being made into a really engaging television documentary too."

Her mother laughed. "Well, we'll see. It might not come to anything."

"Oh, I reckon it will," Sophie said, grinning.

As they'd been speaking, Sophie had noticed an easel with a canvas on it in the corner of the room and the small table beside it which was covered with brushes and paint. "You've been painting?"

"Eh, yes," her mother said as Sophie moved to take a closer look.

The painting was of the cottage and croft fields with Ben Halla mountain in the background. It was all in autumn colours – yellow and orange bracken, the rowan tree with its golden leaves and red berries, and the hedgerows full of crocosmia and rosehips.

"I haven't painted in years, decades actually, but it's something I want to get back into. This is my first attempt. I've a bit of a way to go yet but I am enjoying it."

"It's beautiful, Mum. You really are talented. It's great that you're getting back into it, doing something you enjoy, and it's great you're trying new things like going off to Israel on your own, and your new book idea too."

"Yes, I've been in limbo for far too long and I've been reminded recently that life is for living. And you, my darling girl," her mother put her hand on Sophie's arm, "that's what you need to do too."

Sophie nodded, and she realised yet again, as she and her mother hugged, just how far she'd come in the last few months – when she could not only accept her mother was moving on but that it was also time she did so too.

As her days on Skye passed, Sophie had many more such moments with her mother.

One of those moments occurred one afternoon when her mother had shown her the contents of a small battered brown leather case. The case had belonged to her grandmother, Miriam, and her grandmother had brought it with her when she travelled from Germany to Scotland in the 1930s as a Jewish child refugee on the Kindertransport. Her mother said that Miriam had never let her and her brother see inside it and it remained on a top shelf in her bedroom at Burnside until she died. However, she and her brother had looked inside it after their mother's funeral. And now it was Sophie's turn to see its contents.

There was a doll. It had a china head and a soft body. Sophie had a lump in her throat as she stroked its thin matted brown hair and looked at the rosy-cheeked, blue-eyed face along with the beautifully sewn red velvet coat and bonnet, and tiny, chipped black shoes. There was also a card with a three digit number on it which her mother explained was Miriam's transport number. But by far the most moving things were a handwritten letter from Miriam's parents to their daughter and a black and white photo of a man, a woman and two girls. The letter was written in a mixture of German and Yiddish and her mother told Sophie that in it her parents had said to Miriam how much they loved her and that they hoped to see her again soon. And Sophie and her mother had wept when they looked at the photo, knowing that three of the people in the photo – Miriam's parents and older sister – had died in the concentration camps and that Miriam, the smaller of the two girls in the photo, had never seen them again.

The other incredibly moving event Sophie experienced was when her mother showed her another letter. This letter was from Sophie's brother Finlay and was passed to their mother after his death.

Sophie and her mum were spending the evening curled up on the sofa talking about Finlay, looking at old photos, reminiscing about what he'd been like as a boy, some of the escapades he'd got involved in as a teenager, and his infuriating as well as his lovable traits. They were both wiping away their tears of joy and sadness that the memories brought on when her mother said, "Now seems like a good time to show you this." She went to a drawer in the sideboard and produced the letter. "I only read it recently myself," she said as she handed Sophie the envelope. Sophie took out the letter it contained and began to read.

Hey Ma,

I guess if you're reading this, I must have copped it. And I'm sorry. Sorry that I'll not get to take over the croft or get to scoff your amazing roast lamb again or your magic bacon rolls – or see Hearts win the Scottish Cup. But mostly I'm sorry for YOU – because I know you'll say it's all your fault. You'll beat yourself up, saying stuff like 'I should have stopped him. I shouldn't have let him join up'. IT'S NOT YOUR FAULT. You couldn't have stopped me. It's what I always wanted to do – to be a soldier. I love it, Ma. I love everything about it. I'm with the best bunch of guys, and I think we can make it better for the people we're here to help.

Whatever happened, it's down to me. I probably did something stupid, lowered my guard, forgot to check something, took a wrong turning.

I couldn't have had a better mum than you and I hope I made you proud. Remember me, but don't be sad. Enjoy your life, Ma, and make the most of every day.

I'll miss you.

With love from your boy,

Fin xxx

A wrenching sob broke, shaking Sophie's whole body, as tears coursed down her cheeks. "Oh, Mum," she said. "I miss him so much."

I know," her mum said, crying too, as the pair of them embraced. "I know."

And of course they talked about the pregnancy and about Steven.

"He sounded nice when I spoke to him that time on the phone," her mother said.

"He is," Sophie said. "He's a lovely guy. But I don't … I don't know what to do about him."

"Oh, why?" Rachel said.

"It's complicated."

"Would it help to talk?" her mum asked.

"I wouldn't know where to start," Sophie said.

"How did you meet? You could start there."

So Sophie did. She told Rachel about meeting Steven through her work, and then meeting him again at Dean's party. She told her how he was ex-army and about his injuries and the work he did now. And then she went on to share how their relationship had developed and how, when she got pregnant, Steven had been so supportive.

"Not only supportive," Sophie said. "He wants it all, the full package, marriage, the works. He's told me he loves me and wants to be with me for ever. He was prepared to stay with me if I got rid of the baby – even though it wasn't what he wanted."

"Wow, he sounds amazing and seriously in love. But you don't feel the same?"

"No … that is yes … I do love him … it just took me a bit longer to admit it. He's kind, brave, loyal, everything anyone could want."

"But?"

"But I'm scared, Mum – although not as scared as I was. I think my hesitation is all part of the madness I mentioned before – the madness brought on by grief – and then my fears of being hurt again after how my previous relationship ended."

Sophie went on to tell her mother about the inner conflict she experienced when she first found out she was pregnant, about how she never really wanted to terminate the pregnancy, about the things she talked over with Steven, about the therapy she was undergoing, and about how much better she was feeling about everything now.

Her mother listened sympathetically and when she finished telling it all, Sophie said, "Thanks, Mum," and reached over the table and squeezed her mother's hand.

"What for?" her mother said.

"For listening. Dad was the same. And neither of you told me what to do. You're great parents."

"Both of us?" There were more tears in in her mum's eyes.

"Yes, both of you," Sophie said. And during the shared embrace that followed, Sophie sensed another emotional shift. She felt lighter, more at ease, but most of all she felt healed.

Sophie and Rachel also shared lots of easier times and conversations too. They went to the cinema and to an art exhibition in Portree. They also visited Rachel's dear friend and neighbour, Morag, and Sophie had laughed at Morag's stories of what she and Rachel had got up to as teenagers when they'd been at school together on the island.

Her mother also persuaded Sophie to sit for her so she could sketch her as preparation for a future painting. It was while she sat that Sophie decided to broach another subject.

"So, this Jack of yours, what's he like?"

Her mother stopped sketching for a moment. "What brought that on?"

"Curiosity. I've told you about Steven after all. I just wondered if I'd maybe be getting a bit more information about your guy." Sophie smiled a knowing smile.

"He's not 'my guy'. And there's not much to tell. We're friends like I said."

"How did you meet?"

"He … he rescued me from the burn."

"He what?"

"Rescued me – from the burn – from the river by the house. It was one night back in January. I went out to do a last check on the sheep and one of them had got herself stuck in the burn. We'd had a lot of rain, the water was running high – and long story short – I went into the water to try to rescue her, she freed herself, I got stuck. Bonnie ran off barking and Jack, who'd only recently arrived here, heard her, decided to investigate and rescued me."

"So he hauled you out the river – then what?"

"He … he took me to Morag's holiday cottage. He was renting it at the time while he renovated his new place. He gave me dry clothes, made me tea and toast and yeah, we got talking … and … and we're now good friends."

"He sounds like a proper hero. How romantic." Sophie grinned.

"You're as bad as Morag," her mother said, shaking her head but blushing and smiling too. "She's been trying to pair us off since we met. There's no romance."

"I think you do protest too much. I can tell. Your face is giving you away. At the very least you fancy him. Come on, Mum, tell me. It's more than friendship, isn't it?"

Her mother blushed even more. "Okay, okay, bearing in

mind you're my daughter, I will only say that yes, we have gone beyond friendship and it was just the once and it was just a kiss."

"I knew it!" Sophie grinned again. "And is the 'going beyond friendship' going to move on to a proper relationship?"

"I've no idea. Jack and me, us, the kiss, it was immediately before he left to go to his daughter. She's in Edinburgh. She's just had a baby. So we haven't had a chance to talk about what happens next."

"Right, I see," Sophie said. "When's he due back?"

"I'm not sure. It depends how his daughter is."

"What would you like to happen next?"

"I think I would like it very much if Jack and I moved on to a 'proper relationship', as you call it. But it's … it's complicated." They both laughed as they realised how similar this was to Sophie's hesitancy when it came to Steven. "And I suspect it's not what Jack wants," her mother added.

"Have you told him how you feel?" Sophie asked.

"No."

"Why not?"

"I'm scared."

"Ah," said Sophie.

"Yes, ah," her mother replied.

And, as her mother continued sketching, Sophie acknowledged to herself that she and her mother weren't all that different after all.

Chapter Thirty Two

Steven missed Sophie while she was away on Skye. He was glad she'd gone to sort things out with her mother because it was definitely something she needed to do but it was hard not having her around. They kept in touch with a mixture of texts and calls so Steven knew Sophie's visit was going well.

It was the call from Sophie on the Monday evening at the start of her second week away that proved decisive for Steven. He was thinking longingly about her while trying and failing to distract himself by watching TV. He picked up his phone to call her just as his phone buzzed. It was Sophie on a video call.

"Hi there, soldier," she said, grinning at him, her voice soft and sexy.

"Hi, Soph," he replied, a lump already forming in his throat as his emotions ran riot. It was torture, a sweet sort of torture, but torture nevertheless to see her but not be able to touch her. "What you been up to today?"

"It's been a busy one. I helped Mum on the croft, feeding the sheep and helping with some health checks on the flock."

"Oh, get you Miss Farmer."

Sophie laughed. "Well when I say helped, I walked alongside Mum while she did all the work. And then she insisted me and Bump have a rest."

"And you and your mum, you're still getting along?"

"Yes, we are. We can't seem to stop talking now we've started and it's … it's just so good." Sophie rubbed the back of her hand across her cheeks.

"You okay?"

"Yeah, more than okay. It's happy tears, honestly." She smiled again. "Anyway, what about you?" How was your day?"

"Oh, you know, okay, routine, fine." He shrugged. "With you away, it's like the shine's gone off everything. I know I'm being a soppy git but I miss you, Soph."

"Aw, soppy git is good. I miss you too. I miss … I miss everything about you, about us. I just want to be in your arms." She swiped at her cheeks again as more tears fell. "Bloody hormones," she said with a giggle. "Oh, for pity's sake, now I'm laughing and crying at the same time. You've wrecked me, soldier." She leaned closer to her phone screen and scrutinised his face. "Oh, you're crying too, aren't you?"

Steven nodded. "Yeah, I am. But they're manly tears, of course. None of that soppy, girly hormonal nonsense." He grinned at her. "And speaking of hormones, how's Bump doing?"

"Bump is doing fine. Missing Daddy though. We've had a great time on Skye but Friday can't come soon enough."

And that's when Steven decided. His yearning was off the scale. Enough was enough.

It was very early on the Wednesday morning that Steven set off for Skye. He was two days early and he hadn't told Sophie of the change of plan. He'd spent much of the day before getting organised, arranging the extra time off work, changing his B&B booking on Skye to a hotel one, packing, and doing some important shopping.

The journey north went smoothly and Steven arrived outside Sophie's mother's house in Halladale just after noon. He heard a dog barking as he stood looking around him. The view of the loch, the croft fields and the mountains beyond was stunning and the sign outside the white harled cottage confirmed he was indeed at Burnside. A woman came out of the front door of the cottage.

"Hello," she said, frowning slightly as she looked at him.

"I'm Steven," he said walking towards her, his hand outstretched. "Steven Jackson."

"I thought you might be," the woman said, smiling warmly now as she shook his hand. "I'm Rachel."

"I know you weren't expecting me for another couple of days but I—"

"Steven!" His heart leapt, then started pounding as he looked over at Sophie who was standing on the doorstep. "What are you, why are you—"

"I couldn't wait, Soph," he said as he stepped up to her. "I've missed you so much. I had to see you." He took her in his arms as soon as they reached each other and he held her tight – loving the feel of her and of the bump that nestled between them.

When he eventually released Sophie, Rachel called out, "Right. That's me away." She waved at them both. "I'm having lunch at Morag's."

Sophie looked puzzled as she turned to her mum. Then she smiled. "Ah, right, yes, of course. Bye."

"See you later," Rachel said and then she headed away up the track.

Sophie grinned at Steven. "I think that was Mum's not so subtle way of giving us some privacy. Seems she's just made up a lunch date at her friend's house."

Steven smiled back at her. "I see," he said.

They barely made it inside before they were back in each other's arms and exchanging a long and passionate kiss. When they finally broke apart both of them were breathless.

"Wow," Sophie said as she looked up at him, her eyes full of love and desire.

"You really did miss me." Steven's voice had become a low, lust-filled growl.

"Hmm, a little bit," Sophie said, before running her tongue along her bottom lip.

Steven groaned. "Damn you, woman," he said. "That's too sexy."

Sophie batted her eyelashes before grabbing his hand. "Come on," she said. "Let me show you proper sexy." She seemed to be heading for the stairs – stairs that most likely led to her bedroom.

"Wait," he said, not quite believing what he was about to say. "Maybe we shouldn't … this is your mum's place … we—"

"Trust me, Mum will be at Morag's for quite some time," Sophie said. "As well as all the usual gossip they'll have your sudden arrival to discuss and speculate about too."

"Okay," Steven said, a grin replacing his earlier anxious look. "I'd love to see your room."

But as soon as he'd kicked the guest room door shut, any pretence of looking around the space was the last thing on his mind. He pulled Sophie to him and kissed her. And again his eagerness was more than matched by hers. It wasn't long before their clothes were discarded in a pile on the floor and he was pushing her gently back towards the bed. Their lovemaking was urgent and Steven felt he would never get enough of this beautiful woman. Eventually however, they stopped and lay in each other's arms. Steven was almost overwhelmed as he looked at Sophie as she lay back, her hair spread on the pillow, her hands on her swollen abdomen. She was so beautiful and Bump just added to her beauty. No woman had ever made him feel like this. He was a battle-hardened military veteran for goodness' sake but Sophie could get him crying like a kid.

"I love you so much, Sophie," he said, stroking her face as his eyes watered.

"I love you too," Sophie replied. Then after she kissed him she added, "And much as I'd like to lie here with you for ever, we better make ourselves decent and get back downstairs."

"Yeah," he laughed. "Don't want your mother grounding you after finding out you've been a very naughty girl while she was out."

Sophie lit the fire in the living room and they cosied up on the sofa together. And it was there Sophie's mother found them, Bonnie snoozing on the rug at their feet, when she returned about half an hour later.

Rachel gave them both a knowing smile as she greeted them and Steven could feel himself blush. So, not only crying but blushing too – Sophie had a lot to answer for.

"I'm going out to check on the sheep and then I'll make us all some dinner when I get back," Rachel said.

Sophie gave him a puzzled look when he stood up. But much as he was enjoying sitting there with her, he needed to speak to Rachel urgently.

"Eh," Steven said, "can I come with you?"

"Oh … yes, of course you can," Rachel said.

He glanced at Sophie who now looked even more puzzled. "Sorry," he said. "It's just I want … I'd like to see round the croft."

Sophie shrugged and gave him a bemused smile. "It's fine," she said.

As they made their way down the croft, Rachel pushing a wheelbarrow she'd filled with a couple of feed sacks and Bonnie running in circles around them, Steven was aware of Rachel looking at him. "Sophie told me about your injury," she said. "The ground here is very uneven. Will you manage?"

"I'll be fine," Steven assured her. "The prostheses I have are carbon-fibre. I have different ones for different surfaces and activities – but these ones are pretty much all-terrain."

"I'm sorry," Rachel said. "Sorry that you were injured and I hope you didn't mind me asking."

"Of course I don't mind. It helps if people are direct about it, sort of gets it out of the way. And thanks for your sympathy, but I was lucky to …" Steven stopped speaking as he remembered Rachel's son hadn't been so lucky.

"Lucky to survive," Rachel finished for him.

"Yes … unlike others … unlike your son."

Rachel gave a little nod but clearly wanted to keep the conversation about him.

"It can't have been easy for you," she said. "Recovering, coming to terms with what happened to you."

"No, not easy, not at first, not for a long time actually. There was the guilt that I'd survived. And then there was the grief of losing my legs and my previous life. And then there was some PTSD thrown into the mix."

"And now? Are you okay now?"

"Yeah, I reckon I've come to terms with it – over time – and I got some great professional help. And meeting Sophie, well that's probably what's helped me most of all. And now with the baby coming, I feel even luckier. On top of the world actually."

Rachel smiled at Steven and the look she gave him seemed full of understanding and, he hoped, maybe even approval. Once they arrived at the in-bye field he helped her fill the water troughs and distribute the feed to the ewes and lambs who were kept there. He asked a couple of questions about the sheep and, along with Bonnie, he managed to help Rachel catch a couple of the ewes whose feet she wanted to check.

"I'm impressed," Rachel said when he flipped one of the ewes onto its back so she could carry out her inspection. "Did you grow up on a farm?"

Steven laughed. "No, I'm a city boy but I spent a lot of my summer holidays at my grandparents' farm in Argyll. My uncle has it now and I still like to visit when I get the chance. And my mum's sister married a farmer and they have a farm in the Scottish Borders so that's another place we went to for our holidays."

"Ah, so it's in your blood, then?"

"Yeah, kind of. I was actually telling Sophie I have a bit of a fantasy about maybe farming as a job – just small scale, but I probably don't know enough about it – and I don't know if these would be up to it, day in day out," he added, pointing down at his legs.

"You never know till you try it," Rachel said and the look she gave him made it seem like a dare.

"Yeah, that's what Sophie said," he replied.

It was as they were heading back to the house that Steven realised that he still needed to tell Rachel not only of his plans for the evening but also that he had an important question to ask her. A question he just went ahead and blurted out.

"Would it be all right with you if I asked Sophie to marry me?" he said.

Rachel gasped and her hands went to her mouth. She stopped walking and turned to look at him. He stopped too. Steven smiled. "I hope you're shocked in a good way," he said.

"Not shocked. Pleasantly surprised ... delighted." Rachel smiled back at him.

"So, it's all right then? To propose?"

"Yes, of course," Rachel said. "You didn't have to ask me. But it's nice that you did."

"Good," he said. "And it's okay, I know she might say no. I've mentioned marriage to her before, although I've not made a proper proposal with a ring and everything, but she's not shown any interest."

"And you think she'll be interested now?"

"I don't know for certain. But I do know that during the time she's been up here, it's been awful not being able to drop round and see her. I love her so much. I just want us to be properly together." He paused and cleared his throat. "I have to give it one more try. I've booked us into a hotel in Portree tonight. It looked suitably luxurious on its website and it seems to have a good restaurant too. So I've got a ring and a list of reasons why she'd be daft not to accept, and tonight over dinner I'm going to do it. I'm going to propose properly." Steven let out a long breath as he finished speaking. The earlier confidence boost that his afternoon with Sophie had given him seemed to be fading now. She said she loved him and he believed her – but would she actually want to marry him?

"Good for you." Rachel's voice dragged him back from his doubtful thoughts. "And I do hope she says yes. She told me she loves you and how right you are for her. It's just she's scared it won't work out in the long term, that you and her will fail, end up hating each other. I'm afraid the relationship between her father and me has left Sophie with the very scars I tried to prevent from happening."

"Yeah, life can be messy, can't it?" Steven said recalling everything he'd been through and, as he did so, his resolve not to give up on Sophie and the life he wanted them to have together strengthened. "But if there's one thing I've learned after my injuries, it's that life's too short and too precious to spend it feeling ashamed or guilty or afraid. You have to go to it, embrace it and live it."

Rachel's eyes were now filled with tears. "You're so right," she said softly. "It's what my son Finlay said in his letter. You know the one you military people write to your family in case …"

"In case we don't make it home," Steven said, his voice also soft.

"Yes, and you and him, you're both right of course. I've recently come to truly understand that for myself and I just … I just hope Sophie has too."

After they got back to the house Rachel said she'd leave him to it to tell Sophie about her night away and disappeared into her study. So Steven took a deep breath as he went into the living room, readying himself to put part one of his plan into action.

Sophie was where he'd left her, still on the sofa – but now she was curled up reading – and Steven loved how relaxed she looked. He sat down beside her and cleared his throat yet again.

"The Cuillin View Hotel!" Sophie squealed when he told her the arrangements he'd made for that night. "You've booked us a meal and an overnight stay at the Cuillin View, tonight?"

"I have. Trip Advisor tells me it's Portree's poshest."

"Wow!" Sophie said, clapping her hands together. "That's amazing, Steven. And it really is posh – expensive too."

"Nothing's too good for my woman," Steven said grinning.

Sophie scrambled to her feet. "I need to pack a bag," she said as she left the room.

Part one of his plan had been successful – now for part two.

Chapter Thirty Three

Sophie

"Mmm," Sophie sighed appreciatively. She'd gone straight to the king-size bed as soon as they'd entered their hotel room and after a couple of seated bounces, she lay back and stretched out her limbs like a snow angel. "This is comfy," she said. "You should come and try it for yourself." She rolled onto her side and propped herself up on her elbow, before patting the bedcover and giving Steven what she hoped was a sexy look.

Steven laid down their bags and shook his head as he looked at her. "Stop that right now, woman," he groaned, "or we'll miss tomorrow's breakfast – never mind dinner this evening."

"Spoilsport." Sophie did a fake pout before getting up off the bed and going to take a look at the ensuite.

She smiled at herself in the bathroom mirror as she rubbed her baby bump. "First time me and your father have had a night away together," she whispered. And then a giggle escaped. As it did she glanced at herself in the mirror again and hardly recognised the happy woman she saw looking back at her.

It was Sophie's turn to groan when she came back into the bedroom and saw Steven had started to get changed. He'd taken off his hoodie and tee-shirt and was about to put on a smart, long-sleeved maroon shirt. He'd already swapped his joggers for black chinos. She went to him and ran her hands down his chest, breathing in his unique scent as she did so. Steven took hold of her hands and smiled at her. "Come on," he said. "You need to get changed too. There's a bottle of alcohol-free champagne chilling down at the bar – which I'm assured tastes as good as the real thing – and it's got our names on it."

"Oh, champagne! Why didn't you say so?" Sophie giggled.

She swapped her maternity trousers for the dark green dress she was so glad she'd thought to bring from Glasgow. It was made from stretchy jersey which was fitted around the bust and then draped loosely over Bump. After refreshing her makeup, she added some amber earrings, her black ankle boots, and was good to go.

A young waiter welcomed them to the hotel restaurant and after he'd shown them to their table and handed them their menus, another waiter appeared with an ice bucket and the promised champagne. The wine waiter opened the bottle and let Steven do the tasting. Steven nodded his approval and Sophie noticed he looked nervous as their glasses were filled.

"There you go, sir, madam" the wine waiter said, looking at each of them in turn. Then looking back at Steven, he added, "I'll leave you to it. Just let me know when you're ready to order food." And Sophie could have sworn she saw him wink at Steven before he left them.

After they'd clinked glasses and taken their first couple of sips of what was indeed a delicious drink, Steven reached across the table for her hand. "Thank you for coming away with me," he said. "I'm sorry for depriving you of time with your mum."

"No need to apologise," Sophie said. "I've missed you a lot and it's so lovely to be here with you. Besides, Mum seemed neither surprised or upset when I told her we were going away for the night."

"Ah, yes, well that's probably because I'd already told her our plans – or rather my plans." Steven let go of her hand and looked nervous again and he seemed to be reaching for something in his trouser pocket.

"Right," said Sophie. "Steven, are you okay? It's just you seem … you seem—"

"Terrified?" Steven said. "That's because I am." He took another swig of champagne. "I'm terrified because I have a question to ask you."

"Right," Sophie said again, wondering – indeed hoping – if he was going to suggest again that they move in together. "So ask away."

"Okay," Steven took a deep breath and again reached for her hand. "Sophie, you know I love you. You're the best thing that's ever happened to me – you and now our baby too. And you know I want to be with you for ever. "

Sophie's eyes filled with tears just as Steven's had done and she squeezed his hand as he paused. Then her breath caught in her throat as he placed a small open box on the table and removed the ring that sat inside it. "Sophie Campbell, will you marry me?"

Tears now cascaded down Sophie's face. "Yes," she said. "Yes, I will." Then she was laughing and crying simultaneously as Steven put the sapphire and diamond engagement ring on her finger.

"Yes!" Steven raised his arm and punched the air. "She said yes," he shouted, looking round the room at their fellow diners and the restaurant staff as everybody clapped.

Sophie beamed at everyone as she wiped her eyes and blew her nose. Then as the applause died down and everyone got back to what they'd been doing before, she took a moment. A moment to reflect and to acknowledge that meeting Steven had been truly life changing. Not only could she look forward to a life with this lovely man and the child they were expecting, but she was healed and whole again. There was no more anger, no more guilt, and, yes, although there would always be the grief for her brother, she could now hold him in her heart and move on. And all because of this man. This man who, with his kindness, care and baby steps approach to life, had helped her to find not only true love in the here and now, but also reconciliation regarding the past along with so much hope for the future.

It was then the baby kicked. Reaching across the table Sophie took hold of Steven's hand in one of hers. Then, caressing Bump with her freehand, she looked down at her swollen belly and said, "Yeah, little one, baby steps *are* the best." Then, looking up at Steven, seeing the love in his eyes as he gazed back at her, she added, "And your daddy is the absolute best too."

The End

Note from the author

Thank you for reading *Baby Steps*. I do hope you enjoyed it. As it's a spin off from my Skye series of books, you can read more of Steven's and Sophie's story in the three books in that series – *Displacement*, *Settlement* and *Fulfilment*. As well as reading the romantic story of Rachel (Sophie's mother) and how she meets and falls in love with Jack, you can read all about Sophie and Steven's wedding, the arrival of their baby – and what they do after that. You can see more about these books at the end of this section.

Review Request

I know your time is precious, so thank you for spending some it reading my book. I hope you enjoyed it, and if you did, I'd like to ask for a bit more of your time. Would you consider writing a review either on the website of the book shop where you bought this book, or maybe in an online book group you're a member of. It doesn't have to be an essay – two or three sentences would be great and I would really appreciate it if you did. Reviews really do help authors to reach prospective readers.

Thank you.

Newsletter Subscription and Free e-Book

To keep in touch and get news of my new releases sign up for my monthly newsletter which will be sent to you by email. You'll receive a FREE e-BOOK as a thank you. As a subscriber you can expect:

- Exclusive offers, excerpts and bonus scenes

- giveaways

- sneak peeks and pre-publication previews of my new books

- recommended reads from other authors

- insights into my writing life

To sign up just visit my website at www.anne-stormont.com

About the Author

Anne Stormont writes contemporary, compassionate and thoughtful fiction. Her stories are for readers who enjoy a good romantic story, but who also like romance that is laced with realism on the road to a happy ever after.

Anne can be found on Facebook and Twitter and you can also find out more about her on her blog and on her website.

Facebook: www.facebook.com/annestormontauthor
Twitter: www.twitter.com/writeanne @writeanne
Blog at https://putitinwriting.me
Website at https://anne-stormont.com

Also by Anne Stormont

Displacement

First book in the series of the Rachel and Jack, Skye series of novels.

It's never too late to fall in love,
but the past can get in the way of a happy future.

From the Scottish Hebrides to the Middle-East, *Displacement* is an intense love story where romance and realism, and the personal and the political meet head on.

Divorce, the death of her soldier son and estrangement from her daughter, leave Hebridean crofter, Rachel Campbell, grief stricken, lonely and lost.

Forced retirement due to a heart condition leaves former Edinburgh policeman Jack Baxter needing to take stock and find a new direction for his life.

After the two of them meet in dramatic circumstances on a wild winter's night on the island of Skye, a tentative friendship develops between them, despite their very different personalities. Gradually, however, their feelings for each other go beyond friendship.

But Rachel is about to go to Israel-Palestine where she plans to explore her Jewish heritage and to learn more about this contested land. And Jack is already in what is, for him, the ideal relationship – one where no commitment or fidelity is required.

Will they be able to overcome the obstacles that lie in the way of their deepening love?

Rachel find a way forward and let herself love again?

Can Jack trust himself not to hurt her?

For readers who enjoy a mature, romantic,
and thought-provoking story.

When former Edinburgh policeman Jack Baxter met crofter and author Rachel Campbell at her home on the Scottish island of Skye, they fell in love. It was a second chance at happiness for them both.

But after Jack proposes marriage, it becomes clear they want different things.

Then, as Rachel prepares to return to the Middle East to work on a peacemaking project that's close to her heart, and as Jack's past catches up with him, it seems their relationship is doomed.

Can Rachel compromise on her need to maintain her hard-won independence?

Can Jack survive the life-threatening situation in which he finds himself?

Will they get the chance to put things right between them?

Settlement is the sequel to contemporary romance novel, *Displacement*, but it can be read as a stand-alone.

They both had emotional baggage. Jack helped Rachel cope with unimaginable grief after the death in combat of her soldier son, and Rachel was there for Jack after a criminal with a grudge almost ended his life. There were many bumps along the road but they believed they'd worked through and settled their differences.

However, Jack is struggling. Still suffering from post-traumatic stress, haunted by his past, and taunted by the demons of self-doubt, he feels Rachel deserves better.

Meanwhile, Rachel is busy preparing for the launch of her latest book – a book in honour of her son and aimed at promoting peace. So at first she fails to notice just how troubled Jack is.

Can Jack overcome his demons?

Can Rachel convince Jack he deserves to be loved?

Can they finally resolve their differences and fulfil their dreams together?

A tale of life. A poignant mix of sadness, hope and love.

Be careful what you wish for…

Wife to Tom and mother to four adolescent children, Rosie feels taken for granted as she juggles family life and her work as a teacher. She longs for a change.

When she hits a teenage boy with her car, her life veers into unpredictable and uncharted territory. The boy is Robbie - and Rosie discovers he is part of a terrible secret that Tom has kept from her for seventeen years. Then Rosie is diagnosed with breast cancer.

Rosie leaves home and begins the fight for her life. Meanwhile heart surgeon, Tom, learns what it means to be a husband and father. He struggles to keep his family together and strives to get his wife back.

'A good convincing voice that had me identifying with the characters from the outset.' David Wishart, Novelist

'It's a real emotional roller-coaster of a read. I was completely involved in the characters and their lives.' Romantic Novelists' Association.

www.ingramcontent.com/pod-product-compliance
Lightning Source LLC
Chambersburg PA
CBHW021123190726

48288CB00008B/2466